# Mrs May's Tea and Toast

# MRS MAY'S TEA AND TOAST

A Harrington Family Story

Tamara Martin

The Henry Mayberry Group
Adelaide

First published in Australia 2017 by The Henry Mayberry Group

www.thehenrymayberrygroup.com

Edited by Cathleen Ross



National Library of Australia Cataloguing-In-Publication data:

Martin,Tamara, 1973-

Alexandra Deen / Tamara Martin

1st ed.

ISBN: 978-0-6480250-3-0 (pbk.)

Cover Design: Kristyn McGuiggan, Drop Dead Designs

For Granny – a true lady, creator of generations of strong women (and lovely men!), lover of black jelly beans and the best baker of cakes – sponges, butterflies, swiss rolls, laughing lams and those half cake, half biscuit things with the pink icing and jam – clearly the source of my love affair with cake.

Also by Tamara Martin

Alexandra Deen – A Harrington Family Story (Book 1)

# Chapter 1

I watched the sun trying to squeeze through the gaps in the blinds, the dust motes floating in the rays. On the other side of the curtains the South Parklands would be glistening in the sun. They weren't the jewel in Adelaide's crown, not like the East Parklands or the riverbank, but they were pretty enough. I'd seen it all before, though, loved it once, but it'd been a while since the sun did anything other than make me want to cry. I considered taping the blinds to the wall, squeezing those rays back outside but I didn't have tape and I couldn't seem to make my body work, couldn't throw off the blankets or swing my legs over the side of the bed. So I closed my eyes instead, watched the dark, felt my heart beat slow to steady.

An hour ago I'd considered calling a friend. Did I have any? Maybe one. Maybe Jo, maybe Tash? But not really. There was no one. No one I could call and say hey, my head's fucked, you free? We didn't have those types of relationships. They were busy with men and children and jobs and juggling their own stuff, they didn't need me and my messed up head ruining their day, inconveniencing them and their perfectly structured lives.

The sum of my existence had to be more than this. It had to be more than this, this poor excuse for a human I'd become who couldn't get out of bed, the mere thought debilitating in itself. The pain that stole my breath left me lying here like some vegetable and I couldn't seem to do a damn thing about it.

It had to be more than laughing at bad jokes made by pompous executives, when I remembered to show up for work, if paper pushing in a call centre was work. It was, I knew it was but the robotic days emptied my soul. I had been ambitious once, had goals and dreams. I'm not really sure where they went or when I lost them. Just one day they were gone.

All I knew was I had to be more than this person who couldn't face the daylight or remember to put on pants.

Not that pants were an issue anymore. I'd forgotten them one too many times, forgotten to show up one too many times and my boss, usually a sweet lady, was done with me. Like everyone else who'd seemed to fade into the shadows. No one enjoyed being stood up, no one appreciated the impoverished friend who could no longer afford cocktails or if we're honest they were probably ashamed to stand beside me with my unwashed hair in the cocktail bar. But I didn't know how to stop it, how to change it. Half the time I didn't even realise I'd worn pyjamas all day until I got home. No one said anything, they just began giving me a wide berth. Why didn't they say anything? Why didn't they say, hey, Ains, you doing okay? Hey, Ains, the ducks on your shirt are a little out of place. No one said anything. They just stopped inviting me, stopped calling, now every cent had been auto debited out of my bank account and there was nothing left and I wanted to care but the pain in my chest took priority, it always did.

The darkness sat heavily on my chest, near crushing my bones and stealing my breath. I'd tried to function like everyone else. I watched them, analysed them and I tried but I still made a mess of everything, I still forgot to brush my hair and when I remembered to dress appropriately, the comfort of my pyjamas snug and warm against my skin underneath my clothes is what kept me going, kept me from breaking in two and the tears that constantly pushed at the backs of my eyes from falling. Because I always felt one breath away from crumbling to dust, from fading away into the shadows. It was too much. I needed it to stop. I needed to breathe.

It hadn't always been like this. Not this bad anyway. I'd managed my whole life always feeling a little off centre, masking it with boys and cocktails in the hope I'd somehow feel whole but somewhere along the way both stopped working and when nothing helped, down the hill I began to roll until it became so dark I didn't know the way back. I couldn't do it anymore. The pain of it tore at my insides, it burned and ached and I no longer felt like a person. I'd forgotten what it even felt like to feel something other than emptiness.

Pills were such a cliché way to die. I hated that. Being a cliché. But at this point pride and originality were of such little consequence and I didn't know how to buy a gun and anything involving a knife looked unnecessarily painful and drowning in the bathtub seemed a little dramatic, a little too Hollywood for me. So pills it was. They all did the same in the end.

I jingled the pills in my hand, watching them roll around like shiny pebbles as they crashed against each other. They felt heavier than I'd imagined. I'm not even sure what they were or where they came from, couldn't even say if they were mine. I'd found them in a little plastic tube I didn't recognise in the pocket of a coat I hadn't worn in years. The label had worn off and to be honest, I barely remembered the coat, let alone the pills in the pocket.

I stared at them until dusk became night, until the cars below stopped driving and the footsteps in the hall reached their nightly destinations. I reached for the chipped mug on the bedside cupboard and sipped the stale water, feeling the cool wetness slide down my throat and then, one by one, I swallowed the pills, closing my eyes, waiting, until slowly, finally, everything went quiet and perfect and black.

# Chapter 2

Something touched my head and I woke with a start. My whole body ached and my heavy eyes felt stuck shut but I forced them open. The lighting was hazy, muted. I was in a foreign room, a strange narrow bed and there was something stuck in my arm with tubes stretching out into the shadows keeping me in place. There was a warm soft glow from a night light on the wall above the bed but the room was otherwise dark and the hallway beyond was quiet, eerie middle of the night quiet and only just barely lit. I turned my head slightly and there was my mother's worried face, make up free when it is never make up free, her hair mussed and astray as she hovered right over my face.

'Ainsley dear, are you awake?' she asked, even though she was looking right at my open eyes. A newspaper rustled from somewhere else in the room, Dad I assumed, keeping his usual safe distance from drama.

I could only groan, my mouth and throat sandpaper dry, feeling as though I'd had one hell of a night on the town. Then, as Mum scurried off into the quiet, dimly lit hallway to fetch someone, the night before came crashing down on me with a huge helping of guilt and shame. My stomach sank, my body felt heavy and worn and tears filled my eyes as I realised everyone knew, everyone would be laughing, calling me a silly, silly girl, no one understanding any of it. It hadn't ended, it wasn't over and now everyone knew the miserable human being I'd become.

'It was that nice Sergeant Jack that found you,' Mum told me as she fussed around after the nurse had checked all she needed to check and noted all the necessary details in her folder and left.

Sergeant Jack lived in the flat next door, he'd come home after his afternoon shift, a few beers from the local under his belt with no milk for his nightcap (a hot chocolate for the oh-so-tough Sarge). The stockpile of UHT I'd collected over the years was about all that was left in my fridge and he'd taken to helping himself when he needed. When I hadn't answered his knock at the door, he'd let himself in with my emergency key. Pretty rude if you ask me, I could've been lying there in the nude or riding some hot young stud. The fact that I wasn't doing either of those things is beside the point. The fact the Sarge knew I wouldn't be doing any of those things was also beside the point. Used to finding me on the couch staring at sitcom reruns, he'd come searching for me, found me twisted in a pool of vomit my traitorous body had expelled while I lay unconscious. Forgetting his milk, he called the ambulance and held my hand in the hospital until my parents had relieved him of his community service.

I stared at the ceiling, stuck in the bed with nowhere to go and nowhere to hide while Mum regaled the night before's events as though they'd happened to someone else, as though it weren't her daughter stuck in a bed being hydrated after her stomach had been pumped.

I was glad for the reprieve as the sun rose and a middle-aged man introduced himself as Dr Bailey, my new psychiatrist, before sending my parents up to the cafeteria.

'So, what happened?' he asked.

I shrugged.

He raised his eyebrows and I caved, easy as that. 'It wasn't a thing. Nothing happened. I wasn't sad over a boy, I didn't get dumped or anything. Well, I lost my job but by then, I didn't care. I just couldn't make sense of anything, I couldn't see through the dark and the dark never left. Sunshine made me want to cry. I couldn't stand the thought of getting out of my pyjamas. I didn't have the strength to shower. I just couldn't deal anymore. I couldn't cope with the constant pain in my chest, the ache in my bones, the constant need to cry for no reason. I just wanted it stop,' I sobbed like a five year old. 'I didn't know how to make it stop and I found the pills in an old coat I'm not even sure was mine and I thought it was a sign, a gift, that's how I could make it stop.'

'How long between when you found the pills and last night?'

'A while. I'm not really sure how long. I lost track of days.'

He nodded. 'Do you understand what was happening to you?' he asked kindly.

I shook my head wondering why he was so calm about it, why he wasn't calling to have me strapped in a white coat, but he was so meh, happens all the time, about it.

'Depression is a scary thing, especially if you don't know it's happening to you or why.'

'There's a why?' I asked curiously, feeling a tiny spark of hope that there could be a solution.

'There are a number of reasons why depression happens, for you, there's a wiring disconnect. Like when you turn on your gas stove, and you press the ignitor but the flame won't catch, that's what's happening in your brain, the wires are sparking but they're not connecting with each other. There's a missing chemical pathway. That's why it slowly builds and builds and one issue compounds another and another until you can't take it anymore.'

'Does that mean you can fix it?' I whispered, not quite daring to hope.

'We can treat it, Ainsley but it takes time and it will be something you have to live with and be conscious of for the rest of your life. You'll be on medication. You'll have to treat yourself better. But you can live a relatively normal life. If you want to.'

'What do you mean if I want to? Of course I want to,' I groaned. 'As if I would want to live in the hell I was in, who would choose that?'

'Well that is very good to hear,' he smiled. 'The current state of your health is probably exacerbating the issue. I want to do some blood tests and see exactly what we're dealing with and will probably bring in a nutritionist once we know but it does mean nothing to eat until a nurse can come and do the test, we want a true reading, if you can manage?'

'If it means it will help make me feel like a person again, then do it. Whatever you need to do, do it. I don't care, I'm not hungry anyway,' I lied. They'd pumped the meagre contents out of my stomach with the pills and it felt like my stomach might cave in but if there was a chance to feel better, I was taking it. I'd been unemployed for months and too weary to go to Centrelink, I was used to being hungry anyway.

He smiled again. 'I'm pleased with your enthusiasm to be better. It won't be an easy road to recovery, there'll be rules and a program and you'll be spending a lot of hours with me, but I promise, we'll get there together,' he insisted, holding my hand like a kindly grandpa.

'You're not so bad,' I smiled back. I spent a bit longer talking about the progression of forgetting simple things like my train of thought, groceries, to return a phone call or pay a bill that then became so weighty and overwhelming I couldn't force myself to open my eyes in the morning while he nodded and even occasionally smiled, just a little, at one of my mad life stories. Finally a nurse came in and took some blood before handing me a plate of assorted sandwiches.

Dr Bailey kept me hostage for a few weeks in a small six-bed ward he rented from the hospital. I shared the ward with two other girls, one who wore long sleeves and watched a lot of TV with her headphones on and a beautiful teenager who'd also taken a handful of pills in an effort to escape the bitches she went to school with. The schoolyard wasn't what it was when I was there. Six or seven years didn't seem like a long time but so much had changed in the world and talking about that gave us both some perspective which gave us hope that things could change, circumstances could change.

Dr Bailey spoke with me twice a day, helping me sort through my memories, what had been distorted by my state of mind and what was real and some of the things that had previously preceded downward spirals. We talked about what was calming, I was a retreater, needing quiet and calm to escape the noise of the world. Then we looked at how to incorporate that into my coping mechanisms, how to spot the signs, to catch the change in my state of mind before it started to spiral. He tested out some medications and dosages, some that made me bloated and sleepy, until we got to a dosage that made me feel the most normal. He assured me the pills would sort out the black, help me remember to do basic functions of living, keep my brain working as it was supposed to.

After what felt an eternity of assorted sandwiches, watery soup, flavourless meat and three veg and too much analysis of my broken head and messed up interpretations, Dr Bailey gave me some lectures on being kind to myself, taking it easy, exercising daily and eating a high nutrient diet, then released me into the care of my parents.

Mum handed me a shopping bag with a brand new plain blue t-shirt and a pair of new grey tracksuit pants.

'Where are my clothes?' I asked. She'd already confessed to having given all my furniture to my landlord in an attempt to make up for my missed rent when she cancelled my lease but I'd expected at least my own underwear.

'Oh, Ainsley, really...' she groaned as she fussed with the few accumulated personal things on my side table, an insulated coffee cup, some flowers, half a box of chocolates my nutritionist kept trying to hide from me.

'You didn't throw it all out did you?' I asked, the idea that that was exactly something she would do just dawning.

'Not all of it,' she confessed. She quickly added, 'I kept what

I could, Ainsley. Most of it was too filthy or threadbare to save,' she admitted shamefully. 'There's a case in your old room but it would all be too big for you anyway. You look like you've eaten nothing but nuts and seeds for goodness knows how long.'

If only she knew I hadn't been able to afford nuts and seeds since before Christmas.

'Come on, we have to get home, your father will be waiting,' she told me and suddenly, as a long forgotten repressed adolescence that revolved around my father's dinner time flashed before my eyes, I wondered which version of hell was worse.

# Chapter 3

The rain sprinkled down and I lifted my face to it, enjoying the feel of it as it splashed onto my skin, enjoying feeling something when it had been so long since I'd enjoyed sunshine or rain or happiness.

It wasn't cold though, the leaves were full of their bright autumn oranges, Mrs Parker's roses still showing the last of their blooms. Not much had changed, the magpies warbled in the big tree out the front. Mrs Thompson's lemon tree stretched too far over the driveway. Junk mail hung out of letterboxes and a lawnmower buzzed from somewhere up the street, the smell of freshly mown grass drifting on the air, the sweet smell of suburbia.

'Ainsley, what are you doing?' Mum hollered from the front porch.

'I'm coming, I'm coming,' I smiled as I hoisted some of the shopping bags into the crook of my arms to free up my hands to carry more. After only one night at home, Mum had dragged me around The Plaza like an army sergeant on a mission, forcing me to try on tracksuit pants and jeans, t-shirts, jumpers and jackets and now she'd wandered off leaving me to carry the spoils.

It had been an eye opening experience. I hadn't realized how thin I'd gotten. It was no wonder mum was worried. I'd never been fat by any means, but I'd always been healthy, sporty, athletic, not by effort just by design but now I looked waif-like and bony. She was right, nothing she'd salvaged from my flat was going to fit me for a while but if I kept eating the way I was, it would be sooner than expected. The pills Dr Bailey had sent me home with did more than keep my brain sparking right, they'd given me one hell of an appetite. Mum had shouted me lunch, a steak sandwich with the lot, chips and a latte but already I was wondering what snacks she had hidden in the cupboards.

I let the bags fall to the floor inside the door. Someone would be bothered but I'd take them upstairs as soon as feeling returned to my arm and I'd found another coffee and a snack.

'Hey, you,' my brother called as I walked into the living room.

Two peas in a pod my dad and my brother were, each drinking a beer in a recliner watching a game of football.

'What's cooking?' I asked suspiciously as delicious smells wafted in from the kitchen. Mum had been out all day and it was unlike either of those two to cook anything.

'Dad followed Mum's instructions on how to turn the slow cooker on,' Shaun informed me without taking his eyes off the television. 'Was going to run out and buy him a trophy or something but the game was starting and my beer would have gotten warm,' he grinned as Dad smacked him while mumbling *little shit* into his beer bottle.

'You're looking better,' he smiled, getting out of his chair, hugging me. It was something usually reserved for special occasions; Christmas, birthdays, weddings and funerals, none of which applied here, but we had never covered suicide attempts before so I guess protocol was open.

Shaun had covered a lot of new ground in the past weeks and shown how much of a man, a good man, he'd grown into. He'd come in to the hospital and demanded to know everything, the whys, the hows and what part he could play in making it better. I think Dr Bailey liked Shaun more than he liked me. It was a common occurrence though, he was such a likeable guy.

'I'm okay, Shaun,' I insisted. 'Hungry, but okay.'

'What, again?' Mum asked from the doorway.

'It's those pills, Mum, I can't help it,' I told her, not as sorry as I should be because I knew she was going to find me something to eat. Feeding me seemed to make her feel better so I wasn't going to deny her. It was nice being taken care of after so many months of wallowing alone.

'So what are you doing here, anyway?' I asked Shaun as I sat at the table with a cuppa and a slice of my favourite vanilla cake with the strawberry icing Mum had made for my return.

'Mother has promised me a roast,' he grinned.

'Is that so?' I asked, looking at Mum for a confirmation of this proposed roast dinner on a Saturday night. The Donovan's had their routines, we all lived in accordance with their invisible set of rules, no one ever daring to deviate from them. My brother and I had done a lot of sneaking around over the years for this reason.

In this house you did what was expected, you behaved as was expected and you never questioned why, you just followed along with their grand master plan, whatever that was. It had been the only thing that had made sense to my easily confused teenage self and a roast dinner on a Saturday night was not a part of the plan. Roasts were special occasion Sunday food.

'I thought you'd like it, Ainsley, it's your favourite, isn't it?'

'Sure, but you didn't have to go to any trouble, Mum, you've done enough,' I assured her.

She huffed and went about doing things in the kitchen, tending to the chicken roasting in the slow cooker along with the standard veg, boiling more veg and making a gravy.

When she was done, everyone sat in their usual seats, and that was it, we were a family again. We hadn't all been like this since Mum's birthday almost a year ago. Now it felt like a lifetime since we'd all been together, since I'd seen their happy faces, as familiar as my own. It was nice. I felt safe with them here. I realised then I hadn't felt safe in a long time. I'd been so scattered and miserable and alone for so long I hadn't even noticed I was spiralling out of control until I had and this, this feeling of family and safety hadn't even occurred to me as a solution. I'd been too embarrassed of what I'd become, too ashamed of the mistakes and the darkness in my head. I'd thought for sure people on the street could see and that there'd be no way to hide it from my parents. I'd always hidden it. I'd never thought to tell them, to ask them for help. I always assumed they'd laugh, they'd think I was being dramatic, silly. I never thought that just the familiarity of them could ease the pain. It seemed so simple now.

My brother and I had been great friends once but then we grew up, moved out, moved on, lived in different parts of town. Shaun lived in a fabulously run down clapboard, he shared with two other guys at the beach where the waves reached for the sky before crashing onto pristine golden sand. He taught PE at a prestigious beachside school while I was in the city living my make-do life waiting for something better to come along, waiting for the penny to drop.

There wasn't much distance between us all, really but we got on with our lives none-the-less and the distance grew and grew as time went by and we all soon forgot how nice it was to have each other. But right here, right now in Mum's much loved kitchen where so many memories resided in the shadows and in the creases of the timber dining table and scuff marks on the lino that were now hidden by a cabinet told a million stories. I could feel it. No one needed to say anything or do anything it was just there, in abundance. Family.

It was never supposed to turn out this way, I thought, as Shaun told stories of his fabulously charmed life. We were never supposed to be sitting in this kitchen with its pretty blue cupboards at Mum's beaten and battered dining table avoiding the fact that I had tried to kill myself. Avoiding the fact that I had become so miserable and desperate and alone that I had actually tried to take my own life.

These new pills gave me way too much clarity, too much space to think and wonder. I saw me, my actions as my family might have and I felt like I had somehow let them down. I had failed as a daughter and as a sister and as a friend. I was supposed to be all of those things but I'd done the most awful thing and if I'd died, I could see the hole I'd have left, the devastation I'd have left behind, the torture I'd have put my family though.

Tears began pouring out of my eyes. I couldn't stop them. I

couldn't see. I couldn't breathe. I had no control and the tears just kept rolling. Everyone stopped eating and talking, staring at me confused. They'd never seen the messy side of me. I'd kept it so well hidden for so many years which was what people like me tended to do and the way they looked at me with horror and pity or was it sympathy? Only made it worse.

Mum passed me a tissue and between sobs I said, 'I'm sorry.'

'It's okay, love,' Mum said. 'We all need a cry sometimes.'

'No, Mum, I'm sorry. I'm sorry I took the pills. I wasn't thinking right. I didn't mean to do that to you all,' I said, looking around the table at their frozen, stunned faces.

'It's okay, Ains,' said Shaun sitting next to me holding my hand. 'You're going to be alright now and that's the main thing, yeah?'

'Yeah,' I said, the tears slowing.

'And we're going to make sure it stays that way, okay? I'm not letting you go there again, you hear me?' he insisted with a soft, kind smile.

I nodded, blew my nose, taking big, deep breaths until I could speak again. Shaun had always made things plain and simple. He was that kind of guy. Kind and practical in a no nonsense kind of way.

'It's great chicken, Dad,' I said looking into his sad eyes. I had been his little girl once. It felt like a lifetime ago now. But I saw in his eyes across the dining table how scared he was, how much he loved me in his own dad-like way and my heart broke into a billion pieces for disappointing him, for worrying and frightening him.

Dad looked like he was going to cry with me but instead he

said, 'I know how much you always liked the legs, you used to steal them off my plate, remember?'

I smiled. 'Yeah, I remember. But I always gave myself away, getting gravy all over my fingers.' I laughed.

The memory lightened the mood and the kitchen took on a cleaner, fresher, hopeful air and we got on with dinner and enjoying being together, being grateful we were all still in one piece.

# Chapter 4

Sunday the world returned to normal. I couldn't have taken too much more of the extra nice parents, I needed the stability of what I knew, what was familiar. I couldn't go learning new rules when I was already dealing with so much.

'Ainsley, can you pop to the shop for me, love, I need some more bread and ham for sandwiches,' Mum said.

'Sure, Mum.' It was the least I could do. That's what I told the sulking twelve year old that appeared in my head, anyway. But it was, Mum and Dad had been so good to me, they'd not once berated me for my stupid choice, perhaps that was Dr Bailey's doing, I couldn't be sure. They'd had some meetings with him and even though I was sure he wouldn't betray Doctor patient confidentiality, it was clear he'd given them information on what was happening to me and they'd been with me when he gave me my new prescription for life and I had no doubt Mum was going to follow it to the letter. The walking, the nutrition, the resocialisation, all of it. So helping out and pulling my weight and walking to the shops for bread and ham was the least I could do.

I took the ten-dollar note she offered and the green bag to carry said bread and ham and off I went.

As with everything else in Bob and Jackie Donovan's world, the location of our family home had been perfectly selected. Everything, the kindergarten, primary school, high school, shopping centre, medical centre and bus stop were all within easy reach, just a ten-minute walk would get you to any one of the necessary facilities. As I stepped outside and began the walk to the local shops, taking the route I'd taken so many times during my youth, I marvelled at the bubble in which everything appeared to exist. Nothing had changed. Everything looked the same, the soccer ovals looked the same, the wattles on the corner, number six's dead lawn was still dead. It was strange to think this suburban bubble had kept existing exactly as it always had despite my inner city turmoil. It meant there was hope to find my way back, to maybe start again, to find that point of no return and reroute it.

I turned the corner, passing the row of old cottages with big deep verandahs. Mr Shannahan still sat on his chair, fiddling with some mechanical object he was pretending to fix while offering a friendly neighbourly wave to anyone that passed. I waved back, as I'd done so many times, even though I'd never actually met Mr Shannahan, relying on third hand information that that was even in fact his name. Mrs May sat on her wicker chair two doors down. I knew that was her name because I knew of her son, he'd graduated and was in uni by the the time I started high school, then he got a fancy job interstate, so I heard and off he went, never to be seen again. But still, she sat there every day as though waiting for his imminent return. We shared a wave and I crossed the road, passed the housing trust homes hidden behind the big flowering oleanders, went under the shade of the bridge, ignoring the lifetime of memories hiding in the shadows and up the stairs that led to the carpark, dodged the cars and walked into the cool familiarity of a life I'd forgotten. A life of skipping school, my first radical haircut, meeting up with inappropriate boys after school and sneaking junk food with my pocket money. Everything happened here and it showed me how much had happened since I'd last been here, how much had changed, how much I'd changed. Yet here I was back at the beginning. In the days since I'd been back it seemed the clear theme was the circle of life, the chance to start over, that you could always go back, find that point and begin again.

I walked home with a little spring in my step. It'd been so long since I'd felt any kind of spring, it caught me off guard and I almost giggled at the absurdity of not recognising a little happiness. Happiness for no good reason was a gift I'd forgotten so I smiled.

As I approached the cottages and readied myself for another friendly wave, a gust of wind swept up from behind, knocking me forward as it caught a biscuit wrapper out of Mrs May's hand and floated it to my feet.

'Oh dear,' she giggled as she gracefully floated down the steps. She wore a mint green dress cinched at her tiny waist with a matching belt. I noticed how well put together she was, fully made up as though prepared for more than sitting on her verandah drinking tea. 'Thank you, dear,' she said, taking back the wrapper.

I smiled, it was not a big thing, it was just a piece of rubbish.

I'd forgotten how people could appreciate simple gestures. I'd forgotten a lot but I was glad to be remembering.

'You look better, you looked a little troubled earlier,' she remarked.

'Thoughtful,' I smiled. 'I've had a lot to think about but yes, I feel better, clearer.'

'A lovely walk will do it every time,' she smiled.

'With this sunshine, it's impossible to be anything but happy for long,' I agreed.

'It has come up a bit warm this afternoon, would you like some tea, you look a little flushed,' she offered.

'Thank you, that's very kind. I'd love some but perhaps another time. My mother will be waiting on the bread and ham for lunch,' I told her, hoisting the bag as though evidence.

'Another time,' she smiled before gliding back up the steps and into her house.

I waved to Mr Shannahan who nodded his return greeting and I went home feeling more connected to the world around me than I had in a long time. It was nice to be back.

The novelty of being at home in familiar surroundings, of being waited on by my mother, not having to worry about cleaning or shopping for food or bill paying or any other such mundane adult activities wore off after only a few weeks. I'd returned to the twelve year old me. I was taller, slightly bustier (albeit, probably not much), my hair was shinier (thanks to Mum and L'Oreal 4.0) and I no longer daydreamed about Leonardo DiCaprio popping by to sweep me off my feet or Justin Timberlake serenading me on the front lawn, but the rest was the same.

Mum left a sandwich in the fridge for me before she went to work, took me clothes shopping on her days off, left me lists of chores, made sure I was showered, dressed and fed every day and monitored my daily exercise, either herself or with the help of Mrs Thompson next door.

But having the routine and the rules was good. They felt good. It gave me boundaries and purpose and a reason to get out of bed every day. The pills helped, even though they made me so hungry I was glad the majority of my wardrobe consisted of baggy t-shirts and elastic waisted tracksuit pants. But I still had to do some of the work too, so Dr Bailey kept saying. Walk, begin to take part in life again, give a crap about my life. He said a lot of things. I was just happy the blackness had left, that I felt clearer and lighter and maybe even happy. I didn't even care that I couldn't stop eating, that I slept like the dead, but in a good way because I always woke refreshed and ready to begin again.

The blistering wind whipped at my jacket, flicked hair in my face. I needed to stop, zip up my jacket, tie my hair back but I didn't want to stop, I just wanted to be home and out of the wind, to sit on the couch, drink something hot and eat the cake Mum had left in the fridge. It had been a tough day. I'd been to see Dr Bailey who'd proceeded to dig around in my head, poking and prodding and making me talk about shameful things I didn't want to talk about for an hour while I cried rivers of humiliated tears before getting on the bus and off at the shops to run Mum's errands. Now I just wanted the wind to fuck off and leave me be for five minutes.

I looked up as I passed the row of cottages to nod a hello to Mrs May and Mr Shannahan but before I could, my toe caught a crack in the pavement and I tripped, spilling my groceries as my hands stopped my face from hitting the cement.

Mrs May elegantly descended the steps just in time to see me burst into tears. I was perfectly medicated and had the blackness under control, I was no longer stuck at the bottom of a dark, airless pit, but still, I was jobless, friendless and living with my parents and Dr Bailey had a way of bringing every miserable emotion to the fore. It was his job, I suppose, but it meant that after a session I sometimes walked home on the edge of tears and when your groceries, your shampoo and tampons spill all over the footpath on a cold, windy afternoon, it can all be a bit much.

'Come on, love,' Mrs May insisted, scooping my things back into the bag and leading me by the elbow up her steps and into the spare chair. She poured me some tea and promised everything would be alright.

'Why don't you tell me about it,' she offered kindly.

'You're very sweet to offer a shoulder but quite honestly, Mrs May, all I've been doing this morning is talking about my crap and it's left me an emotional mess,' I said before sipping my tea. It was good tea too, nothing like I'd ever tasted, with hints of floral and spice.

'Well then, why don't we talk about something else, happier things,' she began before gossiping about all the poor, unfortunate passers-by.

'Is that really true?' I asked doubtfully as she told me of the tawdry exploits of the sweet mum pushing a toddler in a pram.

She shrugged with a naughty grin, 'Probably not. How would I know anyway but where's the fun in that?' she winked. 'But that's the point, Ainsley, it doesn't matter what is or what was, what matters is tomorrow and what you choose for it to be. You have all the power to make it anything you like.'

'Anything?'

'Anything,' she grinned.

The next day Mrs May beckoned me up for tea and she was so warm and sweet and full of life, I instantly felt better.

'Where have you been today?' she asked.

'Just around the block.'

'Did you see anything interesting?'

'Anyone, you mean?' I asked with a smirk.

She giggled like a schoolgirl. 'You know I was once the one with all the real gossip. The keeper of everyone's secrets,' she said wistfully.

'Why did that change?'

'Ah, no reason, dear,' she said, pouring more tea. 'Just life happens, I suppose. It's always twisting and turning, this way and that and you never really know what is around the next bend. Sometimes it's frightening, like the scare you've just had and sometimes it's incredible and beautiful. But you never know what you're going to get until you get there and you just have to do the best you can.'

'Was it one of the frightening ones that changed your secret keeping life?'

She smiled. 'But I also got Mitchell so how bad could it have been?' she winked. 'The only thing we can count on, Ainsley, is the river keeps on flowing and we keep on going with it, into the bends, out of the bends and just doing the best we can with what we find there.'

'Do the bends ever end?'

'Do we really want them to? If we get to the end then isn't it the end? Wouldn't you rather keep on going?'

I looked forward to my walks, to seeing Mrs May. She shared her wisdom with the ease of sharing tea. She told stories of glamorous parties and dancing and jazz and love. Mrs May became the highlight of my day and her assurances for life, for it turning around, about dues being paid, became my lifeline of hope.

'What was your dream, Mrs May?'

'Oh, Ainsley, I do wish you'd call me, Ana.'

I smiled. She told me every day but it just didn't feel right. 'You're avoiding the question.'

She smiled. 'You're getting good at this, you know, life, people.'

I frowned at her even though I was secretly chuffed by her praise.

'Okay, okay,' she smiled. 'It's not a big secret. Like a lot of girls, I dreamt of being a ballerina. Of joining the Russian Ballet. That was where I was born, in Russia. Do I still have the accent? I can't hear it anymore.'

'Only a little. What happened?'

'Russia was not always an easy place to live and when I was becoming a teenager, my family, we moved to Melbourne and when I was finishing high school, I met my Henry and we came here and we made a life. It was a good life and then he was gone and it was just me and Mitchell and we made a new life. See, rivers and bends and choices. They all keep coming,' she smiled.

'I wonder what my next bend will be?' I asked quietly not really expecting a reply.

'It will be a good bend. I just know it. I feel it in my bones, Ainsley. All the bad is gone now. If you fight, if you try, if you believe and trust in yourself, the next bend will be beautiful.'

I smiled at the idea of it. I wondered what beautiful looked like.

'Tell me about Henry.'

'Oh,' she smiled. 'He liked to laugh. He liked to make me laugh and we did, we laughed a lot. People said we were like the sun when we were together. I don't know about that but we were happy. There was so much love in our home that when it was gone it was hard to see what was left. But when I looked at Mitchell, at his sweet, sweet face, there was a new love and a new purpose and a new dream.'

I remembered Mitch, he was tall and broad in the way of a swimmer and very handsome. I'd see him waiting at the bus stop to go to uni while I walked to school. I had always thought he was the sort of man I'd marry. I don't know what it was about him particularly because I couldn't remember much other than his handsome face.

As Mrs May became wistful in her memories, I finished my tea and left.


'Where have you been?' Mum asked when I got home from my walk and daily visit to Mrs May's.

I shrugged. 'Walking.'

'You were gone a long time.'

'It's a nice day,' I told her.

'Where exactly did you walk today?'

'Just around.'

'Around where, Ainsley?'

'The block. Up the hill and past Foodland and over the bridge and then down that hill by the nice colonial and past the kindy. It's a big block,' I told her only slightly fibbing.

She nodded, seemingly satisfied.

'What are you doing home so early, anyway?' I asked her.

'I only had a few classes today so I invited Shaun over for dinner. Thought I'd cook spaghetti with the good sauce.'

'I won't be complaining about that,' I told her, just a little excited. 'Is there dessert?'

'Maybe,' she smirked as she began pulling things out of the pantry and cupboards to prepare her feast.

'You want some help?' I offered.

She smiled. 'Thanks, but you go watch some telly.'

I was glad too, because Giada was about to come on the Food Network and I was loving the food network. I liked watching them make fancy food I'd never make while eating cheese toasties. It was like having conversations with friends at the same time each day. They were so cheerful that I always felt good.

# Chapter 5

'Come on Ainsley or you'll be late,' Mum hollered from downstairs.

'Coming, I'm coming,' I assured her, tying my hair back into a ponytail.

'You can have your breakfast in the car,' Mum said, handing me a plate of toast smeared with vegemite and a travel mug of coffee. 'I don't want to get caught in peak hour traffic,' she reminded me.

As Mum deposited me in front of my shrink's office building, she reminded me she was going down to Ikea with Vivi to buy a new hall table and I was catching the bus home and was to pick up a loaf of bread on the way. She handed me a five-dollar note for the bread, kissed me on the cheek and made me promise to behave before merging back into the traffic.

My life seemed to revolve around Mum's errands and visits to Dr Bailey. I knew I didn't have the right to be annoyed after what I'd done but I was annoyed anyway as I waited for the lift in the shiny foyer.

Dr Bailey's office was old school, like him, lots of timber trim, ancient New Ideas and a similarly ancient receptionist. She was proper and put together as she sat behind her shiny black desk, scowling at you over her green-rimmed glasses. You just knew she was reading Dr Bailey's notes as she typed them up.

'How are you?' he asked as he readied himself with his notepad and pen.

'I'm doing okay,' I said, telling him about Mrs May.

'Well that's lovely that you're making a friend. What about your other friends?'

And that was the end of my good mood and refusal to cry. Just one time, one session, I wanted to get through without crying. 'I haven't heard from anyone. But they don't know where to find me, anyway, my phone was disconnected and I didn't really want to pester Mum into one more expense. Although my Centrelink money will come through soon so I'll do something about the phone then. But it doesn't matter, anyway. They didn't notice I'd dropped off the planet in the first place, I hadn't spoken to anyone in weeks so I doubt they even know my phone's been disconnected,' I said, tearing up. I don't know how these sessions continued to break me down and have me crying like a baby every time. You'd think I'd have gotten out all the tears and talked through all the crap there was to get out by now but there was something about being in a shrink's office that made me want to howl, to expunge every emotion I'd ever felt and get it all out, lay it all on the table in front of the psychiatrist for him to sort through and fix.

'That's the way, dear,' Dr Bailey encouraged as he passed me the brightly coloured box of tissues he kept on the coffee table between us.

'Thanks,' I sniffed like a child.

'So, tell me more about these friends,' he prodded.

'There's nothing to tell, Dr Bailey. I was just never going to be good enough for them. They were all so sure of themselves, always so well put together and I was... well, I was just me. It was a miracle if I remembered to brush my hair,' I told him.

'Did they see you as not good enough? What about Jo, she was one of your closest friends, did she see you that way?' he asked.

I shrugged petulantly.

'Ainsley,' he coaxed.

'Fine. No, it was all in my head. Just like everything else. It's all in my messed up head. My brain, it twists things, Dr Bailey, it distorts them like one of those wonky mirrors at the Magic Cave and I just don't know which image is true anymore,' I complained.

'Well, that's what I'm here for, isn't it? And now you have the chemicals balanced, you'll see things clearer from now on. You leave the old stuff for me to help you sort through, alright?' he said, patting my hand like a kindly grandpa.

I smiled and the distant little bell that you could hardly hear at all tinkled that the session was over.

I left Dr Bailey's office with the receptionist's contempt following in my wake, bought a chocolate bar from the nearby service station that lasted about ten seconds and would probably provide all the necessary fodder for my next shrink visit and went back out into the bright sunshine to get my bus back to the suburbs.

I smiled as I got off the bus at my local shopping centre where familiarity was again my comforting friend. I liked seeing the people going about their business. Children running across the car park, parents screaming after them, hipsters zipping into the 24hour gym, the weary foreign guy who was probably once a biochemist, collecting trolleys and having his constant conversations on his mobile phone, it was life. All around me was life, people living, birds and cars and the smell of burgers cooking at Hungry Jacks on the other side of the car park, it was life, all around me. I soaked it up, feeling better by the second and walked to Mrs Mays.

'Oh dear, you look exhausted. Have you been to see that Dr Bailey again?' she asked as I climbed the steps.

'I tell you Mrs May, that man knows how to put a girl through the ringer,' I tried smiling.

'Well, you just sit,' she said, almost pushing me into one of the cane chairs on her verandah. 'A nice cup of tea will sort you out.'

'Oh, that it will, Mrs May, that it will,' I said, already feeling better as she poured the bronze tea into a pretty cup.

'Now, what was that man dredging up today?'

'Oh, just the usual,' I told her.

'You don't need that man pottering about in your head. What you need is a good man pottering about everywhere else,' she proclaimed.

'Mrs May!' I cried.

'What?' she asked innocently as she tucked the shiny red bauble she wore on a chain around her neck, back inside her shirt. 'There's no point pretending neither of us know about such things and what's wrong with you is nothing the love of a good, kind man wouldn't fix,' she declared with a wink.

'I thought in this day and age we weren't supposed to rely on men to fix our problems, being independent women and all.'

'Hogwash,' she smiled. 'Besides, I'm not saying rely on him or give yourself to him completely. A woman still needs to be her own person, that's for sure. But nothing wrong with having some strong arms to keep you warm at night and take care of business, if you know what I mean,' she insisted, matter-of-factly.

I had nothing to say to that. I blushed is what I did, like a schoolgirl learning about the birds and the bees.

'I have a feeling, you know, that things are about to change,' she told me. 'Change they will, my dear, mark my words. You just need to hang in there and keep going as you're going,' she smiled as she topped up my tea.

'Well hello, Arnold,' Mrs May called to an elderly neighbour passing by with his Chihuahua.

'Ana, Ainsley,' he called back, tipping his imaginary hat.

'Not that I'm in the market, mind,' Mrs May said, returning her attention to me. 'I've had my great love and my goodness it was indeed enough to see me through,' she said getting all wistful and staring out to the road as though there was something out there only she could see.

'Now,' she said firmly, changing the subject, 'What is that mother of yours feeding you? You're still all skin and bones,' she said, passing me a plate of homemade honey bread. 'My mother's recipe,' she told me.

It was so good, I couldn't stop at a single piece. 'Mrs May, you know she feeds me just fine and I'm filling out these new pants she bought me already, we'll have to buy more soon.'

'Hmph,' she grunted with a smile as she shoved the plate at me again.

'Speaking of which,' I said, looking at my watch. 'I best get going before this little charade of ours is busted wide open. Thank you for the tea and sympathy, I don't know where I'd be without you,' I said, hugging her before hurrying home.

Mum's car was already in the drive when I got home. Shoot!

'Ainsley, is that you?' she called out when I opened the front door, as though it could have been any number of people.

'Yes, it's me,' I called as I headed to the kitchen.

'Where have you been? I was getting worried.'

'Just out for my walk,' I told her.

'That's another long walk,' she commented, her eyebrows raised, sensing deceit.

'I stopped along the way, chatted to some of the old folk,' I said, not lying altogether.

'What old folk?' she asked dubious.

'Just people, Mum. Old people. It's not like I was out talking to drug dealers and corner hookers, you know.'

'Oh, Ainsley, really,' she scoffed.

'Fine,' I conceded, 'I had tea with Mrs May from around the corner on my way home, alright? Nothing crazy, I promise.'

'Mrs May, Mrs May,' she said, thinking. 'Not Ana May? Mitchell May's mother?'

'Yes, that's her,' I said.

'Well, I'd rather you stayed closer to home from now on,' she said cryptically as she went into the kitchen to put on the kettle, closing the subject. I felt I'd gotten off quite easy considering I'd skipped my shrink prescribed walk for tea with an old lady no one really knew and wondered if it counted as a win? I was sure it didn't, just as I was sure it wasn't quite as over as I imagined. It never was when mum's eyes squinted like that.

# Chapter 6

In the morning, I did as was expected. I got up, showered, dressed and went downstairs for breakfast. I had a sneaking suspicion that my victory the day before wouldn't be without a cost of some sort and was mildly curious to see what Mum had in store. I know she worries when I'm late but it was perfectly innocent and I had to rejoin the world and gain some independence eventually and chatting to sweet old ladies should be a good thing. I know I wasn't supposed to skip my walks to do so and Mrs Thompson was watching out her window for me, timing me or whatever it was she did.

Mum was fussing around with the kettle and putting coffee into the three mugs on the bench in front of her while Dad was straightening his tie, a half-eaten piece of toast smothered with vegemite on a plate in front of him.

'Morning,' I called.

'Morning,' Dad grumbled through a mouthful of toast.

'Good morning, Ainsley. I need you to drive me to school today and come back and get me at three,' declared Mum. 'After you drop me off, you need to go over to Vivi's and take her gro-cery shopping.'

'Fine,' I said, knowing full well this was my punishment for going astray, skipping walks and having tea with strangers and she was trying to keep me busy and out of trouble. But that was okay by me. I needed to be busy and out of trouble and Vivi was a hoot. Spending the day with my mother's best friend would never be a punishment really.

I dropped Mum at school as instructed and as she was getting out of the car she gave me her rules for the day, 'Now no hooning around in my car, you hear. I don't want to be getting any speeding tickets in the mail.'

'Yes, Mum,' I smiled like I was sixteen again.

'No carting around friends or drinking or eating any of that rotten takeaway food in here, the smell takes weeks to come out.'

'Yes, Mum.'

'Don't be smart.'

'No, Mum,' I smiled.

She smirked a little. 'Now be nice to Vivi, take her for coffee and lunch after shopping,' she said, handing me some cash. 'And here's a shopping list for us, the shopping bags are in the boot and don't go substituting brands, you buy what's on the list,' she insisted, handing me her ATM card and giving me the pin. 'And don't go buying anything else because I'll know,' she said.

'Yes, Mum,' I said, taking the card.

'And don't go letting those shop people swipe that card under the counter,' she said.

'Mum, that doesn't happen at Coles, there's cameras and stuff. Your card's safe,' I told her, trying hard not to roll my eyes.

'Yes, well, anyway, just pay attention, okay?'

'Yes, Mum. You better go now or the bell will be ringing and you won't be in class.'

'Or fully caffeinated,' she smiled as she got out of the car and quickly hurried to the admin building with her travel mug in hand ready to refill.

I left before the drop off lane Nazis came to harass me, there's only so much leeway being Mrs Donovan's daughter will get you. I changed the radio station, making a mental note to change it back to Mum's preferred easy listening station later and drove over to Vivi's.

Percy the pink poodle greeted me, panting, his little tail wagging, as I opened the unlocked door. Vivi had him dyed at some fancy dog salon over the other side of town and the poor thing probably lived in constant humiliation but he always seemed happy enough and shoved his head under my hand so I'd scratch behind his ears as I let myself in, calling out to Vivi as I did.

'Back here, love,' she called.

She was in the kitchen filling up her slow cooker with chicken and tinned tomatoes, a bowl of fresh herbs on the bench I knew were from her own garden, ready to mix in. On the dining table was a plate of chocolate chip cookies. Vivi was famous for them. My mum did cakes and Vivi did cookies so it balanced out a person's sugar diet nicely. Beside the plate of cookies was a cocktail shaker and two cocktail glasses.

'What's all this, Vivi?' I asked suspiciously, pointing to the glasses.

'A little starter I was thinking,' she said as though it was perfectly natural.

'Vivi, it's only nine in the morning,' I told her.

'I know what time it is. I also know your mother set this all up just to keep us both out of trouble. I don't particularly feel like being kept out of trouble so I thought we could have a little fun to start our day. I do need some groceries though, so we will still have to go to Coles, but we can do that later. Right now I want to hear about what's going on with you. Just let me finish up here.'

'Okay,' I said, sitting at the table and helping myself to a cookie. 'So why are you in trouble?' I asked.

'Boys,' she said, shaking her head. 'Or to be precise, too many of them. According to your mother, anyway. Never did know how to have any fun,' she laughed.

'Have you become a hussy since I last saw you, Vivi?'

'Oh goodness no, my lady pride is well intact. Well, mostly, but what's wrong with having dinner with a lovely gentleman or popping to the flicks or having a cocktail? None that I can see. Last I checked, I was a grown-arsed woman and if I want to see some men, then I think I have the right to see whomever I damn well please.'

'That sounds fair,' I agreed. After all, she'd raised a child, lost a beloved husband and waved that child off as she moved to the other side of the world. I think Vivi had earned the right to live a little. To live however she pleased.

'Hmph, well not according to your mother. She thinks I'm going to get myself some sort of reputation. But I'm 58 years old, I don't see how that's going to hurt any at this point in my life. It's not like I'm trying to snag myself some eligible husband. I already did that, God rest Archie's soul. A good man that one, the best. But he's been gone a long time and now I'm just happy to have a little fun. Everyone likes a bit of attention, to still turn a head or two, share a sunset now again, what's wrong with that?' she asked as she sprinkled the herbs into the crockpot and gave it a final stir.

'Nothing is wrong with that, you go on and have your fun, you know Mum's just a bit of a stick in the mud.'

'I know. She does mean well. She's a good woman your mum. But a real wet blanket when it comes to having fun.'

'Don't I know it,' I laughed.

'Now,' she said, taking a seat and giving the cocktail shaker a shake. 'What's all this nonsense about you trying to top yourself?' she asked, never one to beat around the bush or mince words or worry about things like political correctness.

I shrugged. What was there to say? The action speaks for itself and one doesn't do it because they're having a jolly time of things.

'Well now, as long as you're on the mend. You're on the mend, aren't you? You're mother says you are, that these pills have you sorted, have things working right again?' she said, giving me her watchful eye over the rim of her glasses as she poured herself a dirty martini.

'You are allowed these, aren't you?' she asked, hesitating above my glass.

'I'm not an alcoholic, Vivi.'

'Good, good, right,' she said, pouring.

'Anyway, you alright now?' she asked being more serious. 'Got yourself sorted a bit. In your head I mean,' she asked.

'Yeah, I'm sorted. The pills have me craving mac and cheese

every day but I have my mother's metabolism and Dr Bailey's fixing the mix ups in my head,' I said.

'Good, good. Yes, that metabolism of hers is an eighth wonder. How are you settling in with your folks?'

'It's hard to be watched all the time. But it's okay.'

She nodded. 'You'll be back in your own space before too long,' she told me. 'Just take your time, you'll be right,' she nodded. 'Come, I want to show you something,' she said, picking up her martini.

I followed her with my own martini into the garden.

'Now I know it's not everyone's cup of tea and you might just think me getting old, but tending to my garden is what kept me balanced all these years. When Archie died and I felt I had nothing in this whole wide world left to hold on to, this is where I came. This is what kept me whole and gave me something to look forward to, something else to focus on other than myself and my own dreadful woes.'

I followed Vivi around the corner of the house and into the pumpkin patch. I knew it was the pumpkin patch because Vivi had taught me gardening things long ago when I was smaller. She'd potter around in her garden and I'd ask a billion questions, some of the answers I still remembered.

We walked through the pumpkin patch, past the potatoes and into the veggie garden proper. She'd had it raised and redone since I was small. It probably helped with her back. Vivi wasn't old, she was the same age as my mother, just a few years older, my mother's cousin to be exact but she'd been like an aunt to us. She had her own daughter who she'd had when she was nineteen but mum had waited until much later. Angie had been living in the UK ever since I could remember so we'd become her surrogate family once Angie had moved.

Vivi bent down, expertly securing her cocktail glass in the dirt and picked up a pot that was sitting between shrubs and herbs and plants, most I could no longer name. 'Here,' she said handing me the pot with a tall green sprout. 'It's a tomato plant,' she told me. 'Nothing tastes better than the home-grown ones and nothing better than knowing you grew them all by yourself,' she said, picking her martini up out of the dirt. 'It'll need lots of water, sunlight and TLC.

'Now,' she commanded. 'Let's go have the last of the martinis before we go grocery shopping and I'll tell you all about the Italian Stallion who took me to dinner last night. But you can't tell your mother because I can't be sure my lady pride is going to stay intact much longer and I don't want her ruining it all with her rules.'

We finished the martinis while Vivi told me about her handsome man who told her she was beautiful and took her to fancy restaurants and got her liquored up and giggly. She was planning on him eating what she had going in the slow cooker and told me to make sure she bought candles while we were out, ones that smelt like vanilla as she'd read in a magazine that candles that smelt like food worked the best for seducing a man. And port. She wanted to offer him port at the end of the evening so he'd feel suitably relaxed and brave to make all the right moves. It was no wonder Mum was worried. But it made me happy to see that you could make life anything you wanted to, no matter what life threw at you and that chances kept coming even when you were fighting gravity. It meant I hadn't missed out, I could still make a life for myself and I got to choose what it was. It meant do overs were real.

We had lunch at a little coffee shop next to Coles where everyone seemed to know everyone before shuffling through Coles while Vivi stocked up as though the apocalypse was coming and she filled me in on all the family gossip, who was changing jobs, changing boyfriends, changing wives and taking extravagant holidays. I helped her to choose candles and followed Mum's list. It was exhausting business.

'Do you need anything else before I go?' I asked Vivi after I'd brought in her shopping bags.

'Nope, that's all of it. I'll be right from here,' she insisted.

'Alright, then, don't do anything too crazy with your stallion tonight,' I said, hugging her goodbye.

'Crazy is just what I'm hoping for,' she winked.

I shook my head and went home, unloaded and packed away Mum's groceries before I found just the right spot for my tomato plant in my room then went to get Mum from school. It hadn't been a bad day of punishment at all, but I wouldn't tell her that or maybe she knew an afternoon with Vivi was enough to fix anyone's woes?

# Chapter 7

Mum stuck to me like glue over the weekend, taking me shopping for new clothes, buying me lunch, taking me to get a haircut, coming on long walks with me as though we were best friends, generally keeping a watchful hawk-eye over everything I did and every move I made.

'What is your problem with me talking to old people?' I asked as she iced a cake.

She sighed like she had the weight of the world on her shoulders and I decided to give her a break and play nice. 'I don't know,' she answered. 'It just feels weird. Maybe it's just because she's old. Maybe you should be talking to people your own age. Reconnecting with some of your friends.'

'I don't know that my friends will want me reconnecting, Mum. Besides, how can I call them now and say what? Oh sorry for not chatting the last couple of months I was busy topping myself.'

'Ainsley!' she chastised and I felt bad. I didn't mean to be flippant but it was a part of me. It would always be a part of me, I had to find a way to live with it and this seemed to be it. It was just something I did but Mum wasn't there yet. I'd have to be more sensitive.

'Sorry, Mum. But it's true. It's not something you can just blurt out to your friends over a cocktail. It's a lot for people to deal with. And to be honest, I'm not sure I even want them to know and if I call them I have to tell them something and I don't want to lie.'

'Well, that's quite a pickle. What does Dr Bailey say?'

'We're getting to it. It's a process. There's stuff to work through before we get to that.'

She nodded thoughtfully but didn't say anything more and I guessed the subject was closed but I was no clearer on her opposition to old people other than the fact they were old. But I let it go. I'd put Mum through a lot and she didn't need me upsetting her any more.

So I hadn't seen Mrs May since the day Mum had caught me coming home late from my walk for the second day in a row and I was desperate to see her, to soak up her beautiful spirit and to tell her about my visit with Vivi. She'd like Vivi. I think in another life they could be friends. A cup of tea with Mrs May was more soothing than any shrink session with Dr Bailey especially as she never made me cry.

There was no leaving the house on Monday until after Ellen though because Mrs Thompson would be keeping an eye out, so I patiently watched morning chat shows, ate my sandwich while laughing with Ellen and then I was free. I gave Mrs Thompson a wave as I walked down the drive and sucked in the fresh air of freedom.

I had the taste of that strange tea she favoured tantalising my tastebuds as I practiced the Russian she'd taught me on my last visit. *Spasibo*, was the word of the day, which means thank you. It was slow going this Russian and don't even think about asking me to write any of it. I had also learnt *privet*, which is hello and *pomoshch*, which is help. 'We will have you speaking in Russian in no time,' she laughed, even when I got tongue-tied tripping over the words.

I walked through the little gate attached to Mrs May's white picket fence and looked up to the verandah where she'd held court surveying the street and road beyond for all these years but she wasn't there. She'd never not been there for as long as I could remember. She must have gone inside for more tea, I assumed. She had to refill her supplies at some time or to pee out all that tea. She'd know I was coming. I always came on a Monday because Mum had her pick of relief work on a Monday. Mrs May never minded my just showing up. She was always there on her verandah watching the world go by so never minded if I arrived unannounced, appreciative even of the spontaneous interruption to her long, lonesome days.

'Mrs May?' I called from the bottom step as I climbed.

There was no response so I tried again 'Mrs May? Ana?' I called, adding the last just to cover bases as I reached the top of the steps. Still no reply came.

A man in a fancy suit appeared in the doorway. 'Can I help you?'

My defences instantly kicked in. I hated surprises. Even before my brain fully malfunctioned, I hated surprises. It was part of my conditioning, I supposed, people like me needed familiar things and order to keep our brains stable.

'I'm Ainsley, Ainsley Donovan,' I said, surveying the man for a moment. He didn't look tall enough or handsome enough to be Mrs May's son, but I hadn't seen her son since I was a kid so my memory may have been distorted by my own lack of height at the time. 'Are you Mitchell?'

'No,' he replied shortly, rather matter-of-factly. 'Her lawyer.'

'Her lawyer? Is everything okay? Where is Mrs May?'

'You better come on in,' he said.

I went the rest of the way up the stairs and followed him into the house. I'd never been inside the house, only ever to the front verandah. I'd never had a need to go inside. We drank our tea and we talked and I went home, that was how it worked.

Mrs May had surprisingly good taste that was for sure. Antique velvet sofas with intricately carved mahogany accents dominated the centre of the small living room along with a large mahogany buffet with glass doors and a bright silver lock against the wall. On another wall was a large window overlooking the front of the house, another held a small TV and cabinet and the other a beautiful fireplace with a mantle crammed with pictures.

I spotted a black and white picture of Mrs May when she was younger. She hadn't changed much. Not that much, anyway. But she was beautiful and radiant in her wedding dress as she stood beside a handsome man that looked a lot like Mitch. Even across the room I could see the sparkle in her eyes, the mischief and stories she was accumulating. I loved her stories, her stories of Russia, her journey to Australia, of dancing at fancy parties and falling in love. There were no more stories of lovely gowns and glamorous parties after her husband was gone. She'd said the stories after that would only matter to her. But they all mattered to me.

I followed this lawyer person to the back of the house and to a small kitchen and a shiny mahogany dining table. 'Tea?' he offered.

'No, thank you. Where is Mrs May?'

He sat in the chair opposite me, shadows dancing across his face as he firmly clasped his hands together in front of him, reminding me of my school principal preparing for a reprimand. 'I'm afraid I have some terrible news,' he started. My heart skipped a beat. 'Mrs May has passed away. She's been very sick but thankfully she died peacefully in her sleep.' He tried a comforting smile but there was too much sadness in his eyes.

'When?' I asked softly, my heart sinking like a rock, more grateful than ever I was perfectly medicated.

'Yesterday morning.'

I nodded as though somehow it made sense. But it didn't. I'd waved to her Saturday when Mum and I had walked past. I'd had tea with her Thursday and she'd been just fine, the same as always, she'd never mentioned anything about being sick. She'd taught me *spasibo*. We'd had tea. She'd talked of her husband and how he took her breath away when he smiled, how she wanted that for me. She said love would fix everything. I'd have no need for psychiatrists or room for sadness when I found someone to fill my heart with joy and purpose.

'Are you okay, Miss Donovan?'

I nodded. 'Ainsley, please,' I offered as though what this man called me made any difference to anything. My friend was dead.

Gone. She'd died all alone when I was just around the corner in my bed. My friend wasn't coming back. No more Russian lessons. No more laughing in the afternoon sun. No one to play hooky from my daily walks with. No more wisdom and kindness shared.

A great chasm opened in my heart and I felt myself falling in. 'Have you contacted her son?' I asked, thinking of all the things that needed doing.

'Yes, all the arrangements have been taken care of. The body is on its way to Melbourne now.'

'Melbourne?' I asked, surprised.

'Yes, she wanted to be buried there with her family, they are all there and her son is there.'

So I didn't even get to say goodbye at her funeral. Nothing. It was over. Just like that. I got up to leave. I didn't know what else to do. There was nothing more to say.

'Ainsley,' the lawyer called as I turned to walk away. 'There's something more we need to discuss.'

What? What more could there be to discuss? My friend was gone. She was going to be buried somewhere else, somewhere too far away for me to say goodbye. There was nothing else.

'Please, sit down,' he asked.

I sat numbly in the chair I'd just vacated. He got up and made me tea anyway and once he'd placed the warm cup in front of me and I'd wrapped my suddenly cold hands around it and taken a couple of sips, he began again.

'Ana had a will. She altered it a few weeks ago to include you.'

'Me?' I asked dumbfounded. 'Why would she have done that?'

'She came to me a few weeks ago and was very clear. She wanted you to have this,' he said handing an envelope to me.

I opened the plain manila envelope, inside was a key attached to a shiny red, heart-shaped ruby like you find in the costume jewellery stores. I took out the piece of paper also inside. It appeared to be a property deed with an address in the city. 'What is this?' I asked, not comprehending any of it.

'Ana had a property in the city. It was something her son had never known about and she was originally leaving it to the City Council, but then she met you. She wanted very much for you to have it. That's all I know, I'm afraid.'

'Well isn't that strange,' I said quietly, almost to myself.

'There was always great purpose to the things Ana did. If she wanted you to have this, then it was for a very good reason,' he said, smiling warmly and meaning it this time. Clearly he, too, had fond memories of Mrs May.

'How long had you known her?' I asked out of curiosity.

'Most of my life. My father had been her lawyer and friend for a very long time until he retired and then I took over the practice. My father is rather distraught over her passing.'

I smiled and covered his hand with mine for a moment of shared sympathy.

'Well, that is all we need to cover now. A moving company is coming to pack up her things and take them back to Melbourne. There are some very sentimental things her son would like to reclaim before donating the rest to charity. You're free to go now. I've taken care of the legalities. There'll be no capital gains because the property was purchased before 1985, so it is now yours to do with as you wish.' He stood, signifying the end of our conversation, perhaps wanting to return to his distraught father or not liking someone seeing his moment of weakness. He was a nice looking man in his late twenties or early thirties, a strong jaw, clearly worked out, had a wedding ring on his left hand and his face now returned to its polite but stern, perhaps his professional façade.

I nodded, stood, shook his hand and thanked him for his time. At the front door I took one last look at the verandah where Mrs May and I had shared so much in the short time we'd been friends and then left, not looking back, already planning an alternate route to the shops so I wouldn't have to see the house being emptied, sold and new people moving in as though Mrs May had never existed at all.

# Chapter 8

'I don't like that Ana May is leaving you things in her will. I didn't think you were that friendly. I thought it was just a one off the other day,' Mum probed. I couldn't tell if it was a dislike she had for Mrs May or if she was insulted that some other person could have thought highly enough of me to bequeath me anything, particularly anything of value.

I tried telling Mum how I'd met Mrs May and how kind she'd been but there was only so much information I could give without incriminating myself. It wouldn't do anyone any good to know I'd been skipping out on my shrink prescribed walks to drink tea and share stories with an old lady no one knew.

'Well, I suppose it's done, isn't it,' my mother said, taking the basket of washing from the dining table into the living room to fold.

She clearly didn't understand or approve of my friendship with Mrs May although I couldn't figure out why. It made no sense. Was it because I was sharing things with another 'grown up' and not my mother, who wasn't interested in the sharing anyway? Did she feel threatened because of it? Inadequate perhaps because she knew she could never have given me the shoulder of support I'd gotten from Mrs May? Whatever her reasons, they were unjustifiable and silly and I chose to ignore them. Between Mrs May's wisdom, the happy pills and the shrink visits, I was getting good at not taking on other people's crap and rolling with the punches. Whatever Mum's problem with Mrs May was, it was her problem, not mine.

'How much is it going to cost?' was my father's only question. When I'd told him nothing, he nodded and turned back to the television.

'It's going to cost her nothing,' Mum said, coming back into the room. 'Because she's going to sell it. Right, Ainsley?'

'Well I don't know, Mum, I'd like to see what it is first.'

'It'll be trouble, that's what it'll be. You're better off getting rid of it and being done with it all.'

'Why? What's the harm in seeing it?'

'I just don't trust anything to do with that woman?'

'Why?' I asked, stunned.

'I don't know,' she said exasperated. 'I just don't.'

'You don't even know her.'

'I taught her son. She came to parent interviews. I know enough.'

'You can't know a person through parent teacher interviews,' I proclaimed.

'I can't explain it Ainsley, there was just something that always felt off with that woman.'

'I think you're off,' I said. 'Off your rocker. She's just a sweet old lady who was nice to me,' I said defending Mrs May and stomping up the stairs to my room where I could cry into my pillow.

Mum wasn't making any sense. I don't think she meant to be ambivalent or jealous or even unsupportive, neither of them did. Mrs May had left me this property in the city and I was curious. What was it?

I cried most of the night. I blamed an unfair universe for taking my only friend. What more did it want from me? I had nothing left to give. Surely it would be finished tormenting me soon? Or perhaps it was angry I'd survived its last attempt to destroy me? Who knew but as I sobbed into my pillow, I was determined to not let it win or the last months, the recovery, my friendship with Mrs May, it would have all been for nothing. I'd worked far too hard to get better, shed too many tears on Dr Bailey's sofa to let that happen.

When the tears dried up, I was trying to figure out what Mrs May was doing leaving me things in her will. It's not like she left me her favourite string of pearls as a thoughtful gesture either. It was a property, a freehold property in the city. It had to be worth way too much for her to be giving it to me. I'd lain awake trying to picture the street it was on. I knew the street but I didn't remember an empty building or anything. It was a street of businesses, boring corporate places jumbled inside the buildings, some new and shiny, some old and rustic. None of it made any sense. Mum possibly had a point to be dubious about it all but I'd never tell her that.

Eventually morning dawned. All I wanted to do was lie in bed and never get out. I'd only had snippets of sleep and shed too many tears for my lost friend and I saw no reason to get up. Surely I could have just one day? But as my parents stomped around outside my door in their not so veiled way to make sure I was awake, I knew that'd never be possible. If I wasn't downstairs, showered, dressed and my muesli eaten before it was time for them to go to work, Mum would be calling in sick and staying home for the day and no doubt shipping me off to Dr Bailey for a bonus session and I wasn't in the mood for that. I wanted to sneak out and see what Mrs May had done, what she'd left me and figure out why me and not her son. It just made no sense. But I had to find out. She'd want me to find out.

I waited, watched a little of Studio 10 on the telly just to make sure Mum wasn't coming back. I left Mum a note in case she popped home on her lunch break or something then remembered some of my teenage escape tricks, jumped the side fence by Mrs Parker's, crept behind some bushes until I hit a back street and went the long way to the bus stop, catching the next bus that came heading into the city.

Having spent so much time in the city, I knew it well. The address was on a street with a bunch of office buildings I'd passed in a daily haze many times so I doubted it was a house or an apartment. Although who knew what was squeezed in amongst the old and new buildings anymore.

I found the address on the deed and stood before it as people bustled around me, coming and going, moving around me, staring straight ahead as though I were invisible. Two big metal doors stood in front of me and a large boarded up window was to the right covered in graffiti. I'd walked past the building a hundred times over the years and it had always looked the same so it had quickly dropped into the unseen part of the street as did most empty, unused buildings scattered here and there amongst the others.

I wondered why it was empty, when Mrs May was only twenty minutes away. Why hadn't she rented out the space? It could have been a nice income for her seeing she had owned the building outright. Not to mention, a beautifully crafted building like this and this old would be worth a fortune. She could have sold it and lived a lot better than she did. Gone to visit Mitch and his family more often. Her keeping it and leaving it to weather unattended and unloved made no sense.

I stepped up to the metal doors and inserted the oversized key into the big lock feeling like Alice in Wonderland, suddenly too small for my surroundings. The lock clicked, I turned the handle and tried pushing the door open but it was stuck.

I pushed against the door with all the strength I had but it didn't budge. It wouldn't move. I was about to give up, sit on the step and hang my head in my hands in defeat when someone called up to me.

'You can't break into doors like that, they're made of steel,' he said smugly.

I turned to the suit who was watching me with a look of clear self-satisfaction at having caught a would be robber. 'I'm not breaking in asshole, I have a key,' I said, my patience wearing thin, waving the key in the air as proof.

He came up the few steps to stand beside me, looking at me with squinty eyes. 'I've never seen any sign of life here,' he said, tilting his head back and gazing up at the windows above. 'Looks like it's been shut up for more than a few years.'

I shrugged, noticing how bright and green his eyes were when he opened them and stopped squinting at me like I really was a robber of beautiful old buildings.

'So it's yours? Did you buy it?' he asked dubiously. Rightly so probably. It was a pretty nice looking old building and I didn't look as though I'd own such a place in my Kmart tracksuit pants and purple V-neck cotton t-shirt.

'It was a friend's,' I said. 'She died.'

He nodded. 'Sorry.'

I shrugged.

'You want some help?'

'Sure.'

So I turned the door handle and together we threw ourselves against the door until it squealed open.

'Thanks,' I said.

'No worries, you might want some WD40 for the hinges,' he replied, dusting off his suit jacket and walking away.

I watched him go. I was a little out of touch with people but that was a really nice thing for him to do even though he didn't seem like that nice a person. Maybe I wasn't ready for the world after all? I was here now, though. I'd just have a look and go home, I decided.

The light from the street spilled into the room, illuminating the thick layer of dust coating the floor, the dust bunnies floating freely in the air and the cobwebs taking hold of a counter on the far side of the room. I looked along the wall for a light switch and hoped there was electricity. It was a long shot but when I found it, I flipped the switch anyway, crossing my fingers.

As light flooded the room I wondered who keeps the electricity on in a building they never use?

'Holy cow,' I muttered, stunned at what sat before me. It looked to be an old café or bar of some sort. Incredibly high ceilings reigned above with intricate cornices and big round pendants hanging from the ceiling with deep raspberry shades. Heavy mahogany tables with matching club chairs inlaid with rich raspberry velvet sat gathering dust across the room and velvet benches surrounded mahogany booths lining the edges of the room. If it weren't for the thick layers of dust coating everything in the room, you'd think Mrs May had only left yesterday. I realised the velvet upholstery and the timber framework was the same as what had been in Mrs May's living room. Perhaps she'd furnished her own home with a couple of pieces from this place before locking it up for good?

I went over to the long counter, wiping my finger through the thick layer of dust and the bright, beautiful mahogany timber beneath shone through as though new. Standing behind the counter, I tried to imagine Mrs May standing in the same place and I suddenly felt my friend all around me. Her essence was everywhere as though she'd come with me from the suburbs and I missed her. I missed her so much I ached and wondered what kind of a bastard universe kept throwing these curve balls at me. Why was life so hard? *Because it's life*, I heard Mrs May whisper in my ear. *If it's not hard or emotional, are you really living? It's just the next bend in the river.*

There was a notebook beside an ancient looking cash register. I opened it, to find columns and rows of records, names, numbers and the sort. There was nothing entered later than 1978.

Bookmarking the page with the last entry was a photograph of a baby, a newborn. Turning the photograph over, the back read: Mitchell, June 3 1978. The last entry in the book was June 10 1978. Had it really been closed since 1978? Why? I knew her husband had died just a week after Mitch had been born but that didn't seem a good enough reason to never return.

It didn't make any sense. Couldn't she have used the money as a single mother? Why would she have shut up shop and never returned, never worked another day? How had she fed and clothed and educated Mitch for all those years with no income? Seeing the property didn't answer any questions as I'd hoped, it just raised more and now there was no one to answer them because my unlikely friend had died and left all the unanswered questions and untold stories hanging in the air like the cobwebs that appeared to be holding together the ceiling roses.

Behind the counter was a swinging door that led into a dated and small kitchen. More of a kitchenette really, one row of top and bottom cupboards with a grey laminate bench in between. At the end of the four cupboards was a big hulky white fridge and a two-burner cooktop built into the bench, no oven. Clearly whatever this place had once been, it had not been a restaurant.

Through an archway there was a staircase in the same beautiful timber as the furniture, the stairs were lined with thick raspberry carpet. Mrs May had done nothing by halves in decorating the place, which made her ignoring it for so long even more perplexing. And why did Mitch know nothing about it? Why hadn't she left it to him instead of me, a person she'd only just met?

The staircase led two ways, up and down. I was still a little too fragile for basements so I climbed the stairs to the next floor. I landed on a hallway with timber floors and a plush raspberry runner down the centre. Three doors led off the hallway. I tried the first door which opened onto a lounge room with big arched windows lining a whole wall and the same furniture from downstairs, the same setting in almost the same layout that had been in Mrs May's own living room.

Closing the door I moved onto the next room, a bedroom with a big, perfectly made bed with turned mahogany posts, the raspberry covers appearing faded under their own thick layer of dust. Two doors sat closed on one wall, I assumed containing a wardrobe and perhaps an ensuite.

I opened the last door, which led to a timber kitchen, mahogany cupboards, matching bench top and dining table and a laundry tucked into the corner, all fitted with the finest appliances of the 1970's. I opened the fridge door to find the little light still happily shone and the insides still perfectly cold. On the top shelf was a glass bottle of indescribable hardened sludge that was once possibly milk beside an egg carton I was too afraid to open. The door of the fridge stored rows of vodka bottles, some open, some full. Canisters filled with tea and coffee, hooks with dust filled mugs still lined the bench top. In other words, it looked as though Mrs May had literally walked out one day and never returned. No one had covered the furniture or emptied the fridge, just left. However, I'd seen no sign Mitch had ever been there, no cot, no toys, nothing.

I went back into the bedroom, curious to see what else had been left behind and opened the wardrobe to find it still full of clothes, not just of Mrs May's clothes but men's clothes too, presumably her husband's. The ensuite bathroom had a shrivelled and cracked, half used bar of soap on the edge of the tub, half empty bottles of shampoo and conditioner, towels still hanging from the rails, a toothbrush and toothpaste still sitting on the sink.

I didn't know what to make of any of it. It made no sense. I sat on the edge of the bed, plumes of dust exploding into the air with the movement. What happened here? I asked the empty room. I opened the bedside drawers, feeling as though I was violating Mrs May's privacy by rummaging through her personal things, but I had to. I had to find out what happened here, the answers had to be somewhere. Inside the drawer was a bible and a large, rectangular gold box.

I put the box on my lap and apprehensively opened it. Inside was a collection of the most beautiful jewels I'd ever seen, glittery and shiny, gems as big as grapes, brooches, necklaces, rubies, diamonds and sapphires. I closed the lid quickly and loudly, almost catching my finger. I couldn't possibly have seen what I'd just seen. I snuck another look. 'Shit!' I had to speak to the lawyer. I had to tell him of what I'd found. It was too much. It had to be a mistake. What if they were real? They looked too real. They looked nothing like the fake jewellery I saw at Diva. If they were real, they'd be worth millions. I'd have to return them. I'm sure Mitch would like to have his mother's things. They were rightfully his.

There was a majestic old black phone on the bedside table, the enormous handset connected to the base with a long spiralling cord. I took the lawyer's business card from the manila envelope in my bag and once I heard the dial tone through the handset.

I inserted my finger into the holes on the base and dialled the numbers on the card.

His cheery secretary answered and promptly put me on hold for an eternity. When he eventually came to the phone he sounded unsure but I went ahead anyway.

'I'm not sure this was all meant for me. There are things here I'm sure Mitch would like returned,' I stumbled, not really sure how to explain what I'd found, even to myself.

'No. Ana was very specific that the property and its contents were to go wholly and solely to you Miss Donovan. The property and its contents, whatever they may be, were of no interest to Mitch, Ana was very clear. He knew nothing of the property or what it was for. In fact, neither my father nor I know anything of the property other than what I've seen from the street. So I assure you, whatever you have found was meant entirely for you.'

I nodded as though he could see me. 'Thank you,' I stammered before hanging up, stunned, still sure it was all a mistake. It had to be.

'Oh Mrs May, what have you done?' I asked the empty room.

As I was getting up from the bed, I noticed a handbag still sitting on the floor beside the bed where Mrs May must have left it, as though she'd just popped downstairs. Inside was a handkerchief, a compact mirror, a near new red lipstick, a small perfume atomiser and a leather wallet. Inside the wallet was a photograph of a man in old-fashioned bathers, more like tight short shorts, at the beach. Her husband I guessed. Some business cards, one for the lawyer with a now invalid phone number, one for an accountant and one for a cheese maker. I opened the fold and there, untouched and forgotten for the decades it had sat in this forgotten handbag in this forgotten old dusty building was a wad of notes as thick as a deck of cards. My heart simultaneously froze and pounded, none of it made any sense at all.

I went to the closet, finding and scouring other handbags and coat pockets, finding more notes than I could hold. At the back of the closet, behind rows and rows of dusty shoes was a row of shoeboxes. Inside the first were more bundles of notes held together with shiny gold clips, some photos of a much younger Mrs May laughing up at the same handsome man from the wallet, his eyes shining back at her. There was a passport in the name of Anastasia Stezhensky and another for Anastasia Mayberry, the last in the name of Ruth Chandler, all different, all with her lovely face smiling up at me.

I was becoming more confused by the minute. Who was Mrs May? Jewels so beautiful but nothing like I'd ever seen her wear. All I'd ever seen her wear was her plain gold wedding ring, a pair of diamond earrings so small you could hardly see the diamonds, a small gold love heart locket and the red trinket on the long chain she kept tucked inside her shirt. She'd told me the time I'd admired it, that Mitchell had picked it out for her from a school fete when he was small. That was all. And all the money? So much money. She lived fine enough, I supposed but not that well and why had she not taken any of it with her?

I didn't even know if the old notes were still of any value. I gathered up as many as I could fit in the envelope with the deed from the lawyer and left, down the stairs, dragging the front door closed and locking it behind me. I'd had enough unveiling of unanswered secrets for one day, my emotional wellbeing wasn't strong enough yet. The day was already getting away from me so I hurried up the street to the bank to see if the notes were still worth anything, my handbag clutched tight to my body.

As I walked, my heart ached for my friend, for her secrets and I wondered why she'd left them to me. What did she want me to do with them? With the money? I just wished we could have some tea and she could tell me.

# Chapter 9

I walked out of the bank with the money situation sorted. The teller deposited most of it into my account and returned the rest in smaller, newer notes.

'There's plenty more,' I'd warned her. 'Crafty old Nanna must have forgotten which boxes she'd put it all in,' I said, telling a little fib but going by the teller's eyes bugging out of her head at all those old notes, I figured I couldn't exactly say I'd inherited this strange old building with handbags full of money and forty year old vodka in the fridge.

Clasping my tote bag close to my body even though it no longer contained all that money, I stopped to pick up a large takeaway coffee from a vending cart and a finger bun that would have to substitute as lunch before catching a bus home. The man in front of me turned and it was the suit that had helped me get the door open.

'You?' he asked.

'Yes, me,' I replied, embarrassed at unexpectedly being recognised while I was clasping my handbag to my chest like a crazy bag lady.

He didn't seem to notice though. 'How did you go in the old building?' he asked.

'Fine,' I said as the vendor gave old nosy parker his coffee.

'Well,' he stammered, 'Nice to see you again,' he added awkwardly and he was gone.

As he walked away, I was relieved. I was out of practice, not that I was ever any good at random conversations on the street and two in one day was pushing my limits. I took my coffee and headed home before anything else jumped on the too hard to deal with pile. I'd had more than enough of that for one day.

I waved to Mrs Thompson as I saw her peeking her head through the curtains as I walked up the front drive, thinking I'd managed to sneak back in without anyone really noticing, until Mum opened the front door.

'How did you know?' I asked.

'You didn't leave after Ellen for your walk. Kelly called me at school. Ainsley, really,' she chastised. 'Haven't you caused enough trouble?'

'Sorry, Mum. But I left you a note just in case. I knew you'd never let me go see what this property Mrs May left me was all about. I didn't mean to worry you. I made sure I was back before school finished for the day.'

'Well I didn't know there was a note until I got here, did I? There are processes and procedures in place for your own safety. When Mrs Thompson called, I was terrified of what I was going to find when I got here. I'd almost had a heart attack by the time

I saw your note. Don't do it again,' she said, her voice laced thick with fear as she walked down the hall into the kitchen.

'I'm really sorry, Mum,' I called. 'I'll sort out my phone tomorrow, I promise.

I left her to stew. She'd settle in a bit when she got over the shock, and I went upstairs to stash Mrs May's money. When I came back down there was a cup of tea on the kitchen table for me and Mum was sitting sipping her own, eating a biscuit.

'I'm really sorry, Mum,' I told her, feeling guilty, realising what must have gone through her head.

She nodded. 'So what was it?' she asked like a jealous girl-friend, not really wanting to know the answer.

'It was some sort of café, fully furnished, as was the apartment upstairs, all covered in dust, that's all I know,' I said, not wanting to tell her of the jewels or the money. I needed to figure those out for myself first because something deep in my tummy told me I had to.

She raised her eyebrows, her lips pursed. 'Well then, isn't she full of surprises?' is all she said as she got up and started unload-ing the dishwasher.

I had no intention of sharing anything more with Mum. She was clearly going to be difficult about the whole thing so it would be better to fully understand what was going on before we discussed it any further.

I shared it with Dr Bailey though.

As I told him of Mrs May's passing and the building she left me, he nodded his head, his big fuzzy white hair moving in rhythm.

'How do you feel about losing your friend?' he asked as he pushed his black glasses further up his nose.

'I'm sad, Dr Bailey. I'm not going to lie, I'm really sad. She was a lovely lady and she was kind to me. She was funny and wise. Although she thought these sessions were all hogwash,' I laughed, remembering. 'She said all I needed was a good man poking around not a shrink,' I smiled.

Dr Bailey smiled too. 'You'll miss her.'

'I will. But I'm okay. Sad, but okay.'

'It's okay to be sad.'

'She left me a property. A building in the city. It's the strangest thing. This café at the bottom, an apartment at the top. Mum's horrified, wants me to sell it immediately but I don't know. What do you think?'

He shrugged in that shrink way of not wanting to really say what he thinks so that I'd talk more. But I really wanted to know what he thought.

'I could live there. I could make it a business. Am I ready?'

'Do you feel ready?'

I scowled at him.

He chuckled. 'Ainsley, I think you're ready. You're feeling good, the talks are working. You have to go back into the real world sometime and it sounds like this friend left you quite a gift she knew you needed.'

'I think she did,' I smiled.

'If you need any extra appointments, if your sadness moves into something else, I want you to call me immediately, okay? But otherwise, I think this is a good thing.'

'Can you tell my mother that,' I laughed as I gathered my things.

'Your mother is just worried about you, she'll come around. Just be patient. You've been dealing with all this a long time before that night, your mum is still catching up.'

I nodded because he made sense. He always made sense.

Thanks to Dr Bailey's endorsement, Mum and I came to an understanding. She would let me go to the café so I could look around a bit more, clean it up, sort it out but I had to be back before school finished and I had to leave the address on the dining table. I picked up a prepaid SIM card for my phone that I found in the bottom of my dufflebag so I also had to send her an SMS every two hours.

With all my permissions in place, I bussed it back into the city with what was left of my bagful of money, picked up a coffee from the vending cart and a coffee scroll thing, thankfully without a run in with the nosy suit, I wasn't up for any awkward conversations, and went to Mrs May's place to see what I could make of it. I'd have to start calling it something else, but it might take some time to figure out what. I had to figure out what to do with it first.

Inside I went on the search for cleaning supplies. There was nothing in the cupboard in the small kitchen and only some old spray and wipe concoction with a ratty old cloth under the front counter. I'd avoided it the day before but now I had no choice, I had to go down the stairs into the basement.

There was a light switch at the top of the stairs, one of those old fashioned ones on the long strings. I pulled it and the light flooded on. I wondered why Mrs May had kept paying the electricity and phone bills if she hadn't stepped inside since 1978. But I thanked her anyway as I went down the stairs.

The basement wasn't so scary, it was large, well lit and really just a storeroom. Piles of wooden crates took up at least a third of the floor space to the right. The other side of the basement was full of shelving with dust-covered supplies, glasses, crockery, fancy teacups and beautiful tea pots. There was a giant powder blue upright vacuum, a sad looking mop and bucket.

I hauled the vac up the stairs, found a power point, dusted it off and plugged it in, surprised and grateful when the old machine sputtered a little then roared to life. I went about sucking up the cobwebs and as much of the dust and who knows what else, as I could before heading up the stairs to the next floor and doing much of the same. It made a lot of noise though so I added a new vac to my mental list of things to buy.

Upstairs I stripped the bed and loaded the linen into the washing machine with washing powder that had probably lost all its strength but it was all I had so I used it, praying everything worked and the kitchen wasn't about to be flooded by the giant machine with its ageing pipes and tubes.

I called Mum when school finished, I was on a roll and I just wanted to finish. After promising her everything was okay, she conceded as long as I was home for dinner and continued to SMS her. Back downstairs I got a fresh bottle of what looked like spray and wipe and some new cloths and went about cleaning every surface I could find. Then I hauled up the crusty mop that took quite some working to loosen and filled a bucket with hot soapy water and mopped the floors.

I still didn't know what I was going to do with the place but as the shadows crept across the shiny timber floors and the foot traffic outside increased with nine to fivers heading home, the place shone and sparkled like new. I couldn't believe it. I'd never cleaned so much in all my life. I left the bedding draped over freshly cleaned dining chairs and shower rails and headed home. Tomorrow I'd return to clean all the crockery and teacups.

Mum was much happier when I returned home. Shaun was sitting at the table drinking coffee while she fussed around preparing dinner. He always cheered her up and usually it'd annoy me that he could do that and I couldn't, that she liked him so much more than me, even though he always cheered me up too but today I was grateful.

'I saw Dr Bailey today,' Mum said, without turning around.

I nodded, 'Uh-huh,' I replied. I wasn't surprised. Dr Bailey had already told me he had once raised a family in our area. Mum had taught his boys for a couple of years before they'd moved to a fancier suburb but now she often came across one of his grandchildren in the classes she relieved. Mum taught part-time at the local primary school where she'd taught for all of my life, these days she mostly filled in for sick and annual leave, so she knew just about everyone. I didn't like the idea of her chit chatting with my shrink, though. But surely doctor patient confidentiality prevented him from discussing much of anything about me?

'I asked him what he thought of this inheritance business.'

'What inheritance business?' asked Shaun.

'That old Mrs May from around the corner left your sister a property in the city. A shop or something, I think,' she told him.

He looked at me with raised eyebrows.

'You know old Mrs May around the corner, Mitchell May's mother, sits on her front verandah all day long as though waiting for someone, watching the world go by,' I told him.

'That kooky old lady? You know her?'

'She's not kooky, Shaun. She's just a lonely old lady. Well, she was before she died the other day.'

'Well why is she leaving you things in her will?'

'I don't know. We were friends. I'd stop by sometimes on my walks. We had tea. We chatted. She was nice.'

'Well it's still strange she left you a building and didn't leave it to her son.'

'I know. I don't understand it either. But her lawyer insists that's the way she wanted it.'

'Hmmm,' he nodded as though processing it all. 'So what sort of property is it?'

'It looks like it used to be some sort of a café. All the furniture's still there and everything. There's a fully furnished residence upstairs too. It's really strange. It looks like she only left yesterday, except for the thick coating of dust that was on everything. I don't really know what to make of it all.'

'What are you going to do with it?'

'I don't know yet. What do you think I should do with it?'

'Well you could run it as a café and live there. It's not like you have a job or a place to live right now.'

'She has a place to live right here and won't that kind of thing be expensive to get started?' asked my mother warily but showing a mild spark of interest now Shaun was interested.

'Maybe,' I said, not sure I should tell them about the money. 'Maybe, I'll look into it.'

I lay on my bed that night thinking, wondering, could I? Could I really make something of Mrs May's place? Is that what she would have wanted? Is that why she gave it to me? I bet she did, that crafty old lady. She'd been saying for the last couple of weeks that life was about to take a turn. *Always keep an open mind,*' she'd been saying. Had she known she was going to die so soon? She probably knew that too. She must have had some idea if she was sick. The lawyer hadn't said what was wrong with her but even though he was sad she'd died, he didn't seem too surprised and she was the wisest person I'd ever met. Nothing ever fazed her, nothing. She was never surprised about what came out of my mouth, never raised her eyebrows like my mother did. She'd just say something wise, often cryptic and pat my hand, so I bet she knew. She'd probably known the date and time. I wouldn't be surprised, I thought, smiling.

But what would I know about running a café? I couldn't cook, not much, anyway, despite how much Food Network I watched. I made half decent spaghetti most of the time and had developed a specialty in cheese toasties. It was about all I could manage after a night of cocktails and what not, not that you could cook much more in that kitchen. Could I really get by serving just coffee and cheese toasties? That would certainly give everyone something to talk about. I fell asleep laughing at my own crazy idea.

I returned to Mrs May's the next day with a stomach full of enthusiasm, hope and another of the coffee scrolls. There was still a lot to do whatever I decided and I wanted to have a proper look at that account book to see what the place had been and see what else I could find stashed away. I'd also have to have a proper look downstairs and really make sense of the place and hope a sensible idea came to me.

I sat in one of the newly cleaned booths with the account book and my coffee, flipping through page after page but nothing made any sense. It was all mumbo jumbo in some sort of code. Mrs May might have just made up her own format or put it in some weird code that only made sense to her. Who knows? Just another of Mrs May's crazy anomalies for the pile.

I was about to head downstairs to see what else I could find when I heard a noise from the back of the building. I went behind the staircase to listen and saw there was a door. I hadn't even noticed it there before buried in the shadows. It opened onto a veranda where there was a clothesline and perhaps space for a car. Well once upon a time there may have been space for a car, before buildings had popped up either side and blocked the driveway in. All that remained was a single laneway on one side of the building. You could possibly fit a scooter through the remaining laneway but nothing more. I didn't have a car anyway so it didn't matter.

On the corner of the building was the electricity meter and a man in uniform was looking in it. 'Hello?' I called to him.

He looked up startled, then after composing himself held up a hand in a wave, 'Hey. Sorry, you startled me. I didn't expect anyone to be here.'

'When was the last time someone was here?' I asked.

'I've never seen anyone.' Which didn't mean much; he was in his early twenties so it didn't surprise me.

'Can I ask whose name is on the account?'

'Oh, I can't say, I'm sorry.'

'No, of course. It's just that I've recently inherited this building and I'm surprised the electricity is even still on.'

He came over and handed me a card. 'This is my supervisor. Maybe he can help you. I just read the meters.'

'Thanks,' I said, meaning it. It was a help. I'd have to sort it all out before long. And then it hit me, the costs would now be mine and I'd have to figure out what to do about the place pretty quickly because I didn't want to go wasting Mrs May's money on such things until I knew what I was going to do with the place.

I said goodbye to the meter reader and went in to phone his supervisor. I begged and pleaded, telling him the story of my inheritance, offering up the name of the lawyer for verification until he eventually conceded, giving me the name and address of the trust on the account. The address sounded familiar but I couldn't figure out why, couldn't quite place it. Assuming it was just because it was a city address I must have been in the vicinity of at some time, I went back downstairs.

I sat on the bench in the little kitchen, looking around, trying to imagine what Mrs May might have used the place for. In the big fridge, there were umpteen bottles of vodka, some open, some brand new just like upstairs. Not much else, just a few containers with unidentifiable contents. In the cupboards there was a bread tin with nothing but the remnants of some waxy paper and lots of green and black dust that I guessed was once bread. I put the tin, paper and all the dust into a rubbish bag I found in one of the cupboards careful not to spill it everywhere along with the containers of sludge and took it out the back door to a wheelie bin I'd seen out there earlier.

There were a few tea pots in the kitchen, some containers

with what I guessed was black tea and a coffee percolator with a hardened layer of black that must have once been coffee remnants and I put them in the sink filled with hot water, hoping that would be enough to loosen what was in the bottom. It really did look as though someone walked out one day, locked the doors and just forgot to come back.

There was no other clue to what went on there. I turned, dumbfounded, looking around the room as though an answer would materialise out of nowhere. Then I spotted it, a business card stuck on the fridge for a cheese maker, the same as what had been in Mrs May's old purse. Then it hit me, the address for the bills. I'd seen it on the business card for the accountant. I raced back up the stairs, bounding two at a time and hurrying down the hall to the handbag. The address on the card was in the city and not far but it had an old phone number so I thought why not take a chance and just go there? I locked up, picked up another coffee from the vending cart, the guy now offering a friendly nod of recognition. I passed the nosy suit at the end of the laneway, groaned at the prospect of another awkward exchange, forced a smile and hurried on in search of this mystery accountant.

# Chapter 10

The accountant's address was in the centre of the city, an easy to find building between a sad looking snack bar and a tailor shop. I stood inside the door, an eerie feeling washing over me and I stood a minute wondering if I should even let the door close or run for the hills. Did I really need answers?

This building was grey, on the outside and even greyer inside. The tiles on the floor were dirty and the foyer was dark, a globe broken in one corner, one of those old metal circular bins with the ashtray on top even though smoking in buildings was outlawed over a decade ago sat empty beside the lift. Against my better judgement, I let the door close, pressed the call button for the lift and waited. I'd come this far, not knowing was worse than the risk.

I stepped out of the lift onto a cleaner, brightly lit hallway carpeted in high grade commercial carpet, but at least it was clean, a big step compared to downstairs. The first door I passed was for a dentist. I caught the eye of a sad receptionist and hurried on to the next door which had the words Miles Addersly, Accountant, in plain lettering on the window.

Inside the reception area was a melamine reception desk with a vase of fake flowers and no receptionist. There was a bell beside the vase so I rang it. Seconds felt like minutes as I waited in the quiet room. I was about to give up and leave when an old man with hair coming out of his ears and nose waddled out of the hallway. He forced a smile and I got the impression Miles Addersly, Accountant, didn't get many visitors. 'Hello,' I said as politely as I ever had.

'Can I help you?' he asked, his voice a little squeaky as though from lack of use.

'I'm not actually sure,' I began. 'I found your card amongst the things of a friend, Ana May and I was hoping you could answer some questions.'

'Ana May?' he asked as though mulling the name over in his head, before something clicked in his head. 'Ah, you don't mean Anastasia Mayberry, do you?'

'I'm sorry, I only know her as Ana May.' I had a light bulb moment then, Anastasia Mayberry was one of the names on one of the passports. 'But yes, I think I have seen the name Anastasia Mayberry in her things,' I told him. Who was this lady with her mystery names and jewels and old money stashed away in shoe-boxes and old coat pockets?

'Well then, you'd better come on through,' said Miles Addersly before walking ahead without checking I was following.

I hurried along behind him and sat in the chair he waved at before he sat in his own oversized leather chair, a desk piled high and wide with papers between us.

'So Stasie's gone, huh?'

'Stasie?' I asked more confused by the minute. 'I'm sorry, I know her as Mrs May.'

He nodded kindly. 'How did it happen?'

'In her sleep I'm told, but she was sick. No one told me with what.'

'Right. And how do you fit into the puzzle, a daughter or granddaughter perhaps?'

I smiled thinking how nice it would have been to be either of those things. 'No, I'm a friend. Actually, I inherited a property she had in the city.'

'Oh yes, the old bank building.'

'It was a bank?'

'Oh, a lifetime ago now. It's been Stasie and Henry's for as long as I can remember.'

It was silent for a moment so I asked the questions I had come for. 'Mr Addersly, do you know who has been paying the electricity and phone bills on the property? Council rates and the sort?'

'Well, I have,' he said, quite matter-of-factly. 'Well, the trust has been. The bills come to me and I write the cheques. I guess that will end now. I suppose I'll have to pay out the remainder of the trust to her children. In fact, I'm sure I did see an envelope from that lawyer of hers here somewhere,' he said as he started scurrying through piles of unopened mail.

'Ah, here it is,' he said proudly as he ripped open the envelope. 'Yes, yes, the remainder of the money is to go by bank cheque to a Mitchell May in Melbourne. Yes. Although, all the quarterlies are due to arrive about now. I'm sure I can hold off paying out the trust until I've paid those,' he winked. 'But then I'm afraid you'll be on your own. Will you be okay?'

'Thank you, I really appreciate it. Yes, I'll be fine, I'm sure. I just need to figure out what to do with the place. You don't happen to know what it used to be when Mrs May was running it do you?'

'Oh, well, um, I think the needs of today's people might be different to those of Stasie's clientele.'

'What is that supposed to mean?'

'Well, to be honest I was never sure exactly what went on in there, some of this, some of that but I had my suspicions. They ate a lot of cheese, I know that, and meat and drank a lot of vodka, had lots of fancy parties. Most of the clients appeared to be friends of theirs, although some a little unsavoury for my liking. But that's about all I can tell you for sure, anything more would be hearsay and I'd never do that to Stasie. I only went there a few times to pick up the books and it always looked like they were in the midst of a party but I just assumed I had bad timing.'

'Do you still have them?'

'The books? Oh no, they're long gone, I'm sorry. I was under strict instructions that if I hadn't heard from Stasie or Henry for three weeks without them letting me know, all the accounting records I had were to be destroyed but the bills were to be paid out of the trust they set up especially. Henry wasn't always around so not hearing from him wasn't a big surprise but until June of '78, I'd heard from Stasie every single week. Without fail she'd pop by, her shoes clicking on the floor in the hallway, two coffees in hand and then one week she didn't come by and she didn't telephone.

'I thought perhaps she'd gone to have the baby but the weeks turned into months and I had no way to contact her other than the café. I went by a few more times hoping Stasie had returned but it was always the same, always locked up and after the window was broken one New Year's eve, it was boarded up and I stopped going. I never heard from Stasie or Henry again.

'I knew someday someone would come. I just hoped it was before I died. They were good people. A little flamboyant, a little eccentric, probably all that money they seemed to make in that café come bar or whatever it was. But they were good people, always happy and so in love you couldn't help but smile. It is sad that they're gone but I suppose it happens to us all eventually, doesn't it?'

I smiled. He wasn't much younger than Mrs May so it was probably a subject on his mind.

I thanked Miles Addersly for his time.  He offered his services should I need any advice and I was back down on the street in the sunshine, grateful the trust would take care of the quarterlies that were about to come due. That gave me three months to figure out what to do with the café and Mrs May's money.

I walked down to the part of town where I used to live, the ghosts of a past life swirling around me. I bought another coffee then walked for a while before sitting in my favourite park with the pond with the rowboats and the grassy hills to try and figure out what to do about Mrs May's. Shaun had a point, I needed a place to live and I needed a job. Mrs May had given me both.

Surely I'd be looking a gift horse in the mouth if I gave it all away for money or out of fear?

Could I really do it though? Own my own business?

I went for a walk until I found myself heading into one of the weekday cafes to sit with a pie and a coke, watching people coming and going. They weren't fussy. They were ordering a lot of sandwiches and coffee. They were too busy with their day to be hanging around eating proper meals and I thought maybe cheese toasties could be enough? It'd certainly be something different.

I looked out the big square window, watching the people coming and going from the fancy tea shop across the road. It was doing a roaring trade and I thought of Mrs May's lovely teapots and decided that was it.

After finishing my lunch, I went across the road to work out a deal with the tea shop. I'd serve the fancy tea and use the business card for the cheese maker Mrs May had left behind to make the best ham and cheese toasted sandwiches the city folk had ever tasted. The more I thought about it, the fancier the toasties became in my head. I was excited. For the first time in years I was excited.

Energy and adrenalin surging through my veins, a spring arose in my step. I had a business. My very own business. It was all just sitting there waiting for me. All I needed was to stock the shelves and open the door and I was good to go and Mrs May had left me enough money to make that happen, too. She really was my fairy Godmother. Not only had she saved my sanity on a daily basis with her wise words and friendship but she was continuing to do so when she wasn't even here for me to thank and there was no way I was ever going to be able to repay her. I just hoped she was up there somewhere looking down on me and seeing how appreciative I was. I would make a go of Mrs May's for her. That's how I'd show her how grateful I was and how much of a difference she'd made to me. She'd saved my life. Now I was going to make the most of it.

As I walked back to the café, I started making a check list in my head of all the things I needed. Coffee machine, some training, sandwich presses, call the council about a business license. It was a lot but for the first time in a long time, I didn't feel daunted or overwhelmed. I just wanted to get started.

# Chapter 11

Over the next few weeks, I packed all of Mrs May's and Henry's belongings into boxes and stored them in the basement with the crates, and then I scrubbed every cup, saucer, mug and plate I could find. I bought a laptop with some of Mrs May's money and filled out all the forms for the council, the food safety people and applied for an ABN.

The lady at the tea shop had been incredibly helpful, not only with recommending teas and preparation techniques but she put me in touch with a coffee guy who was due any minute to install some fancy machine that would make an array of frothy and not so frothy delights in no time at all.

Once the machine had been installed, a barista from the coffee company came to give me some lessons as part of the rental deal. Once she was happy with my concoctions, she left me with a few bags of coffee, a box of takeaway cups and an account form to fill out, leaving me alone with the enormous, shiny contraption humming away on the bench.

The cheese maker on the business card I'd found in Mrs May's things no longer existed but I'd spent an afternoon at the Central Markets and found another who gave me some cheese education and I used some of Mrs May's money to order some of their finest cheddar, camembert, brie and monterey jack. I stopped by a stall selling fancy breads and the smallgoods shop for fine shaved ham then all I'd needed was to pick up an urn for the tea and a few sandwich presses from Harris Scarfes and I'd be all set. The coffee machine was the last piece of the puzzle.

I'd had a heart to heart with Mum and Dad a couple of days before, reminding them Dr Bailey was supporting the move and the cafe and that seemed to calm them somewhat but regardless of his support, they still didn't want me to move into Mrs May's but I did with a promise to message continuously. It was time I believed in myself and stood on my own two feet again.

I caught a bus with a bag containing the few things I owned, the remnants of clothes salvaged from my apartment that might actually fit me again soon and the clothes Mum had bought me from Kmart, a couple of battered books I'd found in my room, some basic toiletries and Vivi's tomato plant. At Mrs May's, I loaded the clothes into the wardrobe that had once contained Mrs May's and Henry's personal affects, my toiletries into the ensuite and carefully placed Vivi's tomato plant by one of the big arched windows in the lounge room that overlooked the bustling street below and let in loads of beautiful sunlight. Then I went and bought a powder blue scooter to park out the back. It turned out carrying supplies around the city was hard on the arms and places like the markets weren't really within walking distance. Well they wouldn't be once I was open for business.

I wouldn't have time to spend hours walking around the city then. Hopefully, anyway.

I invited my family over for Sunday lunch. I thought if I could show off the place, perhaps I could garner a little more support or at the very least leave them happy in the fact I was okay and put their minds to rest. I wasn't much of a cook but I could manage spaghetti bolognese in the stockpot I'd found under the sink upstairs.

Mum and Dad came in, their faces harried as though they'd crossed a desert in a buggy instead of the suburbs into the city. They looked around with dubious expressions. My eyes followed theirs but all I saw were the beautiful ceiling roses and raspberry light shades, the pristine booths I'd cleaned until they shone and the matching club chairs. I thought I'd done a great job. Surely even Mum couldn't find fault with the look of the place. But still they were silent.

Dad patted my shoulder and I knew he was pleased. Mum still had reservations.

'The timber's lovely, though,' she conceded as Shaun bundled in full of life and energy.

I waited for Shaun to look around, run his hand over the old mahogany and the soft raspberry velvet. He looked up with a big grin and I showed them through the kitchenette before heading upstairs.

'This is fantastic, Ains, it's perfect. I can't believe she left you all of this,' Shaun said as they made themselves comfortable in the small eat in kitchen.

'It makes no sense,' Mum added.

'I know. I don't know why she did it, haven't the foggiest.'

'But she did and I think it's going to be a gold mine,' Shaun assured me.

'I hope so,' I said getting out the pasta bowls I'd bought specially.

Mum and Dad left soon after eating amid wishes I'd come back home, that it was too soon. I assured Mum I was doing great and she didn't need to worry before Dad led her out knowing full well we could go around and around with this argument all night long and get nowhere.

'Shall we get started?' Shaun said, brandishing his tool box after they'd left.

'Please,' I grinned like a fool.

Together we took the board off the front window, the glass beneath had been replaced after that long ago New Year's rock had gone through and was still good as new. Shaun was a bit of an artist, not that he'd ever admit it. He used the window paint I'd picked up from Bunnings to paint Mrs May's Tea & Toast on the front window. I hadn't been able to think up any other names nor did it feel right referring to it as anything else so that is what I went with. I didn't need any prizes for originality, anyway, just enough customers to pay my bills and put food on my table.

The paint was bright pink, almost glowing, and stood out for miles, if passers-by didn't see this sign then they were in need of an optometrist. Shaun even painted a beautiful teacup with steam floating out of it. It was perfect.

'There, done,' he said, taking a step back into the street and admiring his own handiwork with a big grin.

'It looks amazing. I'll never understand how you can paint like that,' I told him.

'Ah,' he said waving the compliment away but clearly enjoying it. 'Well, I must go, I have lessons to plan for tomorrow. Good luck. I'll call you after school,' he said, hugging me goodbye. 'You'll do great though,' he smiled.

As Shaun walked down the street with his hand in the air in a wave, I felt a moment of sadness that he was gone. A compulsion to hold him and squeeze him and never let him go washing over me. But I would be okay. I knew I would be okay. I just had to believe, in myself and Mrs May's wisdom. She wouldn't have given me all this if she didn't believe I could do something with it, make a go of it.

Pushing aside the longing, I went back inside, locked up and that was everything. The place was ready to go. I lay in bed staring at the ceiling, listening to the quiet, not really believing any of it was actually happening. I had a cafe and my own place to live, no rent, a job for life if I was smart and now I just had to hope against hope that someone would come in tomorrow and buy a cup of something.

I'd laid in bed most of the night staring at the ceiling worrying if I was nothing but a deluded fool. If Mrs May was up in the heavens looking down at me and laughing, shaking her head, saying, no, no, no, that's not what I meant. If only she was still here to give her wise advice, I thought over and over. But she wasn't and eventually the darkness above made me sleepy and the next thing I knew I was waking to my alarm. The first of the morning light was touching the sky outside the big arched windows, it was going to be a beautiful day. I took that as a good sign that Mrs May was watching, agreeing, that this was indeed what she'd wanted, that it was the right thing to do.

I showered and not quite ready to head downstairs yet, made a cup of instant coffee in my upstairs kitchen and had a piece of toast with peanut butter, my stomach was way too nauseated to eat anything more. With a little of Mrs May's money I'd bought some new jeans and a supply of black polo shirts from Target. I'd decided this would be my uniform along with an apron with lovely raspberry ruffles I'd found in a stack of aprons in the basement. It wasn't very glamorous and didn't do justice to Mrs May's beautifully decorated cafe but I didn't want to outlay too much money before I'd made anything. I'd been poor for so long, I'd forgotten how to be anything else. I pinned one of her beautiful brooches, one as red as a ruby in the shape of an egg with fine gold filigree detailing holding it in place, like a miniature Faberge egg, to my plain black shirt for luck. I'd decided they couldn't possibly be real jewels. They were just too big. No one left jewels like that just laying around in unused dusty cafés. Money, maybe, most of it had been in shoe boxes and old coat pockets so it was reasonable she'd forgotten but giant rubies were prized treasured possessions. I could have had it checked, just in case, I almost did one day as I passed Grahams in the mall but they were busy and I didn't fancy queuing up for half an hour to have the fancy jeweller behind the counter laugh at my plastic bauble. So I dismissed the idea, it was so far fetched. But the brooch was pretty and I liked the idea of having a little piece of Mrs May with me as I went down the stairs to begin my new day.

Downstairs I switched the coffee machine on, filled the urn behind the counter with water, turned on the three toastie machines and got some pans heating on the stove. I made some caramel to go with apple caramel and banana caramel toasties I'd put on the menu for breakfasts and desserts with the strawberry and Nutella toasties and the strawberry, blueberry and cream cheese toasties. I put some bacon in a pan to cook and crisp for the bacon and egg toasties and sliced tomatoes for the tomato and cheese toasties. I began caramelising onions for the deluxe ham and cheese toasties and the French onion and blue cheese toasties, which I expected to sell more of at lunch time, but just in case, I wanted to be prepared for whatever was on the menu. I had a container of leftover spaghetti bolognese in the fridge ready for the lunch-time toasties. I liked it in a toastie with some melted cheese but did everyone else? I'd soon find out. I made a quick cheese sauce in one of the small pots and added a tin of tuna ready for the tuna mornay toasties, shredded and sliced all my cheeses and poured some icing sugar into a shaker from The Reject Shop and I was done.

Everything seemed to be in place. I made myself a coffee with the fancy machine to make sure once again that I had the hang of it and that was everything. It was time. I'd decided opening at 7.30 was a good chance to attract people on their way to work. It mightn't be any success but what did it matter? It's not like I had to go far to work and if no one came I could sit in a booth and read one of the old books I'd brought with me, perhaps the bent and well-read copy of The Outsiders that had been so far under my bed I'd never have found it if I hadn't been so desperate for a matching sock gone astray. That's what happens when you lived with your mother, all your socks needed to be accounted for.

After taking a deep breath and opening the front door, I stood behind the counter, waiting, a fresh pot of French Earl Grey on the counter ready to go, the urn on the bench behind me was hot and ready for any other tea choices, the jars of tea selections lined across the bench looking colourful and pretty and the coffee machine was begging to froth something.

Three people stuck their heads in the doorway, twisted and turned for a minute then kept walking. Another couple squished their inquisitive noses against the freshly painted window and also kept going. I'd at least attracted some interest. That was a start, right?

At 8.15am my first customer stumbled in, a young professional wearing a suit and tie, a little sweaty, a little frazzled and he ordered the biggest double shot latte I could manage. The lady from the coffee company had given me enough of everything to get started so I went about making the latte while the kid stood on the other side of the counter trying to pull himself together.

'You okay?' I asked as I frothed the milk.

'Yeah, first day and I'm running late, had a bit of a session with the boys last night and there's a mile long queue at all the other coffee places I've passed and I'm not sure I'd have made it through the next 20 minutes without the caffeine.'

I handed him his coffee. He handed me my money and my first sale was completed.

At 9.45am my next customer came in. She was as wrinkled as a prune, had flyaway black hair with splashes of grey and only pointed to the tea she wanted. Russian Caravan, a black tea with orange and spices. She shook her head to the offer of milk or sugar and pointed to a pot, put her money on the counter and went to sit in a booth. She sat in that booth all morning, pointing to a caramel apple toastie as her teapot dwindled. I offered her more tea just before lunch and she nodded, put another note on the table and made herself comfortable.

Lunch brought a few people. They didn't seem to mind the menu consisted only of toasted sandwiches. I sold a variety of toasties, savoury and dessert, that kept me busy, buzzing between the front counter, the back kitchenette and the dining tables but they were coming out beautifully and customers were smiling and groaning, which made me feel good and left me beaming. I took an order for a deluxe toastie from the old lady to go with her pot of tea. I don't know how she wasn't peeing under the table.

I stayed open until 6.15. The afternoon had been quiet. Three girls had come in mid-afternoon to talk business and eat dessert toasties when the lady from the booth sloshed out the door but for the rest of the afternoon I'd sat reading The Outsiders and falling in love with Sodapop all over again. One person popped in for a decaf cappuccino at 5.15 and that was it. I waited until the foot traffic had dissipated to nothing and my stomach grumbled its protests before giving it up for the day, making sure all my supplies were refrigerated, lids were on the tea and the machines were all turned off.

Once I'd closed the doors, making sure they were all locked, I turned off the lights and went upstairs, reheated some bolognese in the microwave I'd bought with some of Mrs May's money and had lugged all the way home, then collapsed on the bed, falling into a deep coma until my alarm buzzed in the morning and I started all over again.

Having had a quiet end to the day before meant everything was spick and span to start the next morning so there was no great hurry to head downstairs. I took my time in the shower, had a coffee, ate some muesli and drank some juice before going downstairs to open up. There were already a few early birds making their way to their dull grey cubicles and poorly air conditioned offices. I used to be one of them and I wondered if they were as unhappy as I was or were they living their dream? Maybe like me they didn't know what their dream was and I hoped someday they'd find it like I did but I hoped they didn't have to lose a friend for it to happen.

A couple of stragglers came in on their way to work for coffee and green teas and the old lady who'd sat in the booth all morning the day before but that was it until lunchtime when apparently word about my toasties had gotten out.

There was too much to do. I didn't have enough hands to make all the toasties, the coffee and the teas on order. The medication was keeping my stress levels pretty even, but I knew somewhere deep down, my insides were ready to explode. I was just about to ring through a customer's payment when someone walked in and shouted.

'Ainsley, you bitch, what do you think you're doing?'

My heart stopped, flying into my throat. I looked up, terrified, to see my old friend, Jo standing in the doorway, her hands fastened to her hips, her face scowling with fury. She stormed up to the counter, her eyes ready to pop out of her head.

'I'm working.' I stumbled, my heart pounding, not really sure what else to say. What was there to say, anyway? I hadn't seen or spoken to Jo since before the night of the big mistake.

'Working? That's it? That's all you've got? You stop taking my calls, you disconnect your phone and you disappear off the face of the earth. I go looking for you at your place and I get some goth chick. I knocked on Jack's door and he tells me you're gone and I have to ring every bloody Donovon in three suburbs to find your parents to see if you're even still alive. Then your mum tells me you're here working at some café and that's all you've got to say? I've been worried bloody sick, Ains.'

'Sorry. I've not been myself. Been a bit unwell,' I told her, handing the customer their change.

'Yeah, so bloody Jack tells me. Crap, are you okay, is everything alright now?'

'Yeah, but can't really talk about it now,' I said waving a surveying arm over the café of people watching us.

'Yeah, Yeah, course,' she says. 'You want a hand?'

'Really? Don't you have to get back to work?'

'Nah, I quit that shitbox. Too much trouble.'

'What?'

'Tell ya later, hey? Where do you want me to start?'

'Can you work the machine?' I asked hopefully pointing at the coffee machine.

'Hell yeah, I can.'

I shook my head. Jo was one of those people who could do anything. She was never afraid of trying or of failing, so something like a giant shiny coffee machine was a piece of cake and she jumped straight in.

Jo pulled an elastic band from around her wrist, tied her long chestnut hair into a pony tail, threw on an apron from the stack on the bench behind us and got to work on the list I was using to keep track of everything. She had the crowd waiting for coffee under control in less than three seconds. She also knew the life story of the first two people in line who had been waiting for ages but were now laughing with each other even though they'd never met. That's how Jo did things. People just loved her.

As I was admiring Jo's courage, I caught a familiar whiff of cologne. I smelt him before I saw him. I looked up and saw the nosy suit guy. I was thinking it was too good to be true to have avoided our awkward exchanges the last few days.

'Hey,' he said, examining the menu, turning it over, but it only had one side and he screwed up his face. 'That's it?' he asked.

'Yep,' I said. 'What can I get you?'

'Well, I don't like toasted sandwiches. I don't like cooked cheese. Can I have it untoasted, maybe with some lettuce?'

'Nope, I only do toasties and there's no lettuce.'

'Well how much different can it be? Make it, just don't toast it.'

'But then I have to cut it and stuff and I don't cut bread.'

'What do you mean you don't cut bread,' he asked as though it was the most ridiculous thing ever.

'What do you mean you don't eat cooked cheese?' I asked, no longer in the mood for his weird shit and buoyed a little by Jo's presence. I could feel the old me, the me from before, before wearing pyjamas to work, before not being able to get out of bed, way before any sign of a blackness and paranoia, before censoring every word I considered saying, the me that people loved, the me that went out for Friday night drinks, the me that dated and holidayed and existed like a regular person, that me slowly slid into position, slowly wiggled about, settling and jumping for joy.

'Fine,' he said. 'With the lot then. With Brie if it's no trouble.'

'No trouble at all,' I smiled and went into the kitchen to make his sandwich.

Who doesn't eat cooked cheese anyway? What a prat, with his fancy suit and his squinty suspicious eyes and his long skinny face. And that deep, velvety voice that suggested he should be something other than the awkward bloke who stuck his nose in other people's business.

I took out Mr Nosy's grilled cheese dumping it on the table, loving that I was the boss and could behave as I pleased. As I turned to walk away, he grabbed my wrist. I whipped around with fire in my eyes.

'Would you have dinner with me?' he asked, his face pleading like a little boy.

I shook my wrist free. 'Really? Do you manhandle everyone you want to have dinner with?' I laughed a little at the absurdity of him, my life, as I walked back behind the counter. I rubbed my wrist and watched him as he hung his head and quietly ate his sandwich until I was distracted by the next customer.

The lady in the booth continued to drink her tea and stare into space, not bothered by the growing noise of the lunch rush. Really, the cafe was only a quarter to half full but that was okay, I don't think I could have coped with much more. I don't know what I was thinking. To make any money I had to be busy, to cater for busy, I needed staff. I couldn't do busy as a one-man band. I watched Jo whipping up lattes and cinos and all sorts of frothy miracles and thought she was my miracle sent from the heavens to save me. I felt blessed and lucky and very grateful.

Awkward Mr Nosy approached the register and stood behind a girl who was paying for coffee. What did he want now? It better be to apologise. He'd paid for his lunch. I just wanted him to leave. I suspected he was harmless. He had the look of a misunderstood little boy in his eye, I suspected I saw a little too much awkward familiarity in him than was probably safe for someone like me but that was beside the point. I was fresh out of the loony bin. There's no room for crazies here. This inn is full.

'I love your brooch,' the girl standing in front of me commented. 'It's Russian, right?' she asked.

I barely heard her, still too distracted by old nosy parker fidgeting behind her. I shrugged, 'I'm not sure. It was a friends.'

She nodded. 'My great grandmother had a set of those eggs back in Russia. I've seen them in photographs. There was a ruby one just like yours, a sapphire, an emerald and a diamond one. They were stolen from her home in Russia in March, 1971. My mother would be interested to know there are more. We always thought they were one of a kind. That they were a gift from the Grand Duke.'

The blonde had caught my attention. I thought of the other, similar eggs resembling this blonde girl's description upstairs in Mrs May's jewellery box and beads of slimy sweat crept across the palms of my hands. I nodded, not liking what this girl's tone was implying and as I tried to discreetly wipe the slime onto my apron and told her, 'Well, I'm sure you're mother wouldn't be the least bit interested in this piece of plastic,' hoping that would be enough to placate her.

'I have experience with jewels, I could tell if it's real or not if I could have a closer look,' she said, reaching out as though to unclip it from my shirt.

I stepped back, offended and shocked. Who was this person trying to rip my brooch from my shirt?

Mr Nosy stepped forward, 'I'm sure she'd know if she was wearing a giant ruby on her chest,' he smirked, standing between the girl and me.

'Of course,' the girl nodded, realising the entire café was watching her. She handed over her money, snatched the coffee Jo placed on the counter in front of her despite the waiting queue, took another squinty look at my brooch and left.

'Thank you.' I said absently to Mr Nosy as Jo came to stand beside me. We both watched the girl with the long blond hair leave then exhaled.

'So, dinner?' he asked hopefully.

'Oh you have to now,' Jo chimed in.

'Fine, fine. But no more of that caveman shit.'

He nodded, smirked, or was it a smile? Who knows, and he left.

# Chapter 12

'So what's going on, Jo?' I asked, sitting on the bench after a final swipe of the dish towel.

'Me? What about you?' she asked, opening the fridge. 'What's with all the vodka?'

'Dunno, it was already here.'

'Huh,' she said as she pulled out an unopened bottle and hunted for glasses. 'So some old lady left you all of this, fully furnished, fancy Russian brooches and a fridge full of vodka?'

'Yep, something like that.'

'Before or after you disappeared off the planet.'

'After,' I smiled sheepishly. 'Sorry about all that, my brain wasn't working right.'

'It's done now. As long as you're better.'

'Yep. Medicated, but better.'

'Medicated is just fine. But we'll get to the rest, don't you worry about that,' she smirked.

'Have you seen Tash?'

'Nope. You were right to disappear from her. Narcissistic

bitch. I called her to see if she'd heard from you, you'd basically been missing for weeks and all she could do was make it about her, prattle on about this and that, hubby did this, kids did that, went here, went there, car needed fixing, all crap that no one cares about, not when one of your supposed best friends has gone missing and isn't taking anyone's calls. Seriously. So I haven't spoken to the silly cow since and she hasn't called. Who needs people like that, hey?' she asked as she flung the shot of vodka into her mouth.

I laughed and followed suit, the vodka burning all the way down but feeling good. Too good. 'Why don't you come upstairs, I have pasta,' I offered.

'I'll never turn down your pasta,' she laughed, hopping off the bench to follow me upstairs, the vodka bottle tucked under her arm.

'You don't need to bring that,' I smiled. 'There's more up here.'

'You're kidding?' she laughed.

Jo was one of those people that made your insides light up with happiness. She brought light and cheer into the world. Having her back in my space made me feel whole and stupid for ever discounting her and throwing her into the same bucket as someone like Tash who hadn't noticed I was missing or thought to call. Jo had been the closest thing I'd had to a best friend before everything went to crap and I'd started losing my shit. I'd counted Tash amongst the best too, but Jo was right, whenever you tried to talk to or even email Tash, she turned everything around to herself, not even a 'hope you feel better' before prattling on as though the whole world owed her something.

For what, who knew, but she seemed to think the whole world revolved around her and she was getting the pointy end of the stick, even though she had everything. Sure, things are never as they seem to an outsider, but she was a hell of a lot further along on the happy train than I was and from where I sat, she wasn't grateful for any of it. I can't say if she was always like that, I'm sure she mustn't have been. I can't imagine wanting to be friends with someone like that but that's who she was the last time I saw her and for the couple of years before that, that's about all I can say.

Jo on the other hand was one of the nicest people I'd ever known and I can't believe I'd cut her out and believed for one second she didn't care. She'd never shown any sort of that behaviour. She was busy and driven so sometimes days or weeks would pass without catching up. She'd actually been away at a conference 'that night' and I'd written her off completely along with everyone else. I just didn't see anything clearly, my interpretations so clouded it was one of the many things I was sifting through with Dr Bailey. She tapped a freshly poured shot of vodka to mine as I stirred the pasta sauce I was reheating on the stove and I felt like the worst person in the world for having mixed everything up so wrongly in my head.

'Stop worrying about it, Ains,' she said without even looking at me.

'What?'

'You know what. Don't feel bad. Stuff happens. Just don't do it again.'

She had a wicked grin and I knew we were okay.

'So, a date huh?'

'Oh crap! How did that even happen? The man's a weirdo,' I said, running my fingers through my hair in frustration and telling her about all our other bizarre interactions.

'He doesn't sound too bad and he stood up for you against the blonde bitch.'

'Yeah but he also grabbed at my arm before that like I was a piece of meat.'

'I'm sure he didn't mean it. I think he's just a bit awkward maybe, not too great with the ladies, out of practice a bit?'

'Out of practice with people in general?' I asked, trying not to laugh.

'Cut him some slack. He seems harmless enough,' she insisted.

'Yeah, well if I get cut up into itty bitty pieces and left in a bin, it's on you.'

'Do you really think he's the murdering type, was he that bad?'

'I don't think so. There was kindness and sadness in his eyes. When I told him off, his eyes were like oh crap I've done it again, I'm so sorry. It was kind of sweet. He was quite impressive the way he took charge and sorted out that Blonde Bitch but he's still a weirdo and I'm still fragile and he looks like a ferret,' I said sulkily.

She laughed loud, 'Oh my God, he totally does look like a ferret, his face is all thin and angular. That's hilarious.'

'It's not funny,' I said, trying not to laugh myself. 'I have to have dinner with the ferret man who doesn't like his cheese cooked,' I groaned, serving up our bowls of pasta.

'Well just make sure you go somewhere with lots of people, okay,' she snorted.

'Yeah, ha, ha, it's all good fun for you.'

'You'll be fine. I think he really was okay.'

'I don't even think I'm equipped for a date.'

'You'll be fine, it's not like it's George Clooney you have to impress, is it? It's just some guy who saved you from a crazy blonde bitch. You eat, you leave. Easy. Debt paid. But speaking of the crazy Blonde Bitch, what was all that about the brooch? Is yours really the same one?'

'As if,' I laughed, the idea Mrs May left a giant ruby lying around was ridiculous. They'd have laughed at me if I'd ever made it into Graham's, I'm sure. 'Your turn,' I said to Jo, changing the subject and shovelling a forkful of perfectly spooled pasta into my mouth.

'Nothing to say really,' she shrugged.

'Nuh ah,' I said, chewing. 'I had to talk, now you. Why'd you quit your job? What's going on?'

'I feel silly saying anything about my meaningless shit with all you have going on,' she said pouting.

'Don't be silly, we all have our own stuff. Besides, mine's over with now, let's talk about you,' I smiled.

'I don't know. That's the problem, I suppose. I just don't know what to do with myself. I was so bored. Billy made it clear I was never going to go anywhere in the company and I thought *what am I doing, then*? Why am I putting up with his crap, working my arse off, having my ideas stolen if there's no future? I just couldn't do it anymore. It was sucking all the light out of my soul and even Benny noticed. Benny told me to tell Billy to shove it up his arse and told me to go ahead and bludge off him until I figured out what else to do. So there. That's it. Now I'm here and you get the pleasure of having me brew coffee for as long as you like.'

I smiled. 'The pleasure is all mine, I promise.'

'It was a lot of fun actually. It was good to do something other than sit in an office chair. I might not have been working towards world peace today but I felt more connected to something than I had in ages, like I contributed to something, to the days of people maybe.'

'Oh, that you did. Did you see the smiles they left with? Only you Jo Jo, only you.'

'Ah, that vodka must be doing its thing if the "Jo Jos" are coming out.'

I laughed, she was right and it'd been way too long since we'd been here. I poured us more vodka while she phoned Benny and told him she was going to sleep on my couch. I found a scratchy blanket and a sheet in Mrs May's cupboard and made a bed for her on the couch.

'What's with the tomato plant?' Jo asked. 'That wasn't left here too was it?'

I laughed. 'It'd be ten foot high or dead if it had been. No, it's from Vivi.'

'Ah, Vivi. She still as kooky as ever?'

'Yep. She's got herself some Italian Stallion as she calls him. She thinks caring for a plant might help me in my recovery. Mind you, she gave it to me at nine in the morning over a dirty martini.'

'Geez! God, I love her,' Jo laughed.

It was just like the old days having Jo sleep over after a night of drinking and laughing and sharing all our darkest secrets. I told her everything and she didn't run, she hugged me and poured more vodka. It was probably going to react horribly but it was nice and just knowing she was in the next room made me feel better as I snuggled down into my bed.

# Chapter 13

'That forty year old vodka can still kick butt,' Jo declared as she walked into the kitchen the next morning, her usually well-kept hair looking like a bird's nest, her clean face furrowed in pain.

My head pounded and throbbed, vodka still swirled through my digestive system and all I could think of was roast chicken, chips and gravy. I'd given up on my muesli, chewing was too much of an effort and it just didn't satisfy the need for stodgy food to soak up all the vodka. We barely spoke as we slowly descended the stairs. I made us bacon, egg and cheese toasted sandwiches and we ate while setting up for the morning.

With a head full of cotton wool and a stomach still churning its way through its half of a bottle of premium vodka, it wasn't a day for the café to be busy, but it seemed we had no choice. People flowed in for their morning brew and fruit filled toasties as soon as I opened the doors.

The first through the door was the lady who had spent the last two days sitting in the booth. Today she was dressed in all black with a black hat and veil as though she was in mourning. She walked straight up to the counter and pointed at my chest. 'No more egg,' she declared. 'Ladybug, yes, egg no,' she said, waggling her finger. She looked me dead in the eye until I nodded my understanding then nodded and left, her homypeds squelching just a little on the floorboards as she went.

I'd forgotten I was even still wearing the egg. I'd accidentally thrown on the same t-shirt as the day before. It's bound to happen when your shirts all look the same and you're too hungover to pick through the pile for a clean one. It was just easier to grab whatever was on top. I took the egg off and popped it in the cash drawer for safe keeping. Then I wondered, how did she know I also had a ladybug brooch in Mrs May's jewellery box?

'What was that about?' Jo asked.

'I don't know,' I said, watching the lady walk out the door as more people came in to join the queue.

'Do you think we could sell them all tea?' Jo asked.

'Tea? Why's that?'

'That machine's too loud,' she groaned as she headed back to her station and I served the next person in the lengthening queue.

We had a steady stream until lunch when it seemed the toasty word of mouth had continued to spread while we digested our vodka and the queues and orders continued to grow. It reminded me I was going to have to do something about extra help during the lunch rush. Could I afford the commitment so soon? The customers were growing and at this rate, who knew how the books would balance at the end of the week but I didn't want to get ahead of myself and offer someone a job only to have to take it back next week when the novelty wore off and no one showed up for lunch. Everything was popular when it was new, sustaining the lunch rush was going to be the trick and who knew at this point if we would be able to do it. And on top of all that, Jo could get herself a fancy new job at any second. She was used to being a big wig, earning the big dollars, making cappuccinos for what I was paying her wasn't going to sustain her in the lifestyle she'd become accustomed to for long. The fun of making coffee was bound to wear off and once word got out through the business community that she was a free agent, someone would surely come calling with a big fat offer, so I had to start thinking of contingency plans. But it'd have to wait until after I'd served the queue of people before me.

The couple of girls in front of me, clearly gossiping colleagues, paid for their sandwiches, took their table number and went to find a table. Who knew how I was going to find time to actually make their sandwiches, I thought as I dropped some of their coins onto the floor. I bent, collected the coins, standing back up, coming face to face with my mother.

She had on a green cotton dress with a black cardigan and sensible black court shoes with the smallest of heels. She was wearing her city clothes, like one's Sunday best for my parents' generation; they had nice outfits reserved especially for the rare occasion they had to go into the city.

I quickly composed myself, 'Mum, what are you doing here?'

'Well, I was in the city to see Vivi, she had a fall and is in the hospital, so I thought I'd stop by and see how things were going.'

'Is Vivi okay?' I asked, suddenly a little panicked, not to mention annoyed that this was the first I'd heard of it and I have to say, hoping it really was an innocent fall and had nothing to do with her Italian Stallion or Mum would have her convalescing in that convent at St Josephs.

'Oh she'll be fine. Hurt her hip doing goodness knows what but she'll be fine.'

'Well, good,' I said, annoyed they were all the details she was going to give me. I'd have to phone the hospital later and speak to Vivi myself.

'Well it looks like you're rather busy. Who do you have cooking?'

'Me?'

'But you're out here serving.'

'Yes, well, I didn't expect to be so busy.'

'What can I do then?'

'Really? What about school?'

'They've cut back on subs, put in an incentive to make people show up every day, so I have some time. What can I do to help?' Mum always did know just when to come to the rescue. It's like she had a sixth sense.

'Can you work a register?'

'Of course I can. I'm not a fool.'

I smiled, showed her the process we were using and went out the back to make what felt like a million different toasties where it was quiet and I could finally get some sort of a toasty making process going.

When I'd filled the last toasty order on the bench I went out the front to check on the chaos. No chaos though, perfect organisation. Mum and Jo were sharing a laugh over coffee while the last of the lunch rush ate and chatted amongst themselves.

'Great work today, Boss,' Jo laughed, handing me a coffee.

'Nice work to you, to both of you. Thanks, Mum, I don't know what I'd have done if you hadn't shown up when you did.'

'Oh, it's fine,' she said, almost blushing. 'It was kind of fun actually,' she admitted sheepishly.

'Really?' I asked, a little surprised.

'Oh yes, chatting to all those people, who are loving your toasties by the way, and not having to harass some bored eight year old to pay attention, it was a refreshing change. I felt so productive, part of a whole other world.'

Jo and I shared a look of amusement. Jo had said almost the same thing the night before. 'Well, I'm glad we didn't bore you.'

'Not at all. In fact, I'm free the rest of the week if you want some more help.'

'Really? Oh Mum, that'd be fantastic.'

'No problem then. I'll be able to keep an eye on you while I'm at it,' she winked with a smile, taking off the apron she'd found. 'I'll see you then,' she said, giving me a quick peck on the cheek.

'Say hi to Dad,' I called to her departing body. She smiled and waved a hand in the air and was gone.

# Chapter 14

Everyone returned the next day and we fell into a nice rhythm, Mum putting through the orders, Jo whipping up the coffee and teas and me out the back where it was quiet making toasties, the hum of a filling café sounding like sweet music.

Just as the lunch rush was finishing their sandwiches, I was getting a coffee from Jo when in walked Mr Nosy with his absurd cheese issues. Before he even opened his mouth I told him, 'I'm not not toasting your sandwich.'

'That's okay, I'll just have the same as last time. It was actually really good.'

'Of course it was good,' I said, smiling triumphantly as Mum rang his order through the register and I went into the kitchen to make it.

'Alright, love, I'm off. You'll be alright, then?' Mum asked, while I waited for Mr Nosy's sandwich to toast, the smell of cooking bread and melting cheese filling the room.

'Yeah, sure, the rush has gone so we'll be right. Thanks again, Mum.'

'No worries, love,' she said, hurrying off to visit Vivi before getting home.

The problem with toasted sandwiches is you can't delay their delivery, a cold toasty is not nice so after Mum left and the Ferret's sandwich was toasted to perfection, I had to go and deliver it.

'So that date?' he asked as I put his sandwich on the table. 'How's tonight, say seven?'

'Tonight? Well that's short notice, isn't it?'

'Do you have something else on?'

'That's beside the point. It's rude to assume I don't.'

'Huh,' he said as though only just considering it. 'Well next time I'll be more considerate. But this time, can you do tonight?'

'Next time? Be thankful you have this time,' I said, walking away, my brain screaming, shit, shit, shit. I'd thought I'd have more time to prepare, not half a day. People like me need time, we need therapy visits and consultations with our inner circle, sticky notes with conversation prompters in our purse, time to get our heads around such things, even if it was only a date with Mr Nosy, The Ferret.

He hurried after me, his sandwich getting cold on the table. 'You didn't answer me,' he called over the counter where I'd gone to hide.

I looked at Jo for help. 'You might as well get it over with,' she suggested.

She had a point. The sooner I went on a date with The Ferret, the sooner I could forget about him and move on. 'Fine,' I said. 'Tonight, seven o'clock. Where should I meet you?'

'Well, I thought I'd pick you up, isn't that how dates work?'

'I don't know you from Adam and the café will be closed. Where should we meet?'

'Fine,' he said as though offended. 'Chiantis?'

'Fine. Chiantis at seven. What will the booking be under?'

'My name,' he said confused.

'And that is?'

'Oh,' he said blushing. 'Christian. Christian Harrington.'

'Fine, Christian, I'll see you then.'

As he left, I realised I hadn't told him my name. What was wrong with me? Then I remembered I had a name badge, which would explain why he hadn't asked.

Jo offered to watch the café while I popped over to Myers to find something to wear, but I refused to spend any of my hard earned money impressing Christian bloody Harrington. But I had some self-respect and other than my work wear of cheap jeans and a black polo shirts, I only had the Kmart casuals Mum had bought me that no longer fit very well. So I left Jo minding the café and went down stairs to the basement to rummage through some of Mrs May's old things. It was all old but wasn't vintage back in style? I was sure I could find something that could do the job for a fancy restaurant, some nice pants and a shirt or a dress. I'd have to do something about my lack of wardrobe supplies before too long, but not for a date with Christian Harrington. He had no business asking me out, I wasn't equipped for an awkward man like him with all his weird contradictions.

I found a short-sleeved fuschia satin shirt with a tie at the neck in amongst Mrs May's old clothes that I put with my black jeans as her pants were too small in the waist. It was a little librarian, but it was nice, it was respectable, it would do. It's not like I was trying to land a husband with my fashion sense.

'Would you at least let me do your hair?' Jo begged.

'Fine,' I said, going into the bathroom, even though I knew bothering with my hair was pointless. I was only going to ruin anything she did when I put on my helmet. But if it kept her happy, it was fine by me. 'What was with the blankets?' I asked, referring to the bed she'd made on the couch with the blankets from the night before.

'Well I'm not going to have you go out with a stranger then come home to an empty place now, am I? What kind of friend would that make me?' she asked as she fired up the blow drier. She's good people.

'Right, then,' I said when she was done and I shrugged into one of Mrs May's old black trench coats. 'Guess I'll be off,' I groaned.

'I'll be here waiting for all the juicy details,' she grinned.

'Don't be ridiculous. There'll be no juicy details. Not unless it's about the juicy steak I plan to order,' I said as I reluctantly walked down the stairs as though walking to my death.

Christian was waiting in the front of the restaurant, looking around nervously. I watched him a minute from across the street where I'd parked the scooter before putting him out of his misery. He looked up from his watch, just as I dodged a passing car and reached him.

'I'm not late, am I?' I asked, not really caring if I was.

'You can be as late as you like when you look that good,' he smiled, looking me over like a piece of meat.

He reached for my hand. I pulled mine away and he instead

placed his hand on the small of my back. It actually felt good, for just a moment, if I pretended it was someone other than ferrety Christian Harrington. It'd been a long time since I'd dated, even longer since I'd felt safe with a man and for that split second as we walked through the doors of the restaurant, I felt safe. Then he spoke.

'Harrington,' he spat at the waiter that greeted us.

The waiter masked his scowl, nodded and led us to a table by the window. He handed us menus and recited some specials, but before he could walk away, Christian ordered a bottle of red wine without even looking at the wine menu or asking what I'd like, then proceeded to prattle off a range of requests in perfect Italian even though the waiter spoke perfect English.

'Are you ordering food?' I asked. 'I haven't had a chance to read the menu yet.'

He half-heartedly waved his hand at me, dismissing me like my opinion was nothing. It was like waving a red rag at a bull. Dr Bailey and Mrs May had taught me a lot over these last weeks, I wasn't standing for anyone's bad behaviour ever again.

'I can order my own food, Christian.'

'Trust me, I know what you'll like.'

'How could you possibly know what I'd like? I just met you and all we've discussed is how you can't break into a steel door and that you don't like cooked cheese.'

The waiter was stifling a smirk.

'Well I want a steak,' I told him, huffing and slumping in my chair like a child.

He stared at me as though I'd ordered one of my cheese

toasties in his fancy restaurant, but I'd seen a steak on the small amount of the menu I'd read and I really wanted a fancy steak.

He rolled his eyes, 'Fine, you can have a steak, but can I at least order the appetisers and entrees, I promise, they really are good,' he said pleasantly.

'Fine. Deal,' I agreed. Why couldn't he always be the nice version? Why were there so many personalities in him? I was starting to wonder if he was crazier than me.

The waiter raised his eyebrows in surprise at my win and started reading back Christian's requests from his notebook and off he went.

'So how'd you end up with your friend's old building, anyway?' he asked, after we'd had a few sips of wine and the awkward air settled.

'It's a long story,' I said, unsure what I did and didn't want to get into with Christian Harrington.

'I've got all night, you know,' he smiled.

He was a whole different man when there was no one around to impress and he behaved like a regular person. His face changed, his tone changed. He was kind and honest, his face was soft, he wasn't trying to be anything, to impress anyone, to hold up some façade he thought he needed to. He just relaxed and let himself be.

As I took a sip of wine, I told him how Mrs May had died suddenly and left me the café, with no reason, she just did, no one could tell me why. He listened quietly, politely, nodding, sipping his own wine, sympathising over the loss of my friend.

'So what were you doing living with your parents?' he asked.

I shrugged. 'I had some issues. It suited.' I could have told him everything. I'd started the night not caring if he thought I was mad or a fool, but suddenly I didn't want him to look at me like people who found out you had a mental illness looked at you, with pity, concern, fear. And what did it matter, anyway? He didn't need to know about the whole sordid mess, beside you don't discuss such things in lovely restaurants like Chiantis.

The array of entrees landed on our table, saving me from having to say anything more for the minute. When Christian poured us more wine, I diverted the attention to him and asked, 'So, how about you? What's your story?'

'Well,' he started. 'I work in the family business,' he said, pausing as though waiting for me to say something. But I didn't, so he continued. 'I was my father's right hand man for a while. I'd thought I was doing a pretty good job too. I'd had to learn on the hop. There'd been a mess with my brother that needed fixing, so I jumped in and did whatever Dad needed me to do. But then my older brother finally decided to face up to his responsibilities and in doing so I got shafted down here to the sticks where no one had to bother with me anymore, not now the chosen one had returned to his rightful position at the top of the family tree,' he told me, his face returning to its harsh lines, the anger and contempt thick in his voice.

The waiter returned to clear our plates and Christian cleared this throat, perhaps uncomfortable at sharing so much, at being vulnerable.

'Anyway,' he said after the waiter left. 'That's me. I live here now and I run the local operations, the west coast and up the centre and just do what I'm asked.'

'Well that doesn't sound very inspired,' I said.

'What do you mean?' he asked.

'Well, shouldn't you be doing something you love? You don't sound like you love what you do?'

He waved his hand dismissively. 'I'd never thought I'd do anything other than work for Dad. Everything I did at uni, it was all for the business. I don't know what else I'd do.'

'Well, what do you do for fun?' I asked, thinking surely there'd be something a bit more inspired in that. But he just shrugged.

'What about the movies, what was the last movie you saw?' I asked, trying to head us into easier territory.

'I think there was one of the Ocean's movies on telly the other weekend. I was reading some contracts so I didn't catch which one.'

'Right,' I said, trying to think of something else to ask. But it was no use, he did nothing but work at fulfilling his family obligations. It was sad to see a person with nothing else to cling to. I'd been that person and my heart broke for him. I thought my family had me locked into a bit of a box at times but they were nothing compared to these Harringtons. 'You gotta give me something here,' I begged, smiling, trying to lighten the mood, help him to relax again.

He actually seemed to blush a little. 'I've really become a boring old man before my time, haven't I?' he said.

'I'm sure you're not,' I told him. 'What about before you left Melbourne?'

'It was definitely different then. There was always a party to attend or drinks with mates or a game of tennis or golf to play or a band to see.'

'There you go. What sort of bands did you see?'

'There was a great one called *The Snow Kings* that was doing the rounds for a while, not sure what happened to them but they were pretty awesome.'

'I know them,' I said.  'They've been killing it on the charts.'

'Really?'

'Yeah. You should download their album from iTunes, it's a great album.'

'I will,' he nodded. 'I'm just glad we found something in common, I was worried you were going to walk out for a minute there,' he said.

I laughed, 'Not before my steak arrives.'

As the waiter placed my steak in front of me a few minutes later, I oohed at how delicious it looked and how amazing it smelt. Christian smiled wryly. 'Shut up,' I laughed, realising I must have sounded like a homeless person with a hot meal.

As I sliced into the steak though, Christian almost ripped it from under me.

'What are you doing?' I demanded.

'That is not medium. I'll get the chef to cook you another one.'

'Don't be ridiculous. This one will be fine.'

'He won't mind redoing it,' he insisted, losing some of the scowl.

'I don't care. It's fine,' I said as I took my first bite and groaned, not just for affect, it really was one of the best steaks I'd ever eaten, although my opinion may have been swayed by my lack of restaurant food in the last year.

He smiled, an honest, warm, genuine smile, it wasn't crooked, he didn't look like a ferret and for just a second his face lit up and a beautiful warmth crossed over his face and his eyes almost glowed.

By the time we finished eating dessert, it'd disappeared, the waiter returned, topped up our glasses with the last of our wine and Christian snapped, 'bill,' with a look of sour distaste covering the warmth in his eyes.

'I just have to go to the bathroom,' I said, forcing a smile, unimpressed with the way he was treating people he thought were beneath him.

Walking through the restaurant I smiled at our waiter who was behind the bar giving me a tight smile in return and a distinct look of pity. I didn't blame him. Christian hadn't turned out to be as torturous as I'd expected, we'd even laughed, found some things in common, it hadn't been too bad at all. But he'd been so rude to the staff, I'd have pitied me too.

I was appreciating the ambience and how lovely it had been to dine somewhere with white linen, silver freestanding wine buckets and a proper wine list, when a woman cried from across the room, 'That's her!'

I stopped, looking around, who is who, I thought? Then, before I could even comprehend that they were referring to me, the Blonde Bitch from the cafe was standing before me in some hideously low cut black dress with a guy the size of a mountain beside her.

'We want to talk about the egg,' he said, the words strained as though they were struggling to escape from his enormous neck.

I tried to speak but nothing came out. I wanted to say get nicked, bugger off, Mrs May's things are none of your business.

But a vein was pulsating on the mountain's head and I was afraid it'd explode if I said the wrong thing, if I said anything.

The Blonde Bitch stood smirking, far too buoyed with the mountain by her side for my liking. She had crazy eyes. They were almost exploding out of her beautiful head. I couldn't understand all this fuss she was making over her stupid great grandmother's eggs from some stupid Grand Duke. As if Mrs May was going to have some giant stolen diamonds and rubies and emeralds just sitting around in a jewellery box untouched in a forgotten building for a few decades while she and Mitch lived a simple life in the suburbs. Mitch hadn't even gone to a private school; he went public like the rest of us middle class misfits.

I realised my hands were sweating when Christian slid his hand into mine and almost kept sliding. 'I think that's enough, you're upsetting my date,' he told them authoritatively, not the least bit afraid of their pulsating veins and bulging crazy eyes.

'Like I care,' said the mountain. 'Like my sister here, we just want our great grandmother's brooches back.'

'Well, like my friend told your sister,' he said pointing to the Blonde Bitch. 'The chances of those brooches being real is next to none. The old lady she inherited them from had nothing of value, they have to be copies. I'm sure she wouldn't have just left them lying around if they were real jewels.'

Christian squeezed my hand, turning to leave but the mountain grabbed his arm, 'I don't think so. We want to have them checked.'

'Is everything okay here?' Two guys burly enough to take on the mountain and then some appeared beside Christian and me. 'Christian?' the same one asked when Christian hadn't answered.

'Everything is fine, Sam,' Christian said, shaking his arm free from The Mountain who was as surprised as I at the back up that had arrived.

Our burly back-ups escorted us out the front. A black chauffeured sedan sat at the kerb waiting. 'Can I give you a lift?' Christian asked.

'Thanks, but no, my scooter is across the street,' I said, my hands shaking as I reached for my keys.

'That's okay, Sam can drive it home, you can come with me in the car,' he suggested with a kind, take charge, no fuss tone.

I turned and saw the Blonde Bitch and her mountainous brother watching us from the doorway of the restaurant and suddenly, I didn't fancy riding my scooter alone across the city and handed over my keys, telling Christian I lived above the café.

He placed his hand in the small of my back and led me into the waiting car, keeping his arm across my shoulders while we drove in silence. I was too confused to speak. Who was this man with his bodyguards and chauffeured car? Hadn't I had my share of people with secrets? I wanted to ask him about it all but the altercation with the Blonde Bitch and her brother had shaken the words out of my mouth.

The car pulled up in front of the café as Sam drove my scooter down the laneway. Christian got out of the car with me and we walked through the dark laneway. I was secretly glad his hand was protectively guiding me by the small of my back, and secretly glad for Sam as we passed him with a stern nod, but I wasn't telling Christian that and I wouldn't be telling Jo.

'You really didn't need to come this far. I have a friend waiting inside. I'll be safe now,' I told him when we reached the back door.

'It's okay,' he said. 'I'd hate for something to happen to you on my watch,' he smiled, that strange, beautiful warmth from earlier crossing his face again. And then he softly stepped forward and his lips melted on mine.

My initial response was to push him away, to flee but I'd had a tough night. The Mountain and the Blonde Bitch had scared the crappers out of me and Christian's lips were surprisingly warm and soft, his embrace strong and safe and I just wanted to hide in his arms for a while where I knew no-one could get to me, no crazy blonde bitch, no dark shadows, no self-doubt, none of it.

I could taste the blackberries from the wine as his mouth moved gently, barely touching mine as though he were breaking a rule, tempting fate, but unable to resist. I melted into him, into his warmth and the perfection of his kiss. My knees went weak and my blood pumped so fast I was losing all sense of control. I was lost in the foreign feeling of powerful desire, craving him. I had to pull away, to catch my breath. Instantly regretting it the second I did, wondering if I'd ever feel that connected, that alive, that perfect again, not sure how it had even happened at all.

Christian's face remained only centimetres from mine and it lit with a smile as he watched me staring, breathless. He softly kissed my forehead, leaving an incredible searing imprint and was gone as Jo opened the door to let me in.

'What was that?' she asked.

'I don't know,' I said absently as I stumbled inside trying to comprehend how The Ferret had made my head spin with pleasure and why I wanted desperately to do it again.

# Chapter 15

The kiss plagued my brain all through my restless night and then all through the next day. My mouth tingled every time I thought about his mouth on mine, how it'd felt, how soft and warm it'd been, how perfect the kiss had been, how my entire body had tingled from his mere touch. But how? It was The Ferret. How could he do that to me? How could he upset my entire equilibrium? It made no sense but I couldn't get him or that kiss out of my head or stop the tingling running through my insides and the goose-bumps running up my arm when I thought of it.

I managed not to stuff up any orders or chop off a finger, which was a miracle in itself with the visions playing inside my head when I was supposed to be focussing on making cheese toasties. I was just thankful for being able to hide out in the kitchen for a large portion of the day where I didn't have to face any customers or look Mum in the eye and give away what was going on because I was sure she'd have something to say about it.

Mum left at two after the lunch rush to pick up Vivi from the hospital and take her home to recuperate with her and Dad for a few days. Jo left at four to run errands and spend some time with Benny. She'd been out a couple of nights in a row and he didn't mind at all because he was a good guy but she was cooking him a nice dinner so had gone to get started.

It was pouring with rain outside, all the foot traffic too busy racing for the cover of bus shelters, wanting to get home as early as possible, to be warm and dry and fed, to bother coming in for a coffee to see them through their journeys. So now it was just me, alone behind the counter waiting for the after work customers that weren't coming, trying not to think of The Ferret and chastising myself for my stupidity every time I did and making a mental note to make an appointment with Dr Bailey.

I was grateful I'd seen nothing of the Blonde Bitch or her mountainous brother as I took the last of the dishes into the kitchen before locking up for the day. When I came back into the main room to close the doors, Christian was standing in the doorway like a very wet apparition. Dripping all over the beautiful hard wood floors, he looked like a drowned rat. His fancy suit was ruined, his hair stuck to his head, his shoes squelching on the floorboards as he walked towards me. I tried stifling a smile, the usually perfectly groomed ferret looked nothing like his usual dapper self.

'Stop laughing,' he said, now stifling his own grin.

'What are you doing here?'

'I wanted to make sure you were okay after last night. I'd have come over sooner but I was stuck in meetings all day. I was worried sick through them all, too.'

It was the sweetest thing I'd ever heard. This awkward contradiction had been worrying about me all day while doing his big wig business, so worried he'd raced across town in the pouring rain, regardless of his fancy clothes, just to make sure I was okay.

'Come in, come in,' I said waving him forward. 'I was just about to lock up.' I walked past him, closing the big doors and locking them. 'Coffee or something?' I asked.

His lips quivered as he tried to speak.

'Oh dear, let me get you some dry clothes. Just stand there,' I told him, not wanting him to drip on the velvet seating.

I raced down the stairs and opened the box of Mr May's clothes. I found a blue pinstripe shirt and a pair of navy blue trousers. They'd be too big for Christian but they were dry.

At the top of the stairs, Christian was standing right where I'd left him, shivering like a leaf. My heart leapt as I watched him trying to be strong but nothing could hide that much shivering.

'Come upstairs,' I smiled.

I stood him in the living room, got a towel from the linen closet in the hallway and handed it to him with the clean clothes. I left him to change while I heated some food but as I was walking away I couldn't help turning back, still amazed he'd run through the rain to see me, just as he peeled his wet shirt from his body which turned out to be surprisingly beautiful. His body was tanned and toned just nicely, not too muscly but well cared for. I looked up and our eyes locked. He held my gaze for just a moment, a moment that had my head spinning, then the memory of the kiss came forth and I walked away before I tackled him to the ground.

I distracted myself putting the kettle on, dishing up two bowls of casserole that Mum had left in my fridge and put the first in the microwave. What was wrong with me? It must be the medication, the emotional turmoil, something. I was lusting after The Ferret. I'd wanted to touch those muscles. I'd wanted to put my mouth on that beautiful, tanned skin. I'd wanted to hear him groan with pleasure.

I took a bottle of vodka out of the fridge and poured myself a shot, downing it almost as quick, feeling the heat surge through my body, taking the edge off the panic, the desire, the whatever it was that was taking over my brain and my body.

'Can I have one of those?' Christian asked quietly from the doorway.

'Ahuh,' I said, unable to look at him for fear of blushing.

I poured his shot and turned to hand it to him, willing myself to maintain some pride. I couldn't be lusting after ferrety Christian Harrington, he was awkward and snippy and sweet and kind and I just didn't know what to make of him or these feelings. I was busy regaining my mental health and his contradictions were a bad idea. He was no good for me, Dr Bailey would agree. Perhaps that's all I needed, a visit with Dr Bailey to make sense of things, where I was at, what was going on in my head. I'd never even had a healthy adult relationship. Was it even possible for someone like me? Dr Bailey would sort me out. I'd speak to Mum tomorrow morning about covering for me one morning or afternoon.

Christian stood at the bench beside me, his body so close I could feel his muscles moving beneath the cotton shirt. He put his shot glass in front of me so I poured him another. Poured myself another while I was at it.

'So,' he said.

I gulped, suddenly afraid of where this could lead. The microwave beeped, I turned away from Christian Harrington trying not to see his glistening green eyes, returned handing him the hot bowl with a tea towel underneath. From the corner of my eye, he smiled, not the crooked smile, but a warm, sexy, knowing smile. He lent across me to reach for a spoon in the canister on the bench, sucking all the air from my lungs, then sat down at the dining table to eat. I put my bowl in the microwave and all I could smell was his cologne, or was it his soap, it was faint but rich and warm and musky. It was buried beneath the musty smell of Mr May's old clothes but it was still there, stuck to his skin and all I could think of was how he would taste.

I got a hold of myself and sat down to eat, ignoring his gaze, refusing to meet his eyes while I spooned casserole into my mouth.

'Are you going to look at me at all?' he asked.

I shook my head and kept eating. I could see him smirking though out of the corner of my eye as he, too, kept eating.

We finished our bowls of casserole, downed a couple more shots of vodka and I was at the sink washing the bowls, the kettle warming beside me, my head spinning, torn between wanting to throw him out now and wanting to rip Henry Mayberry's shirt off his body. I knew Dr Bailey would insist on the first option for the good of my mental health but my heart was begging for the second.

Without warning or a single sound, Christian's arms snaked around my waist and he buried his face in my neck, his warm mouth, his warm tongue, tantalising my skin, setting my blood on fire, the decision made.

I don't know what happened after that, my brain was working too fast for me to control it so my body took over and did as it pleased. I groaned, turned and our mouths met in an explosion of heat. He kissed me hard, his tongue searching, his hands roaming, desperate, hungry. My hands went straight for the buttons of Henry's shirt, I wanted so badly to feel Christian's body but my fingers shook and I couldn't get them to work so I grabbed hold of the fabric, ripping it open, gasping then smiling at the treat before me.

We caught our breaths, our eyes meeting for an intense moment and I could hear nothing but his panting breath and my beating heart before his mouth caught mine and his body pushed me against the cupboards.

I led him to the bedroom, falling onto the bed in a tangle of arms and legs, full of urgent need. Our clothes fell where they were thrown from bodies or thrown out of the way.

The heat was too much, we were going too fast. He groped and nipped, licking, here and there, all over the place as though there was a race to be won. He was a kid in a candy store and wanted everything at once.

I edged him onto his back, whispering, 'Shhh...' before making my way over his body, slowly, methodically, exploring every sculptured, tanned muscle that awaited and twitched with pleasure beneath my touch.

He must have gotten the hint because from there he took the lead, slowly, strongly, suddenly knowing or maybe remembering all the right buttons. He meticulously made his way over my body before finally filling me, moving, doing this thing with his hips, until the exquisite joy ripped through me, connecting me to him in a way I hadn't expected, until I saw stars, until I near screamed down the flat, grateful the neighbouring businesses were vacated for the day or I'd have had the police on my doorstep and knowing my luck I'd have gotten good old Sergeant Jack.

I lay with a smile spread across my face, Christian's arms wrapped around me holding me close. I felt safe again. There was no sense in it. He was so many different things and I was afraid of which one was his natural truth. But just now, once he'd found his groove, he'd brought me back to life and now in his arms I felt so safe and happy, I never wanted to leave. It was ridiculous. How had I found myself here in bed with this beautiful, awkward, snippy man who treated me with so much kindness and adoration? How had it even happened, how had I ended up feeling so perfect in the arms of The Ferret? That was never meant to happen. It was meant to be dinner. One dinner.

He lay staring at the ceiling as though just as surprised any of it had happened himself. Surely he couldn't be any more surprised than me, though. 'You okay?' I asked.

He smiled, kissed my forehead, 'Never better.' He held my eyes for a few moments, brushed away a stray strand of hair and kissed my forehead again before throwing back the covers and getting out of bed.

'Where are you going?'

'Home,' he said as though it were a given,

'Really? After that you don't want to stay?' I asked surprised and suddenly deflated, a hole opening up somewhere deep in my stomach, terrifying me. I know it had been a while for me but I was pretty sure that had been the best sex of my life. I'd never felt so alive, so needed, so whole. How had he not felt that too? Surely I wasn't in this alone. I couldn't be in this alone.

'You want me to stay?' he asked curiously.

'Yes,' I whispered, feeling stupid. I certainly didn't want him to stay if he didn't want to but here I was admitting I wanted him to, being vulnerable. I didn't like vulnerable. I added it to the list in my head for Dr Bailey.

His face lit up like a Christmas tree and he folded his naked body back into the bed, pulling me to him, wrapping his arms and legs around me. I felt him grinning as he cocooned me against him and we spooned until the sun crept in through the big arched windows.

Christian was still asleep when I rolled over to look at him in the morning. He looked like a little boy, his face peaceful, soft and handsome. He lost the angular, harsh, concentrated ferret-ness in his features, the hardness of his tone while his face was soft in sleep. It had been a long time since I'd last woken beside a man. It was nice. But I didn't need him seeing me with smudged eyeliner and my hair on end. I carefully slid out of the bed and showered.

'How's the water?' Christian asked from the doorway as I rinsed the last of the conditioner out of my hair.

I was stunned silent. I didn't know what to say and before I could consider the proposition any further he'd stepped over the lip of the bath and was standing in front of me, naked, his face unsure but wishful. Who could resist?

We steamed up the bathroom in seconds, no longer caring about morning breath or smudged eyeliner. I just wanted, needed, to feel that searing heat flow through my body again, to know that I could please a man with such little effort because he fancied me to bits. To have him hold me tight. To have his hot breath whisper how beautiful I was in my ear. To believe him. To believe that I could be the most amazing person in someone's world, even for just a moment.

I heard bashing on the downstairs door but ignored it. Then the phone was ringing in the bedroom but I couldn't move. I was lost in the moment of passion, of ecstasy. The phone stopped and he thrust harder. I couldn't help but cry out. Then the phone rang again as his release erupted among orgasmic cries of pleasure.

We lent against the wall as the bashing and the ringing continued. Eventually I caught my breath. My legs that had near turned to jelly regained their strength and full consciousness returned. I put on a robe and went down to see who the hell was bashing at my door at the crack of dawn.

Jo stood on the other side with a questioning look. 'What time is it?' I asked her.

'Time for you to have the coffee machine on, not scaring the bejeezus out of me by not answering the door or phone.'

'Sorry,' I offered sheepishly.

'What were you doing?'

'Nothing, I was in the shower.'

Christian came down the stairs, buttoning his shirt which had dried on the back of one of the kitchen chairs, his hair damp, his stupid mouth whistling as he walked. Seriously, whistling.

Jo looked at me, eyebrows raised. 'You didn't?' she whispered.

'Shut up,' I said, letting her in.

We followed Christian into the cafe where he'd already begun firing up the machine, totally ignoring Jo's bemused eyebrow raises.

Once Christian had poured his coffee into a takeaway cup, he kissed me on the forehead, sending bolts of electricity through my skin as my body remembered all the things that mouth could do and then he left through the back door and I was alone with Jo and her questioning eyes.

'I don't think I even want to know!' she said, waving her hand in the air and setting up the coffee supplies for the morning onslaught.

'Good, because I don't even know if I could explain any of it,' I told her.

'I don't need to call your shrink, do I?' she asked.

I laughed, 'I don't think so.'

'Good,' she smiled, shaking her head as she bent down to get some milk out of the under counter fridge. 'You scared the shit out of me, though. What if something had happened, does any-one else even have a key?' she asked.

'Um, no.'

'Well, sort that out, would you?' she said as she poured coffee into cups.

'Sure, I'll get you one this afternoon.'

'Thank you,' she said smugly, handing me my coffee. 'I promise I won't walk in on any business. Now would you go and get dressed?' she smirked.

I opened the doors to the world and the cocoon Christian and I had created during the night was gone. Reality waited on the other side, people bustling up and down the street none the wiser, the sun sending shards of rays at me piercing the perfect bubble we'd created. What if that was it? One night of accidental, sensational, life altering, searing pleasure? What if he arrived at his office, sipped his coffee and decided the whole night was nothing but a quick, easy shag? How could I have been so stupid? How could I have put myself in that position? Dr Bailey was going to have a field day with this one.

The old lady was back, squeezing past me as I stared into the sun scolding myself for my stupidity. She was no longer in the black funeral garb I'd last seen her in. She nodded at me but made no further mention of the brooch or her admonishment of it. She ordered her usual pot of tea and sat in her usual booth and that was that. Everything was back to normal and I'd have to be too, besides I had no way of even contacting Christian to beg him to reconsider.

'What do you reckon she knew your Russian friend?' Jo asked watching the old lady sip her tea.

'Why do you say that?' I asked, wondering why I hadn't considered it myself.

'Just the way she sits there, she looks thoughtful in a pining, longing sort of way. Don't you think?'

'Maybe,' I said, watching the old lady, perplexed. 'Who knows? Now, how was date night?' I asked, changing the subject.

Jo told me of her date night, the usual couple business, nice chicken chasseur dinner, Jo's speciality, a few glasses of wine finished by a little sexy business. But all that was crowding my head as she spoke were images of Christian's perfect body, the sound of his voice heavy with need, the feel of his breath on my neck, his touch on my skin, his arms wrapped around me and wondering if I'd ever feel that completeness, that contentedness again.

Then, as I went to serve a customer, I saw the long stretch of quiet that waited for me over the next couple of days. What would I do for an entire weekend? The corporate world would be closed. There'd be no customers to distract me from the fact Christian wouldn't be coming in for lunch or standing in the doorway dripping, that he'd be off living his life, doing whatever he did because I'd be closed and he didn't have my number. It'd just be me, all alone, with all those hours to think about what I'd almost had.

# Chapter 16

I'd closed the front doors, showered, put on some warm jammies and was thinking about what I could scrounge up to eat while I tried not to self destruct in front of Mrs May's ancient television, which I'd hooked up to an old set top box Shaun had dropped off when someone began banging on the back door. I put on slippers and a robe and went downstairs.

'Who is it?' I called, thinking I'd have to invest in one of those camera doorbells.

'Christian,' he called back.

I opened the door, holding back the relieved smile that was threatening to burst forth as I saw Christian standing in front of me wearing dark blue jeans and a navy polo shirt with a red Polo Ralph Lauren logo. He held up a plastic bag with takeaway containers. 'I was thinking food and some Netflix?'

'Come on in,' I said, making way for him to come in. 'The takeout is most welcome but I'm afraid I don't have Netflix,' I told him as we climbed the stairs.

'What? Who doesn't have Netflix?'

'Me, asshole' I laughed while trying to scowl at him but failing miserably because he was here with food and looking immediately sorry for his faux pas.

'That's okay, I'm sure there'll be something on TV,' he conceded guiltily and I wondered if the awkwardness was a lifelong personality flaw or something new.

Thai food was a luxury I hadn't had the joy of experiencing for a long time, since before I'd lost my job and and all my money had been auto debited out of my account, and it was heaven. On a cold autumn night with the wind picking up outside, nothing beat a bowl of pad thai, warm pyjamas and a man to keep you company.

'Cute jammies,' he said, raising his eyebrows with a smile as I snuggled up against him.

I flashed back to my old life, to the times I'd been unable to change out of pyjamas not too much different to these for work, some days I just forgot, some days I didn't have the strength and some days I just didn't even notice, in such a dark place I was only able to focus on putting one foot in front of the other, everything else was too much, too overwhelming. Those had been pretty generic, checks, plain t-shirts that really could have been anything. These had a few green frogs on a white t-shirt with long green cotton pants with white frogs. Mum had chosen these, they were cute and soft and serviceable. Remembering struck a chord, made me realise how far I'd come in such a short time. I was dressing for work every day without even having to think about it. I was showering every day, being productive all day long, talking to people, functioning and laughing and snuggling up to a handsome, successful man in my frog smothered jammies on a Friday night.

'What's with the thinking?' he asked.

I smiled. 'Nothing, I was just thinking how nice a turn my life has taken, that's all.'

'Yeah?'

'Yeah,' I said, snuggling further into his warmth as a romcom began on the telly.

The weekend continued like that. I didn't want him to leave on Saturday. He didn't want to leave so he didn't. We popped out to the mall, to Coles for some snacks, Myer for a new smart tv he expertly installed and we came home to find an overnight bag by the back door, courtesy of Sam, he said. We ordered pizza but were mostly naked, wrapped in each other's arms for the rest of the weekend. Thankfully my mother didn't know how to video chat so couldn't see us when she called to check on me.

The rain pelted down outside late Sunday afternoon and Christian lay spent beside me, grinning like a madman. Perhaps all the sex had driven him crazy and I needed to send him to Dr Bailey?

'You know, we probably should get out of bed sometime,' I suggested.

'Really? Why?' he asked, nuzzling my neck.

I laughed. 'Good point. But you know, there's something I've been meaning to do but have been too chicken. I could use your manly support before you disappear on me tomorrow.'

'Well I can do that,' he said, kissing the top of my head.

He followed me down to the basement. I'd been meaning to go

through the crates in Mrs May's basement but the fear of uncovering more secrets I'd have to contend with had kept me upstairs and out of her last unexplored corners. At this point, who knew what I was going to find and I just didn't know how many more surprises I could take. Not to mention I had a mild fear of mice and cockroaches and spiders and so far I'd been lucky to not encounter either but that was sure to run out soon, it was a basic probability that something was living amongst all those crates. But I figured while I had someone to hold my hand and squash the bugs and share any burdens we uncovered, I should make the most of it.

The crates piled against the far wall took up a good third of the room, a few rows high and more rows deep. 'These?' queried Christian as we approached the neat pile covered in dust.

'Ahuh,' I nodded from behind him as though something might jump out of them.

Christian tested some, trying to pull off the lids before saying, 'They're all nailed shut.' He went back upstairs with his phone to his ear and a few minutes later returned with a crowbar and began prying open the first lid.

After pushing aside the strips of paper used for packaging, we uncovered a number of fine, bone china teapots, carefully wrapped with reams of fine paper and protected with bubble wrap.

'This looks pretty fancy,' Christian said, unwrapping an incredibly beautiful teal green teapot with painted pink flowers, a black, almost square handle and black spout. He turned it over, carefully holding its lid in place. 'Royal Doulton,' he said. 'It's a really old one, too by the looks of it,' he added.

Christian started jimmying the lids off more boxes and inside were more teapots. They were beautiful and elegant and some so fine I thought they'd crumble in my clumsy hands. More crates, more intricately painted pots, buddas adorning some of the lids, some with elaborate, Asian landscapes in the most amazing colours painted on the sides.

'What's with all the teapots do you reckon?' Christian asked dumbfounded. 'Some of these must be worth a fair bit.'

'I dunno,' I said as surprised as he. 'Who would need this many teapots? Even a collector would struggle to source this many and if Mrs May was a collector, why hadn't the crates at least been opened?'

Box after box revealed more from various parts of the world. Some of the boxes on the bottom of the pile, furthest in the back had already been prised open, some of the teapots unwrapped, some still wrapped. Christian became more and more fascinated, examining some closely as though he had some idea of antiques, which I suppose he could have for all I knew, but he definitely had an inkling about their value. He pulled out one with a dragon mouth for a spout and something hard inside rattled against the fine china. Carefully removing the lid, he reached inside, bringing out an emerald pendant as big as a rock.

We stared at it like it was a bomb.

'Do you think it's real?' I asked.

'I don't know,' he replied, holding it up to the light. 'But I think so.'

'Shit,' I stammered.

We went back to the other boxes, taking out more teapots, giving them a little jiggle finding more pots rattled where either there hadn't been enough tissue paper stuffed inside or the paper had degraded over the years and was no longer able to provide the pots any protection from the jewels hidden inside. Meticulously opening all the lids, we found all the teapots had something inside, if there were no jewels, we found rolled up wads of money heralding from all parts of the world, big, fat rolls of money.

I sat back on my haunches, dumbfounded, not knowing what to make of any of it, annoyed I hadn't investigated on my own instead of being such a chicken, before Christian became involved. But it was too late. He was here now and there was nothing I could do to go back in time and change it.

'What's going on, Ainsley?' he asked. 'What is all this?'

'I don't know,' I whispered. Which was the truth.

Sitting in the dust, I filled him in on all the other strange things; the electricity being paid, the vodka in the fridge, the jewellery upstairs, all the money I'd already found in handbags, coat pockets and packed away with the passports in the shoe boxes.

'It was like she just got up one day, walked out and forgot to come back,' I said shaking my head. 'What do we do?' I asked him, praying he had some answer.

'I don't know yet,' he said sitting beside me. 'We might need to do some googling, I think. Find out who the hell this Mrs May really was.'

I nodded. Still staring and the crates and the teapots and the jewels. We packed the jewels and the money and the teapots we'd pulled out back into the crates, restacked them so they were safe and out of harm's way and went back up to the living room where Christian's laptop sat.

He loaded up the computer while I made us coffee and then we sat on the couch side by side. His home screen flashed up, a black background and a bright, lime green crest with the words Harrington Industries underneath it.

'You're one of those Harrington's?' I blurted without censoring myself. 'That's why those guys and the driver were right there when you needed them?'

He didn't speak for a moment. 'I am,' he whispered as though wishing he were anyone else.

'Huh,' I nodded. 'How closely related to Richard Harrington, are you?' I asked, my heart sinking as I dreaded how over my head I was as I pictured the billionaire property mogul in my head.

'He's my father. Changing your mind now? Ready to kick me to the kerb?'

I was afraid to answer, my voice was lost somewhere in my throat. He wasn't just a random Harrington, a distant relation who shared the surname, he was right at the core of the billionaire's empire and I didn't quite know what to make of it.

'This doesn't changes us, Ains. Who my family are doesn't change me. Kick me to the kerb if you have to, I wouldn't want to be mixed up with him either, but it doesn't change how I feel about you,' he said.

'Hey, if I didn't change my mind after seeing you treat sales staff like they're dirt beneath your feet, I think you're safe for now,' I said, wondering what the hell I was doing.

He raised his eyebrows high in surprise.

'Yes, it's a bad habit. Waiters, sales people. You treated that nice lady at Myers like the hired bloody help from a bad old movie. The man at Chianti's the other night too, it was really uncalled for.'

'Really?' he asked as though he hadn't noticed doing so.

'Yes,' I replied amused at his complete lack of understanding. 'You were pretty bloody rude to me when you came in, with all that hoopla about not liking your cheese cooked and grabbing my arm like I was a thing to own. You're lucky I didn't punch you in the bloody nose.'

'Shit, Ains, I'm so sorry. I'd never hurt you, I promise,' he apologised, kissing me. 'I don't mean to be like that. It just happens. Sometimes I just, I don't even know. It just comes out that way.'

'Is that how your father is?'

'Worse. But my brother's not. My sisters aren't. Just me.'

'And where do you fall in the family scheme of things?'

'There's my older brother, Tom, and Lydia, they're twins, and a younger sister, Jasmine.'

'So you're always in the shadow of your older brother? Always trying to impress your father and get his attention but never succeeding? As well as being the forgotten, ignored middle child?'

'How do you know that?'

'Pretty classic really, doesn't take a genius.'

'Huh,' he said. Now he was the one nodding in thought. 'Not so complicated after all?'

'Fraid not. You're just as messed up by your family as the rest of us,' I said, planting a kiss on his lips, pulling away before the kiss could become something else. 'So what exactly do you do for Harrington Industries?'

'I used to do a lot of things working side by side with Dad, managing some of the big developments. Then Tom came home, there was practically a freaking parade, he took over and I was sent here. It was all over the news, you really didn't see any of it?'

'I've been a bit distracted with some of my own stuff,' I admitted. 'Go on,'

'Well, now I'm running a few things here including the redevelopment of the Old Regent Hotel.'

'Oh that's a beautiful old building. You're not going to ruin it, are you?'

He smiled, perhaps a little proudly. 'No, I'm not going to ruin it, I'm going to make it beautiful.'

I liked seeing the pride on his face and the quiet confidence in his voice. 'Well, I look forward to seeing it. Now, let's get googling,' I grinned, deciding he was right, who his family were didn't make any difference to who we were. We were just a couple of messed up people figuring things out.

Christian, kissed my cheek then typed Ana May into the search bar and waited to see what came up.

A number of results came up, Facebook pages, Wikipedia pages, an IMDB page for an actress, photos for women who weren't my Ana, none of them led anywhere. Nothing we opened had anything to do with my friend.

'What if that's not her name?' I said, telling Christian about all the passports in different names and what the accountant had called her.

'But which one's the real name?' He typed in the first then

another but still, nothing came up that related back to my friend. It was as though she had never existed. When he typed in Anastasia Stezhensky, it came up with a marriage record to Henry Mayberry dated 1969 but that was it.

'What about the husband?' Christian suggested before typing Henry Mayberry into the search bar.

Christian clicked on a link to a news article topping the list of results. A small picture of a young lady with big questioning dark eyes smiled out at us. The by-line telling us she was Connie Shrew reporting for the Daily News. The article was hard to read, it was a scanned copy of the original, which was dated June 17, 1978.

'Wait, the last date in the journal I found was June 15th. That can't be a coincidence, can it?'

'No, I don't think it is,' he agreed.

The print was small, but there was a picture of Henry that I recognised from the shoebox. It was him. I leant into the crook of Christian's arm, snug against his body as he read what he could of the article.

*The Bauble Bandit*, the story headlined. *Henry Mayberry couldn't help himself,* Connie Shrew began. *He was a Magpie, attracted to and distracted by anything shiny. He didn't restrict himself to shiny expensive baubles though. He'd happily take your cash and any other valuable treasures that caught his eye. People say he had a good eye too, he could tell in a moment a fake from the real thing.*

*Famous for stealing from the homes of the rich and famous from all parts of the world undetected, it is thought he worked as a chameleon, living and partying amongst those he thieved from but no one could catch him red handed and his disguises varied from job to job and even to this day, no one knows how he got his treasures back into the country or what happened to them.*

*No one really knows what happened to Henry Mayberry, his last sighting was a couple of days ago when a Texan rancher, famous for his oil wealth, was photographed holding a shotgun to Henry Mayberry's head in the middle of the desert while Henry smiled for the camera holding a handful of jewels up for the world to see.*

*The photograph was printed in every newspaper around the world and that was the last anyone saw of Henry Mayberry, famous for his extravagant vodka parties and his beautiful Russian wife, once a promising ballerina. People had been only too happy to point their fingers at the Mayberrys, until then, Henry had been a ghost no one could name or catch.*

*No one knows exactly what happened to Henry Mayberry, his beautiful wife or the jewels. It is destined to be a mystery for a while yet.*

'It's all stolen?' I asked.

'It looks that way,' Christian whispered.

'What about the stuff in the bedroom?'

'I don't know,' he said, pulling me into his arms.

We sat that way, quietly contemplating the incredible loot down in my basement. Millions of dollars worth of stolen jewels and money, soooo much money. It was all so ridiculous it was hard to comprehend.

'You okay?' Christian asked.

'I don't know,' I told him. 'I really don't know.'

'Shall I make us some tea?' he offered.

'I think I may need a shot of that vodka,' I said, still disbelieving I was living with the hidden remnants of Henry Mayberry's thieving. Had Mrs May known? Had she left it all to me for profit or to sort and return? None of it made sense. How could lovely old Mrs May have been involved in such a sordid life?

Christian brought in a bottle of vodka and two shot glasses. We had one shot, then another. After the third, I was much less horrified as the numbing warmth spread through my veins and Christian's hands began to roam over my body.

I forgot all about Henry Mayberry then. Something inexplicable happened whenever Christian's mouth met mine. I lost all control, all sense of reason as I lost myself in the perfection of his mouth and the pleasure of his touch. I didn't even feel bad about the things we did on Mrs May's fine furniture.

After moving to the bed, tangled in each other's naked limbs, warm and safe for the night, Christian said, 'I'll have someone look into Henry Mayberry some more during the week, okay? See if we can find out some more details, see if any of it's true and find out what happened to him.'

He kissed my forehead and I nodded, grateful, before falling asleep.

I let Jo in the next morning as I let Christian out.

'You spent all weekend with him?'

'Yes. Yes I did. And it was bloody nice,' I laughed.

She laughed too. 'Well good for you. 'Bout time you got back on the horse. Not sure I'd have picked The Ferret for your re-entry into dating, but hey, if the glow you're touting is anything to go by, it's lucky I wasn't doing the choosing.'

'Shut up and make coffee,' I said nudging her with a ridiculous grin I couldn't control.

# Chapter 17

I was just short of whistling while I worked in the kitchen throughout the morning. Life happened around me as though I were in my own Teflon bubble of happiness. The cheese man popped by and I smiled at him like a Cheshire cat until he near ran out of the kitchen from fright. I happily worked through the orders that continued piling up with a smile and a whistle. Even when I burned my little finger on one of the sandwich presses lined up on the bench, I just shrugged, ran it under the tap and went back to stirring the onions caramelising on the hot plate, humming to myself. I was in a happy daze of post-coital delirium, too happy to even worry about the basement full of stolen jewels beneath my feet.

'You doing alright out here, Chuckles?' Jo laughed.

'Just fine, thank you very much,' I laughed, making a poor attempt of whipping her with the tea towel.

'Well, I just thought you'd like to know there's a ferret all alone out there not looking quite as cheery as you.'

'What? Christian's here? How long has he been here? Why didn't you tell me? Why didn't he come through?'

'I don't know, Ains, don't shoot the messenger, yeah? Your mum must have served him. I only just noticed him staring despondently into his cooling coffee.

'Oh shit,' I said, walking out.

I stood in the doorway, surveying the café until I found him, my heart dropping all the way to my toes at the sight of his sad face.

'What's wrong?' I demanded, flopping into the spare chair.

He looked up, his face wrinkled and almost grey, a sad looking toasted sandwich before him. 'My dad phoned.'

'And?'

'And he's telling me I have to go to a thing on Sunday. Tom got engaged on the weekend, so Dad says I have to go. I haven't seen them since they sent me here, Ains. I was demoted and practically kicked out of the family when Tom came back, I just don't think I can but knowing Dad, he'll drag me there if he has to, just for the photo op.'

I'd never seen him look so sad. I couldn't stand it. I hated that someone had hurt this beautiful man so much that the pain was consuming him. I knew what it was like to be consumed by pain, by disappointment, by feeling as though you weren't enough and he didn't deserve that, no one deserved that.

'Do you want me to come with you?' I offered.

His face brightened instantly, warmth returning to his cheeks, a slight sparkle returning to his eyes. 'Would you? You would do that for me?'

I laughed. It was by far the sweetest thing I'd ever seen. 'If you want me to, of course I'll come,' I said, reaching over and putting my hand on his. 'Now why don't you bring your lunch out the back and talk to me, I've got sandwiches to make.'

He nodded like a lost little boy grateful to be found, to be seen.

The lunch rush carried on as normal after Christian left and the smile returned to my face. Until Mum stuck her head around the corner, anyway.

'Ainsley, love...'

'Yes, Mum?'

'That boy earlier, is there something going on?'

'Might be. Why?'

'Well, is that wise?'

'I don't know. It feels wise,' I smiled mischievously, knowing it would irritate her.

'When did you last see Dr Bailey?'

'A couple of weeks ago. Why? What are you getting at, Mum?'

'Well, I think I'd just feel a bit better if you went and saw him and talked about this boy.'

'He's not a boy Mum and I'm not a child, you know.'

'Ainsley, really?' she huffed.

'Fine, Mum, I'll call him.'

'No need, I already did. He has a spot at 9.30 tomorrow. I'll come in early and help Jo so you can go over and see him.'

'Right, then. Thanks, Mum.' I rolled my eyes and went back to cleaning up.

'I'm just trying to help, Ainsley. You made it clear you needed some help so don't condemn me for caring now.'

'Fine Mum, you're right. I'll go see Dr Bailey in the morning.'

'Don't get smart, Ainsley.'

I kissed her on the cheek and smiled, 'Me? Never!'

'Now that sounds more like our Ainsley,' she winked. 'I'll see you both tomorrow,' she called as she let herself out the back door.

'Not a moment of freedom, hey?' Jo asked.

'She's right, though. I brought it on myself with those stupid bloody pills. I can't get shitty with her being bossy now, can I?'

'Guess not when you put it like that. That will teach you,' she laughed, nudging me and keeping the mood light.

'Whatever,' I rolled my eyes. 'I need a drink, you coming?'

'You bet. But just one, we can't keep making a habit of it or we'll both be off to see Dr Bailey.' We both laughed our way up the stairs, joviality was getting out of control here. Perhaps that's what I'd share with Dr Bailey.


Mum arrived the next morning just as we were opening the doors for the morning rush. I hadn't expected her so early and stepped back to let her in a little reluctantly as she walked through the door, kitted out in her black skirt, black button through shirt, court shoes clicking on the floor boards, nude sheer stockings and her hair and makeup in perfect place. Her sensible handbag hung in the crook of her arm and she carried a pink Tupperware container I couldn't see through.

'What's in the Tupperware, Mum?' I asked, after a quick peck on the cheek.

'Oh, nothing, just a little something I thought we could try selling for morning tea.'

'We?' I asked dubiously, unsure when this whole operation had become a we.

'Now don't go getting testy, Ainsley, it's just some cake for goodness sake.'

'Which cake?' I asked, suddenly interested. 'Is it Granny's sponge?'

'Maybe.'

'It is, isn't it?' I asked, my eyes growing wide with excitement.

'It's to sell, Ainsley, not for you to eat.'

'Oh, come on, Mum, I can have one piece, can't I? It'll keep me alert for my appointment with Dr Bailey. Besides, we can't go selling stuff you made at home in your kitchen, there are rules, you know.'

'Oh, Ainsley, don't talk like I didn't spend fifteen years as a home ec teacher, I'm not an idiot. I know there are rules. Besides I got all those approvals when I did that wedding cake for Mrs Parker's daughter.'

'Oh right, then all her friends kept calling for cakes. Fine then. But I'm still having a piece,' I said smugly.

'Fine, fine,' she surrendered, perhaps feeling a little guilty about sending me off to see the good doctor.

I didn't wait for her to change her mind, ripped open the container and helped myself to a slice before scurrying back behind the counter like a naughty mouse to where my freshly brewed coffee waited.

'Well I have to see what the fuss is about. How about I go find a plate or something for these, Mrs Donovan?' Jo said, helping herself to a piece and disappearing out into the kitchen with the whole container, her groans of pleasure echoing through the empty café.

Mum's cake was ready to go by the register at morning tea so she could personally see to their selling as I raised a hand in a wave and exited through the back door to my scooter to ride across town to see Dr Bailey. It wouldn't be the same seeing Dr Bailey without later debriefing the whole session with Mrs May over a nice cup of tea. I missed her. I missed her wisdom and her kindness and her tea.

The coiffed lady manning Dr Bailey's reception desk watched me like a criminal for what felt like an eternity before Dr Bailey came out and called my name as though I wasn't the only person in the waiting room. Inside his office, I flopped in the patient chair, suddenly feeling like a petulant child and waited for him to start the session.

'How are you?' he asked.

'Fine,' I replied.

He smirked, he was used to me now. 'I saw your mother yesterday, she says you have a boyfriend.'

'That doesn't sound very professional, to be discussing me on the street,' I smiled.

'Ainsley,' he chided.

'Sorry, I don't mean to sound sulky. Yes, I do, well kind of, I suppose. We haven't exactly discussed labels.'

'Right, why don't you tell me about it?'

'What's there to tell? We met, I like him and we're just going along and seeing what happens.'

'Well that sounds smart, you don't need too much pressure right now.'

'There's no pressure with Christian.'

'That's his name?'

'Yep.'

'Right, then.  And how's the café going?'

'Oh, fine, making some money. It's kind of fun actually.' I told him about Jo working there and Mum helping out and how much fun she was appearing to have and how she was now bringing in cake. He seemed more pleased at Mum's headway than anything happening with me.

'Well, it seems like you're doing just fine. What's your head telling you? Any thoughts we need to discuss?'

'You know, there's nothing, there's no anxiety, there's no stress, I'm feeling pretty bloody good to be honest, even the compulsive consumption of carbs has eased off.'

'I'm glad to hear it,' he smiled. 'Keep taking the medication, and just take it easy with this boy. I'll see you in a month but if you need me beforehand, you know where I am.'

I thanked him, left, made an appointment for a month's time that I was working out how to cancel even as the judgmental receptionist and her annoying scowl wrote my name beside the time slot and I went out to where my scooter patiently waited.

Back at the café, Mum was busying herself with a customer, clearly more relaxed just knowing I'd been over to see Dr Bailey, she even smiled when she saw me come in.

All the slices of cake had sold, so I gave her the entire cake takings out of the till and she beamed with pride. She hadn't yet realised I'd been transferring her daily pay into her bank account after she'd refused to take it.

'I best go home and make some more then,' she smiled as she left to go cook Dad's dinner.

# Chapter 18

Mum started coming in earlier and earlier each day, loaded down with baked goods, muffins, cakes, cupcakes, slices, she was having too much fun, smiling more than I'd seen her smile in a long time. She always sent a slice of something out with Christian's toasted sandwich, perhaps trying to butter him up, keep him on side so she could keep a better eye on me? Jo and I were endlessly amused by whatever she was up to.

'A little help, Ainsley,' Mum called as she tried struggling through the door with her arms full of Tupperware.

'That's a lot of stuff, Mum,' I told her.

'Oh it's not all for you. Vivi goes back to her own house today, your father wanted me to make sure she was well looked after so he doesn't have to see that dog again. It growls at him while he's watching the news and there's pink dog hair all over the house. Anyway, I've just dropped her off at physiotherapy and have to pick her up in an hour. Can she come back here and rest upstairs? Your father will come and get us later.'

'Of course, Mum.'

Mum found homes for her treats, put some food in the fridge upstairs for me and some for Vivi, set up a place for Vivi to rest on the couch and eventually returned, slightly short of breath and declared, 'I just have to go get Vivi, will you be okay while I'm gone?'

'We'll be fine, Mum. Go, just worry about Vivi.'

'Alright. We'll be back within the hour.'

A taxi delivered Mum and Vivi not long later to the front of the café. We could see them through the open door squabbling as Mum tried to help Vivi, who didn't want any help, out of the car and up the few stairs.

Vivi stood in the doorway, frozen, looking around. 'You alright, Vivi?' I asked.

'Sure, sure. I just didn't know *this* was the place your mother's been telling me about?'

'What do you mean? Do you know this place?'

'I sure do. I came to a party here once with a guy named Gilbert. What kind of a name is Gilbert? Isn't that what you said at the time, Jack?' she asked my mum.

'Oh that guy. I did. He had a bushy beard and long hair. You just knew he was no good,' Mum concurred.

'Well that was the truth, for sure,' Vivi said, shaking her head.

Jo bought over some tea and we sat in a booth to hear Vivi's story while we had no customers.

'Gilbert said he just had to drop something off to a friend on our way to dinner. We walked in and this place was crammed with people. They were all dressed in beautiful gowns and suits. The ladies swilled fancy champagne like it was water and the men sat around tables playing poker drinking shots of vodka and smoking cigars. Gilbert introduced me to some people, got me some champagne and left me with some ladies who were talking diamonds of all things.

'He returned a little while later, introduced me to some over-sized, loud man with a moustache who slapped him on the back before walking away. Then he says there's something I want to show you and he leads me up those stairs through there and through the panel in the stairwell and up to the third floor where there was boudoir after boudoir filled with people up to unlady-like shenanigans.

'Vivi, really? No, that can't be right,' I said, sensing this was all way off base it couldn't have anything to do with Mrs May. Not my sweet, dear friend.

'I just thought, wow why are they all doing that here? And he opened a door and said this one's for us, it's a gift from Frank. I go, but I don't think I want to, and he goes what do you mean? I say, it's only our second date and he says but you didn't protest when you came in here and I say what's that supposed to mean? He goes that's what happens here. You're just lucky some other fella didn't scoop you up here. I thought this would be your thing, he says, you're such a party girl. I thought you'd be up for it for sure.'

'I told you all that partying would get you into trouble,' my mother admonished.

'What happened then, Vivi?' Jo prompted.

'Well, I hightailed it out of there, didn't I? He went to get drinks and I ran. I jumped in a taxi and went to your mother's house. I didn't even have my purse with me so I had no money or anything to get home. That was the last time I partied or went out with a strange man. Archie was already in the wings and he was kind and lovely and would never have done such a thing and I grabbed a hold of that beautiful man and never let go.'

'Yet, look at you back to your old party ways with the boys, Vivi and now you've got a busted a hip and a broken toe to show for it.'

'Vivi, exactly how did you hurt your hip?' I asked.

She smirked. 'It's not what you think. I was dancing with my Italian Stallion, he dipped me and that was it,' she shrugged. 'Nothing like any of this and it's not nice of you to suggest otherwise, Jackie,' she scolded Mum.

'Did you know about this place, Mum? Is that why you hated Mrs May?'

'Who's Mrs May?' Vivi asked.

'Ana May, that's who left me this place in her will.'

'No,' Vivi said. 'This place was owned by Anastasia Mayberry, one of the most prestigious madam's in the country.'

'A madam?' Jo and I blurted.

'That's what I was just telling you. All the boudoirs, they were for the prostitutes in the fancy gowns downstairs waiting for the men playing poker to decide they needed a little recreational relief between hands,' she added.

'Crafty old lady,' I said, shaking my head.

'I always knew there was something not right about that woman,' Mum added. 'That's why I didn't like her, Ainsley. There was just something not quite right. She was always too hoity toity, wouldn't talk to the other mums or do her canteen duty, barely even spoke during parent teacher interviews and so secretive. No one knew her. No one knew anything about her and it was just strange and her boy was always too well dressed for a non-working single mother. It never made sense and I just knew there was something I didn't like.'

'Okay, Mum, we get it, you've made your point. You hate her, move on,' I smirked. 'Now Vivi, what's this panel doorway in the stairwell? We haven't seen a door there.'

When Vivi had finished her tea, she slowly led us all up the stairs. We followed like sheep and their shepherd.

'See, there's nothing here Vivi,' I said as we stood on the landing. 'Are you sure this is the same place?' I asked, wondering if her memory had been distorted by life or too much fun with Italian Stallions.

'Oh, I'm very sure, Ainsley Donovan. You do not forget nights like that, I promise you,' she chided as she began pushing on the timber panel on the wall until it popped open to reveal another set of stairs. 'Didn't you even notice the building proportions were all wrong? That this wall didn't end where all the others ended or the ceiling was too low?' she asked.

Jo and I just shrugged. We hadn't paid it much attention, really. There'd been so many other things to deal with since I'd got here.

Vivi pulled the string hanging from the ceiling to the doorway of the stairwell. Light flooded down and up we trooped.

'Are you okay with the stairs, Vivi?' I asked, thinking surely this was more than she should be doing.

'I'm fine, stop fussing,' she scolded.

There was a long hallway the length of the building with cheap, threadbare carpet and six doors, three on each side, numbered like hotel doors. We opened each of the doors as we went, each revealing small rooms just big enough for a sumptuous bed, beautiful rugs and linen and not much else. Some of the beds were unmade, the covers still rumpled or askew, a pair of hand-cuffs still hung from a bedpost as though someone had only just finished using them.

'You need to close this place down, Ainsley and come home,' Mum insisted.

'Mum! I can't do that now. I've put in too much time and effort and we have customers and everything.'

'But you can't live here. You can't live amongst all this tawdry history.'

'Why not?' I asked. 'I'll just close this floor back up and forget it even exists,' I said, as we all made our way back down the hidden stairs.

Mum and Jo went back down to see to the lunch rush in stupefied silence while I set Vivi up in my living room with some tea and food and the television.

'Sorry I don't know any more than that,' Vivi said.

'That's okay, I think that's enough to take in for one day,' I laughed.

'You really never guessed anything?' she asked.

I didn't want to tell her about the jewels in the basement and handbags full of money so just shrugged innocently. 'Nope, no idea. She was just a sweet old lady who made great tea and helped me deal with my shit.'

'Well, I'm sure she'd seen just about everything so she probably had lots of practice,' she grinned.

'I'm sure she did,' I laughed, leaving her to recuperate while I went to help Mum and Jo with the customers.

Christian came in later for his lunch and kept me company in the kitchen while he ate and I told him about the hidden boudoirs upstairs.

'You're kidding?' he said. 'Show me, I have to see it.'

'No way, I'm not going back up there. You go, just push on that timber panel and it'll pop open.'

He returned a little while later shaking his head. 'I just can't believe this place.'

'I know. It's too much. We need to call the police, don't we?'

'Probably. But I'd like to wait and see what the guys I have looking into Henry come back with first. I want to know what we're dealing with before we call the police.'

'Okay,' I nodded, trusting him.

'What are you going to do with the upstairs?'

'Nothing. I'm going to pretend I never saw it, that it was never there,' I said.

'Will you be alright? I gotta get back, but I'll see you tonight.'

'Yeah, yeah,' I insisted as he leant in and left me with a delicious, toe-curling kiss.

We spent a nice, naughty, Saturday night in with takeaway Thai food and downloaded a movie we didn't actually watch before making a mockery of Mrs May's marital bed. Although who knows what that sneaky old lady was like back in her day. It seemed she was full of secrets. We were still waiting to hear back from Christian's investigator people but were easily distracted from the subject once we started ripping clothes from each other.

I'd never needed someone like I needed Christian. I'd never craved and consumed and been consumed with such desperation. Heat filled all the space and surged through my veins when he touched me and he touched me in a way no one ever had. He saw me. He sensed every emotion running through my head and followed it. I felt connected to Christian in a way I'd never known you could be with another human being. He made me smile and laugh and feel the most incredible sense of satisfaction and calm.

I could no longer imagine a life or even a day without Christian. He made everything, he made me worthwhile and whole. Everything would be fine as long as he was there to wrap his strong arms around me at the end of the day, to hold me close in bed at night, our skin fusing us together under the blankets in sheer perfection. Turns out Mrs May's theories were right, after all, and it was bliss. Total and utter bliss and we indulged in it, filled ourselves with it until we could take no more and slept.

The coffee machine was buzzing downstairs when I woke on Sunday, the sun barely kissing the sky outside the arched windows. I usually woke with Christian's arms still wrapped around me, his manhood standing to attention, ready for action. But instead he was up at the crack of dawn running the coffee machine.

I threw on a robe and went in search of my man.

Christian stood behind the enormous, shiny coffee machine in nothing but boxers. His beautiful tanned body exquisite in the dappled early morning light, his hair still mussed from sleep. If only our morning patrons got to see this. Perhaps business would increase, I thought to myself with a smile, before realising, he hadn't even noticed I'd come down. I'd never seen him so distracted.

I put my arms around him, feeling his muscles flex slightly at my touch. I kissed his neck and asked, 'What's wrong?'

He put down the milk jug and turned, taking me in his arms and kissing me. 'Sorry, didn't mean to wake you. I'm just a bit distracted and we probably should get going soon.'

I kissed him, harder. 'Don't you worry about today,' I said, pressing my forehead to his. 'We can do anything as long as we're together.'

He smiled tightly, 'You say that now, but you haven't met my family.' He finally smiled and kissed my forehead. 'Go back to bed, I'll bring coffee up in a minute.'

I smiled sympathetically and kissed him on the cheek before going back to bed and giving him the space he needed.

We had our coffee in bed, me nestled against him as we talked about inane things, a distraction on both our parts, I suspect, before showering and getting ready, which seemed to take Christian an inordinate amount of time to complete when he was usually done in ten minutes.

'You ready?' he finally grumbled, shoving the last of one of Mum's muffins in his mouth.

I opened the front door to find an Audi RS Quattro sitting at the kerb. 'That's yours?' I asked.

He smiled.

I rolled my eyes.

'You'll be glad for the luxury in a little bit. We're going to the country house. It's about a five-hour drive. But don't worry, we won't be staying long,' Christian promised with a satisfied grin.

As I slid into the perfectly moulded leather seat, I no longer cared how ostentatious the car was.

The car barely hummed as it started. Soft jazz drifted out of the stereo and cocooned us in our own little bubble of perfection as we headed out of the city.

A road trip with a new boyfriend can be an intimidating experience. All that alone time in a car, just the two of you, no food or drink or sex to distract you, nothing to do but talk. It could go any which way, especially with a man like Christian. The relationship might not survive, it might die a slow and painful death or it could flourish like an apple tree full of blossoms in the spring and be better than you ever imagined. You can never really tell though until you get into that miniscule space and begin the journey.

But we seemed to be managing fine enough with conversation, a few laughs and I was as comfortable as I would have been in my own car if I still had one and began poking around to see if I could learn more about my man from the hidden corners of his car. I opened the glove box to see what I could see.

'What are you looking for?' he asked.

'Nothing, just seeing what you have stashed in here, you can learn a lot about a person by what they stash in their glove boxes and consoles,' I said smartly.

'Is that right?' he asked, smirking. 'And what have you found?'

'There's next to nothing in here. What kind of person are you?'

He laughed.

I shifted the car manual and underneath was a battered and

loved copy of Hunter S Thompson's The Rum Diary. 'Well, I found this, looks well loved.'

'Ah, you cannot beat The Rum Diary.'

'And you keep it in your car for emergencies? In case you're stuck on the side of the road waiting for the RAA or something?'

He laughed. 'No, of course not. When life gets too hard I'll get fish and chips, a few beers, go to the beach and read it cover to cover and it never fails to transport me, to who I was, where I was and how I felt the first time I read it. Which, by the way, was at one of Tom's surf carnivals that I'd been dragged to when I was a miserable twelve year old wishing I was anywhere else. I think that's why I always read it at the beach which is kind of perfect for the story too, I guess.' He smiled wistfully before turning to me and asking, 'What about you? What's your go to book?'

'Nothing as prolific as The Rum Diary. Depends on my mood though, I read Marian Keyes when I need to feel like someone out there gets me and all my madness. If I want to feel powerful and have a laugh I read Janet Evanovich and pretend I'm Stephanie Plum with two hot guys to lust after while I kick ass. Sounds silly I suppose but hiding in a corner and losing myself in these worlds, it just makes it better.' Now I was smiling wistfully as I remembered how I got through so many hard times before I got lost in the darkness that led me here, to now, to this moment, riding in Christian's ridiculous Audi sports car discussing the books that changed us. I made a mental note to see if Mum had packed the books in one of the few boxes of things she'd taken from my flat.

As a Michael Buble song filled the car, Christian asked, 'So tell me, if you could go anywhere in the world, where would it be?'

'Paris,' I said without even needing to think about it.

'Really? Isn't that a bit clichéd?'

'Maybe, but I'd still like to go, stroll arm in arm along the bridges as the sun goes down and the lights come up, it seems very romantic to me.'

He turned and smiled at me. 'Romantic is good,' he winked.

'What about you? I bet you've already travelled everywhere.'

'I've travelled. But if I could go anywhere, it'd be Russia. Drink vodka in some ridiculous Russian bar, walk the streets completely anonymous with just you and me.'

'Me? You've thought about that since you met me?'

'Oh, I think about running away with you every day,' he smirked.

'Ana was Russian you know. Did I mention that?'

'You did,' he smiled kindly. 'We'll find out what's going on, what happened to Henry, I promise,' he said, squeezing my hand.

Thankfully Christian and I were turning out to be the flourishing sort of road trippers, growing closer with each conversation, falling more in love as he told me of his dream for us to move to a quiet beachside town where nothing much happened and we could have a big estate like property where we could raise our babies. Apparently, this was the only thing he coveted of his parents' life. He told me so many of his dreams and I loved hearing them. Where we could drink martinis at sunset and spend Sunday afternoons watching the quiet ocean and he could design beautiful buildings and I could do anything I wanted.

It occurred to me that while he was making all these plans for our future, I hadn't shared with him the most important thing he needed to know about me, about the darkness and the shame and the blackness I had to work hard at every single day to keep from coming back. I wondered if he'd still want me at his lovely estate in the quiet seaside town if he knew. Fear rippled through my veins as he pulled into a car park in front of a pub in a small country town.

'You alright?' he asked.

'Yeah, sure, why wouldn't I be,' I said, forcing a smile.

'You just paled for a minute.'

'I must be hungry,' I said. 'Come on, let's find somewhere to eat, hey?'

He nodded but I'm not sure he quite believed me. He took my hand, squeezing it, kissing the top of my head. 'We won't eat until late when we get there so how about an early lunch? The pub okay?'

'Sure,' I said and he led me through the doors.

I found a table and Christian went up to the bar to order us both schnitzel, chips and salads and get some soft drinks. It was an average country pub, a few old blokes at the bar, a couple of young blokes playing pool, a few girls giggling as they watched, a few middle aged lunchers, perhaps farmers taking a Sunday off, helping themselves to the salad bar.

While Christian waited at the bar for our drinks, a couple of the boys who had been quietly sipping their beers and watching a football game on the big screen on the wall started chatting animatedly with Christian about the Audi. Christian beamed, but not in a self-centred, egotistical, centre of attention, yes, go on, look and admire my fancy car that you'll never afford way, but just like a bloke talking cars with other blokes who loved them. Not a single sign of the obnoxious pig that sometimes came out, in fact, I hadn't seen any sign of that guy in a while. I smiled. Christian laughed as he chatted with the boys like he was a whole new person. He was more relaxed than when we'd first met, I thought as I looked up from checking Facebook on my phone. His face was softer, smoother, calm, happy. Seeing him like this made me love him more, this person I'd somehow accidentally stumbled across, as though he were one of the hidden gems in my basement covered in dust, now shone in all his fabulousness. I couldn't help but love him. It terrified me. Suddenly I had something to lose that I didn't think I could bear losing.

He joined me with a giant grin as our schnitzels were delivered. How did I get so lucky? I thought as I looked across the table, begging God or the universe or whoever was controlling this life of ours that I'd stay lucky and that after I told him just how crazy I was, he'd still be mine and not rung for the hills or hide out in his Russian fantasy without me, where I'd never be able to find him.

I tried putting it out of my mind. Christian kept asking if I was okay and I did my best to change the subject, trying easy topics like movies because now wasn't the time to shatter his perfect fantasies.

With our tummies full, we were back on the road and suddenly there was a change in Christian. The further we drove, the tenser he became, this lovely tranquil, happy man from the pub disintegrated before my eyes. I figured we must be getting close to our destination. I reached over, pried open the fist he'd made and held his clammy hand. He didn't even look at me, his eyes hard and focussed on the road ahead. I didn't know how to help him, how to take away the fear and the pain, other than to squeeze his hand to show I was there and bring it to my mouth and kiss it. I looked over at him and he gave me a tight smile of appreciation. This was harder for him than I realised. I wanted to make it better, to make it easier, to make it all go away, but all I could do was be here and hope it would be over soon.

# Chapter 19

We'd turned off the highway and been driving down a wide, tree-lined road that appeared to lead to nowhere for almost half an hour. I hadn't seen any houses for a while. Either there weren't any or they were buried so far back behind the trees, away from the road and prying eyes there was no way to see them. I should be very concerned about where Christian was taking me, I thought.

We seemed to have been driving for an age. I had no idea it'd take this long. I was just as concerned about the long drive home and thought we probably should have made arrangements to stay somewhere, to have Jo open the café. The way Christian's jaw locked and his eyes went the darkest green as he turned the Audi off the road to nowhere, there was no way I was going to even speak until he was ready.

He drove through a pair of very grand, intricate white gates that had been opened wide to reveal acres of perfectly mani- cured green grass. He followed the curving drive, the house getting bigger and bigger the closer we got and Christian's face became tenser and harder.

The front of the big white house was swathed in blue from the mass of hyacinths. We kept going down the drive, past the side of the house where the drive was edged with strawberries, followed the curve almost to the back where Christian stopped the car with a jolt between a shiny black Range Rover Evoque and a cute blue Volvo hatch, near ripping the door off its hinges when he opened it, clearly wanting to be anywhere else.

We got out and he stood a minute, taking it in, sucking in a deep breath. He took my hand and then we followed the gravel drive up to the back of the house, Christian gripping my hand as though it were all that was keeping him upright.

To my left was an enormous resort style swimming pool, complete with a Bali hut in the far corner and enormous frangipani trees providing shade over some of the pool lounges that went the whole way round the pool.

Next to the pool was a grass tennis court, the net absent but the court perfectly manicured and marked out, an umpire's tower stood tall in the centre and floodlights stretched up in the corners.

Beyond the tennis court was a beautiful grassed area just waiting for children to run and play, surrounded by more frangipani trees and flowering shrubs dividing one space from another hidden from view, only an arched walkway nestled in the middle indicating there was more.

Where was I? Who were these people? This couldn't possibly be a home. It was like a resort. Who lived like this? Even with all Mrs May had left me, this kind of wealth was incomprehensible. All the properties we had passed now made sense, the trees, their seclusion, they were all homes like this.

A large deck was on the right. The big doors pulled wide joining the deck with the family room inside. I could feel Christian's tense body shaking beside me as his sweaty hand continued to grip mine like a vice as we stepped into the bright room. On the sofa to the right sat three girls deep in conversation. On the left were two men by the pool table and a very chic middle-aged lady was walking between the two groups carrying a tray of drinks. They all stopped mid action, their mouths open, their eyes bugging out of their beautiful heads and Christian gripped my hand so tightly, I thought my knuckles might crumble to dirt.

I tried squeezing his hand in return with the little strength and movement I still retained to let him know I was there for him. I wanted to let him know I'd always be there as long as he wanted and to not fret, not anymore. He relaxed the intensity of his sweaty grip but only slightly, just enough that I might retain the use of my hand.

The lady carrying the tray of drinks unfroze and shoved them at the older of the men by the pool table and hurried to Christian, embracing him in an all-consuming hug. I took the opportunity to take in the scene before me. The three girls sat close, intimate as only best friends do, their frozen conversation still hanging in the air. There was a beautiful, girl-next-door brunette, a captivating girl with wild black curls and bright green eyes that shone from across the room. The third was a petite redhead with fine chiselled features and dark eyes, as equally beautiful as the girls beside her.

The two men standing beside the pool table, although no

game was in play, watched us warily. I recognised Richard Harrington from the newspaper and magazines but the photos didn't show just how intimidating he was in person. He was a little shorter and a little greyer than his younger counterpart who I assumed was Tom with his sun-bleached, unruly hair. But even though Tom was handsome and enigmatic in a warm way, Richard Harrington was just frightening, and I saw where that coldness and harshness I remembered from the earlier version of Christian came from, what he could have turned into.

'Darling, it's good to see you,' the lady who'd just been hugging Christian gushed as though she hadn't seen him in a hundred years.

'Hi Mum,' Christian stumbled uncertainly. He coughed nervously before turning to me, 'This is Ainsley.'

'Hello. It's very nice to meet you, dear,' his mum smiled warmly. 'Come, come, I was just making drinks, what can I get you both?'

'Scotch?' Christian said, asking rather than telling. He looked at me, 'Red wine?'

'Sure,' I nodded. 'That would be lovely, thank you.'

Mrs Harrington nodded, her grin too big as she hurried off to fetch our drinks.

Tom strode forward, he was quite captivating up close. He shook Christian's hand, 'Good to see you,' he smiled warmly before shaking mine. 'I'm Tom, it's very nice to meet you, Ainsley. Let me introduce you around,' he said, leading me by the elbow.

Christian kept so close he was almost standing on me as Tom led me across the room and introduced me to the girls on the sofa. Tom pointed to the brunette, 'My fiancée, Alex.' You could feel the electricity sparking between them as she gave me a cautious wave of hello.

'This is my sister, Lydia and her girlfriend, Andrea.' They each stood in turn and shook my hand. Lydia's girlfriend was French, her 'nice to meet you' sounding more like poetry than a simple hello.

Christian led me away and introduced me to his father who had not moved from the pool table where he'd stood maintaining a strangely suspicious look in his eye.

'Don't worry about him, he always looks like that,' Christian whispered in my ear as we moved across the floor.

His father was perfectly polite, intimidating, cold, even a little frightening and I was thankful Mrs Harrington returned with our drinks and suggested we all head out into the sunshine on the patio.

Another lady followed us out with a drinks trolley with a bucket of ice filled with beers like a flower arrangement, a couple of bottles of red wine and an ice bucket with a bottle of white wine and a bottle of scotch and quietly left without speaking a word.

The air was tight and we stood awkwardly, me in Christian's death grip while he made polite conversation with his brother.

'So, tell us how you met,' his mother insisted.

Everyone suddenly paid attention. 'I thought she was trying to break into this old building in the city. I told her you couldn't break into a building like that, it has steel doors. She called me asshole because she had a key but the door was stuck, so I helped her.'

'I was very grateful, it had been closed up for a long time and the WD40 you suggested worked a treat,' I smiled nervously.

He smiled back, squeezed my hand. 'After that we kept running into each other while getting coffee from the same vending cart. Then I passed the old building on the way to a meeting and it had come alive. It was this beautiful café and I just had to go in and see if it was her doing. But you know me and my people skills are not the best. I made her mad again and she yelled at me but somehow she agreed to go on a date with me and the rest is history,' he told them, smiling.

'And how exactly did he get you to agree?' his father asked suspiciously.

'Oh, I had a customer who was causing a bit of trouble and he helped me out, told her to get lost. My friend said I owed him dinner. I really didn't think this would happen. I thought it would be one date and that was it but he turned out to be lovely and sweet under all that brashness.'

His father hmphed and walked away. The girls looked at each other suspiciously and slinked away into their own conversation.

'Well, I think it's all very lovely and romantic,' his mum said, squeezing his hand.

I thought their reactions were a little rude. It was a perfectly good story. I drained my wine. This was going to be a long afternoon. After forcefully extricating my hand from Christian's grip and doing my best to assure him I would indeed return, I went to replenish our drinks.

Standing at the drinks trolley pouring another wine, I could hear the three girls who stood nearby with their backs to me whispering. I didn't mean to listen in but couldn't help catching a fragment of their conversation.

'But she actually looks nice,' said the French girl.

'I just can't believe anyone would actually date him, it has to be the money,' said the newly minted fiancee.

'Alex,' giggled Andrea.

'What? It's true. My brother is not known for his charm, you know,' Lydia agreed.

'Maybe she's one of those brow beaten masochists who doesn't mind being treated like dirt,' added Alex.

Were they seriously talking about me? I glared at them, waiting for the punchline, sure it was a mistake, a joke, a misunderstanding, that they were talking about someone else and a whole other situation. My eyes locked with Alex's, her face instantly reddening like a beetroot, her mouth frozen open in mid speech as she realised her mistake.

Red hot anger flowed through my veins at their cruelty. I looked over to Christian, my body frozen between the desire to lash out at those girls and to protect Christian. But I was dumbfounded, their cruelty incomprehensible in my polite brain and my feet refused to move.

'Shit, Ainsley,' Alex said, nudging Lydia. 'I'm sorry...'

I opened my mouth wanting to say something, defend Christian but nothing came out. I just couldn't believe his own family could be so mean. There were no words. White fury raged inside me as though it might burst out of my skin in a flow of volcanic hate but I couldn't get any of the words to come out. There were too many.

'Ainsley, wait,' Lydia called as I turned to walk away. She

caught my arm and I had to wait, turn, hear her out, or cause a scene and I didn't want to upset Christian. It was hard enough for him to be here as it was.

I looked at her, waiting, waiting for an apology for her to say you misunderstand, I'm sorry, something. 'You don't know Christian the way we do,' is all I got.

'Clearly,' I spat.

'It's just that, Christian is not really known as Mr Charming or Mr Personality or even Mr Nice,' she said defending herself, hanging her head in shame as well she should. I knew his people skills weren't always the greatest. I'd experienced it firsthand that day in the café with the carry on over cooked cheese and the way he'd grabbed my arm but this was his sister, she was supposed to love him anyway.

'He made a pass at Alex once too, and he wasn't very nice about it. Tom would have killed him if he'd been in the country.'

'Enough, Lydia.' Christian seethed from behind me.

'I think I need the ladies room,' I said, looking for someone to direct me, desperate to escape the disgustingness of the situation. Why would they even share something like that? They'd just met me.

'I'll show you,' Christian said, all the air and pent up anxiety expelling from his body with one exhalation as though finally defeated.

We walked back into the house, through the room we'd just been in, down a small hallway that bended out of view from the patio and stopped in front of a door.

Christian rested his hand on the handle but stopped, 'I'll wait here and take you home when you're done,' he said, not looking me in the eye.

I put my finger under his chin and tipped his face up. 'Clearly they don't know the same Christian I do,' I smiled, kissing him softly.

He smiled tentatively in return.

'Did you really make a pass at Alex?' I asked.

'Yes,' he said, hanging his head. 'I was angry. Angry at Tom. Angry at Dad. I was just angry. This is actually the first time I've seen her since.'

'Why do I sense there's more?'

He let out a huff of air. 'I wasn't exactly polite about it, Ains.'

'What does that mean?'

'I was more like that guy you met at the cafe, the guy who grabbed your wrist.'

'Oh.'

'If Dad hadn't interrupted, I don't know...'

'Well, clearly he did,' I smiled, not really sure what to think. He looked so broken, so ashamed and I wanted to love him, care for him, make everything okay, make all the sadness and misery go away. I knew he'd never actually hurt anyone, it wasn't in his soul. He was a good man, a kind man just looking for someone to understand him, to get him, to love him. Like me, we'd both come from a dark place where we'd been so lost we didn't know if we'd ever be found.

He looked at me dubiously, words were clearly only having a mild affect and as I had really only asked for the bathroom so I could escape those horrible people and their insensitive gossiping before I did something I regretted as opposed to actually needing to pee, I looked down the empty corridor, before pushing the door open, dragging him inside with me.

He gasped, his eyes wide as I forced him up against the wall, knocking a beautiful outback painting askew as my lips met his, hungrily forcing his open, our tongues desperately meeting, entwining as my hands made their way under his shirt, roaming inside the waistband of his jeans as our breathing increased and our need for each other catapulted us out of our surroundings, out of reality. His erection pressed against me and I unbuttoned his jeans, hastily, accidentally scratching his tender skin as I went, causing him to gasp loudly, his erection ready to burst from the contact.

Heat pumped through my body as we switched places, my back against the wall, my legs wrapped around his waist and Mrs May's pretty sundress hitched up to my waist. In moments we were panting, sated and flushed as a giggle erupted from somewhere within. I could feel Christian smiling as he kissed my hair, nuzzling my neck, himself trying not to giggle.

Eventually my breathing and my heartbeat returned to normal and I looked at him smiling down at me. 'I really needed that,' he said smoothly, that deep after sex tone to his voice.

'Well, anytime, Mr Harrington, anytime,' I smiled, kissing him softly.

Straightening Mrs May's sundress, running my fingers through my mussed hair, I couldn't believe what we'd just done and the thought made me smile. I helped Christian button his shirt, unable to resist kissing him quickly before opening the door and checking the hallway was clear.

I'd never been so bold in all my life. I don't know what came over me, where the impulse had come from but I liked it, it felt good to let loose and do something fun and crazy, not looney bin crazy but regular person crazy. Briefly I wondered what Dr Bailey would think. He said I needed to be strong, independent and take control of things. I think I just did that and from the smile stretching across Christian's face, I think it was a good move.

We walked back out onto the patio, Christian's arm stretching protectively across my shoulders, reclaiming our drinks and each taking a long, necessary gulp before our eyes caught and I was unable to hide the mischievous smile that erupted.

I caught a confused look from Lydia but ignored her as Christian took my hand, tenderly kissed my hair and led me over to his mother who was brushing lint off of Tom's navy blue polo shirt.

'We're going to go, Mum. Congratulations, Tom, it was good to see you,' he said, shaking his brother's hand.

'But darling, you just got here and we haven't eaten yet.'

'I know, but Ainsley needs to get back. We both do and it's a long drive.'

'Of course,' she smiled tensely. Perhaps because of Christian's not so veiled comment about being shafted out to the backwaters as Melbournians always thought of Adelaide. 'But please, go inside and say goodbye to your father, or I'll never hear the end of it. He's just gone into his study to take a call.' She leant forward and kissed Christian on the cheek. 'Ainsley, it really was lovely to meet you, dear.'

I smiled and nodded as Christian led me inside. I stood just outside the door to his father's study while he went in to say goodbye. On the wall was a family photograph, it was old, maybe five years or so, but even then Christian looked uncomfortable, awkward, 'ferrety,' I heard Jo laugh. But yes, ferrety, although Christian was looking less and less so by the day. It was all the cheese toasties he was eating, I thought. His face had filled out and he was looking more like Tom now, I thought as I studied the photograph in front of me. A little shorter, his hair was darker and he was not quite as stocky. More refined and classic, but just as handsome.

Lydia and Tom appeared to be sharing a joke in the photograph, lost in some strange world no one else was able to share as twins often were. But there was another girl, long dark hair, beautiful big, rich sea-green eyes and a megawatt smile holding onto Christian's elbow. His other sister, I assumed. She was beautiful with the kindest, sweetest, most innocent eyes, clearly imploring him to behave, to be strong, to be present. It was as though she was all that was anchoring that lost, sad boy to the earth. I wondered if I'd ever be able to be that for him or where on earth she was if he'd been dragged here kicking and screaming.

Christian came out of his father's study, his mouth in a tight straight line. 'Ready?' he asked. His hand snaking over my hip to the small of my back as he looked at the photo. Then his eyes glistened as he looked at the picture properly before he smiled. 'My sister, Jasmine. The only one smart enough to go where he can't find her,' he said, proudly. 'Jaz disowned the family a long time ago, not too long after this photo was taken, I guess. This was probably the last time we were all together, before all the crap with Tom happened. She just couldn't stand Dad trying to control her life anymore. Ran off with her security guard,' he smiled as he told the story.

'You look close,' I said.

'We were. We are. Sort of. Not so much now. No one actually knows where she's living. I get an untraceable email once or twice a year,' he smiled tightly. I imagined it was just another reason for him to be furious at his Dad, at Tom who'd stolen his job and forced him to uproot his life where he found me, fumbling my way in the world. I'd have to remind him there were advantages to having been sent off to my little city.

'Come,' he smiled, kissing my head. 'Let's go home.'

I nodded, linked my arm through his and we left through the patio. He called a 'See ya' to the masses rather than doing a proper goodbye, not that any of them deserved one anyway and we hurried to the car. He screeched out of the driveway, flicking up stones as he went as though he was an angry teenager, perfectly controlling the car from fishtailing as though he'd done the same thing many times before and my heart broke a little bit more for him just as it swelled a little bit more with love for this beautifully broken man.

# Chapter 20

'Why don't we stop somewhere for the night?' I suggested. It had already been a long drive to get to that mansion they called home and it was a long drive back to the cafe, even in the luxury of the Audi and after the trials of the day and the couple of drinks we'd had at his parents' house, I thought it would be safer for us both.

'But we need to get back, we both have work tomorrow,' he protested.

'It's fine. I'll call Jo and get her to open up and I'm sure you can be late one day, can't you?'

He smiled. 'You're very wise, you know,' he said, pulling my hand to his mouth to kiss.

Christian pulled into the first Comfort Inn we passed in the next country town and booked us into the best room they had while I sent Mum a text to let her know what was happening and Jo a text asking her to sort out the opening of the café in the morning.

With the Audi parked safely in the front of the room and

the rest of the world locked away on the other side of the door, Christian finally exhaled as I snaked my arms around him and breathed him in.

'I couldn't have done that without you, you know,' he said, kissing my hand.

After freshening up as best I could in the bathroom with the lack of supplies, I came out to find Christian propped up on an elbow watching a *How I Met Your Mother* re-run on the small television, laughing, already looking more relaxed than he had an hour ago.

I climbed onto the bed beside him, happy enough to watch inane television with him, but he drew me to him. 'You're amazing, you know that,' he said, looking at me intently.

'Well,' I said, kissing him lightly. 'I'm pretty impressed by you, too.'

'You really don't hate me after what Lydia said, after what I did to Alex?'

'No. That wasn't who you really are,' I told him.

He looked unsure.

'How about I show you how fine I am about it all?' I suggested.

He raised his eyebrows.

To drive my point home, I pushed him onto his back, straddling him, snaking my way down his body and beginning a night of pure unadulterated bliss, a night of things I'd never be able to discuss with Dr Bailey but proved once and for all how much I loved Christian.

He gasped for air, we both did before he pushed me on the bed, a naughty grin spread across his face and showed me just how grateful he was for my support and I responded easily and loudly, already planning an early departure before having to show our faces to those in the room next door. I was so used to the remoteness of the café's living quarters that I'd forgotten to censor myself and the way Christian made love to me made it damn near impossible not to cry out from the sheer and utter glorious pleasure that rocketed through me, shaking me to my core, bonding my heart and my very soul to his, fusing us together like an electrical circuit, one piece no longer effective without the other.

We arrived at the café late in the morning, during the quiet in between time, the morning rush done, the lunch rush still to come. We entered through the back door and Christian ducked upstairs to put on a fresh shirt from the collection that appeared to be growing in my wardrobe. Mum was in the kitchen prepping for the lunch rush, humming happily to herself. After calling a quick hello to her, I went into the café to see Jo who was just finishing up with a couple of very serious looking blokes in the middle of the room.

Jo turned as I walked in, her face was white, tears streaming down her face, her eyes were big and red and terrified. My heart dropped to my toes and my breath caught in my chest for just a second before I raced to her.

'Jo? What's the matter? What's happened?'

'Benny,' she whispered so faint, it was barely audible.

'What about Benny?' I asked, panic rising from deep in the very pit of my stomach.

'He's gone.'

'Gone where?'

'Gone. Just gone.'

'Jo, sit down,' I commanded. 'Mum, could you bring Jo some tea?' I ordered, as Mum came in with a plate laden with cakes to sell.

'What happened?' I asked the policeman.

'There was an accident on the freeway this morning. There was nothing anyone could do. I'm so sorry for your loss,' he said, his face clouding. 'Joanne was in his phone as his ICE, his in case of emergency, and we traced her here.'

One of the men Jo had been speaking to handed me a card. 'Will she be alright, do you need us to call anyone?'

'Maybe just Benny's parents,' I said, getting their details out of Jo's phone.

He nodded. 'Again, we're really sorry for your loss,' he said before they left.

Jo wrapped her hands around the warm cup of hot sweet tea Mum handed her. Once she'd taken a few calming sips, she lifted her tear-stained face, her eyes a dark red, her face puffy and blotchy. She took a deep breath but when she spoke, again, it was only the softest of whispers. 'He's dead.'

'I know, honey,' I said, pulling her to me, neither Mum nor I really knowing what to do, the shock still rolling through our systems.

Christian burst into the room as only Christian can before taking in the scene before him, instantly sobering his abrasive demeanour. 'What's going on,' he asked almost fearfully.

'There was an accident. Right now, I just need you to help me get Jo upstairs.'

He nodded, not arguing perhaps for the first time in his life.

He scooped Jo up as though she were a feather and carried her upstairs, laying her gently on the bed. 'What else can I do?'

'What do you need, Jo?' I asked.

She barely shook her head, just stared vacantly at the wall as tears streamed down her face.

'I think we just need to give her some space.'

He nodded his agreement and we went into the living room. Mum had already closed the front door and put up a sign apologising for the early closure. She was in the living room with coffees and was slicing up the banana cake she'd brought with her.

Christian and I sat on the couch, not speaking, there was nothing to say. I couldn't believe Benny was gone. Just like that.

'What do we do? How do we help her?' I asked no one in particular.

'I don't know,' Mum said as Christian squeezed my hand. 'Perhaps we should start by calling her parents?' we really were in trouble if even perfectly organised and structured Jacqui Donovan didn't know what to do.

Once Mum had sorted us with coffee and cake and called Jo's parents and told them we'd touch base again when Jo was ready, she kissed me on the head, tenderly touched Christian's arm and let herself out the back door.

I was in a state of shock myself. The sugar in the banana cake helped get my brain ticking. Christian went down and turned the lights off in the café and I went in to check on Jo. She lay on the bed, fragile and broken, shaking, crying, unable to speak or move.

'I'm going to call my doctor, see if he can give her something to help her sleep,' Christian said quietly, heading into the living room.

I lay on the bed beside Jo and wrapped my arms around her letting her sob into me, absorbing the shaking and the pain as best I could.

She hadn't stopped crying, she wouldn't eat or drink. She refused to go with her parents when they called. She kept looking at us as though begging us to tell her it was all a misunderstanding. But mostly she stared at the wall, tears falling from her vacant eyes.

Christian returned after a while with a very proper and formal looking doctor. Only a Harrington could get an important doctor to make a house call. They spoke quietly in the doorway before he came over and spoke softly to Jo who only sobbed, making no sense at all.

'I won't give her much, just a little something to take the edge off and hopefully she'll be able to sleep. She'll be stronger then. Is she staying here?'

'Yes,' I said, without even looking at Christian to see if he minded being booted out of my bed because there was no way I was putting her in one of those beds upstairs.

I got off the bed and went with Christian to see the doctor out. After Christian had closed the door, I asked him, 'You don't mind, do you? If Jo stays here?'

'Of course not,' he said, wrapping me in his arms and holding me tight. 'Do you want me to stay? I'll be fine on the couch,' he offered.

'No, it's okay,' I said, not sure if I'd be fine at all if he left but needing to focus only on Jo.

'Okay,' he said, kissing my forehead. 'I'll stop by first thing in the morning, okay?' he tilted my face up and looked into my eyes. 'Okay?' he asked again.

I nodded and then kissed him hard. 'I love you, Christian.'

He smiled timidly, 'I love you more than I ever knew I could love a single human being. You are my air, my purpose, my very reason for existing. Without you I'd fade to dust.' He said matter-of-factly, then he kissed me, softly, lovingly. 'Call me if you need anything, anything at all, even just to talk, okay, no matter the time.'

I nodded and he left. I stood leaning against the door a minute, everything sinking in, not liking the feeling of any of it, except that Christian loved me. That bit I liked. That bit made me strong. That bit helped me up the stairs and onto the bed with Jo. I took off her shoes and jeans and pulled the covers over her shaking body.

There wasn't much else I could do so I made some tea, did some accounts at the table, absently watched some television until it was late enough to lie on the bed with her, wipe her silent tears and do the only thing I could do, hold her as tight as I could in an effort to keep her together, to keep her whole, because if it had been Christian who'd died I don't think I could have continued breathing.

# Chapter 21

I couldn't keep the café closed another day. I didn't want to open but I couldn't risk losing all my new customers. Jo insisted she was fine, even though she lay on the bed staring vacantly at the wall, not touching the coffee I'd made her. That was fine though, I'd expect no less.

Christian's doctor had left some Valium. It was a low dosage but it would help. I insisted she have one before I would shower. She rested then and I headed down stairs to fire up the coffee machine and prepare for the day.

It would be strange working it all alone again. We'd become such a team. I only hoped I could keep up with the morning onslaught. I should have phoned Mum but I hadn't really planned on how the day would take shape and there wouldn't be a bus to get her in on time now.

I needn't have worried. Before I even opened the front door, there was a knock at the back door and Mum stood beaming with Tupperware containers in her hand. She was out of control. But I was too grateful to do anything other than smile and welcome her in with a big hug.

I opened the front door while she found a plate for the muffins she'd made. She put the container of what I assumed was cake out the back for later, cake was not breakfast food, it was one of Mum's many rules.

The morning went as fast as Mum's muffins. I ran upstairs every chance I got to make sure Jo was okay. She was mostly just asleep. Christian had called in on his way to the office to make sure everything was okay and then at eleven, just as I was wondering how on earth I'd get through the lunch rush with just Mum and I, a young girl walked in wearing jeans and a black t-shirt. She had clear skin, her thick blonde hair pulled back in a soft ponytail. She stood a moment looking around and on spotting me behind the counter, bee-lined her way to me.

'Hello,' I said cautiously.

'Hi,' she replied brightly. 'Are you Ainsley?'

'I am,' I answered apprehensively.

'Oh good. Christian Harrington sent me, he said you could use some help.'

'Christian sent you?'

'Yes. I used to work as a Barista when I was at uni.'

'Right. And what is it you do now for Christian?'

'I'm a junior accountant.'

'And he sent you here to make coffee?'

'I make really good coffee and he said you could use a hand. I don't mind,' she smiled.

'What about your real job?'

'It's okay, it's the middle of the month. It's our quiet time.'

'Right,' was all I could answer.

'Do you have an apron or something? Shall I get started?' she asked enthusiastically.

'Um, sure, okay,' I said as Mum handed her an apron, clearly as shocked as I was because she hadn't said a word.

The girl smiled and tied her apron then looked up and said, 'I'm Kelsey by the way.'

I introduced myself and Mum and as Kelsey headed behind the coffee machine, I said, 'Kelsey?'

'Yeah?'

'Thank you.'

She smiled sweetly, a good, wholesome, honest kind of smile, 'No problem.'

I excused myself and went out the back, pulling my phone from my back pocket and dialling Christian.

'You're mad, you know,' I said when he answered. 'But thank you.'

I could hear the smile in his voice as he said, 'No problem. You can have her as long as you need.'

'But Christian, she has a real job.'

'Don't worry about it. She'll still do mornings and afternoons here and then help you out during the lunch rush. It's middle of the month, I can spare her, don't worry.'

I laughed. She was a very expensive Barista I suspected but thanked him again before getting everything ready for the upcoming lunch rush.

I was working my way through the last of the order pile when Shaun walked in and startled me.

'Hey, you!' he cooed as he walked around the corner making me jump.

'Hey yourself,' I said, ripping the gloves off my hands and pulling him into a hug. 'What are you doing here?'

'We have a student free day and our staff meeting finished early so I thought I'd come check the place out and see how it's all going. Can't believe you've got Mum smiling behind the till. She did nothing but crap on about this place when I called earlier to see if you needed any help with what's happened to Jo. You know she's not going back to the school?'

'Ever?'

'Doesn't sound like it. I thought she was just keeping an eye on you but seems she's fallen in love with the place. I see why. You've done a great job. How'd you manage it?'

I laughed. 'Dunno, think this place just has something that you fall in love with and it gets under your skin.'

'Now,' he said, as though about to go on a tirade. 'Who's the blonde making coffee?' he asked.

I laughed. 'Now I know why you're here. Mum told you about Kelsey, didn't she?'

'Maybe,' he smirked. 'So, can I ask her out?'

'Do what you want, she doesn't work for me. She works for Christian.'

'Ah, the boyfriend Mum's so concerned about. Do we need to talk about that?'

'No. We do not,' I said, leading him into the other room and over to where Kelsey was manning the machine.

'Kelsey, my brother, Shaun,' I introduced. 'He'll have a double shot latte if you can.'

She nodded, her face slowly registering how handsome he was.

'Mum has cake over there,' I said pointing to the register and leaving him to make his moves in private.

I was happy to send him Kelsey's way if it meant I could avoid talking about Christian with Shaun. That was never going to happen. I loved that my brother was there for me, but there were just some things you don't discuss. I wasn't sure Christian's take would be the same, not sure he'd be too happy about me palming his staff onto my brother, but I'd worry about that another day. Besides, I was sure Shaun could handle Christian. When Shaun turned on the charm, people, his students, strangers on the street, they were all putty in his hands. It was quite funny to watch.

I peeked around the corner as I slid on a fresh pair of gloves and Kelsey was melting right where she stood. I shook my head, smiling and went to make the last of the sandwich orders.

On the day of the funeral, Kelsey arrived at seven in the morning with three matching friends in tow.

'Christian said you'd be out today and needed the help.'

He was quite the organiser, that man of mine. Mum arrived just after the girls, loaded up with Tupperware containers of cake, along with soup and a casserole that she took straight upstairs to the fridge.

'Will you be alright, Mum?' I asked, concerned about leaving her alone for the day.

'Oh, Ainsley, we'll be fine, stop fussing. Go, take care of Jo, she needs your fussing, not me.'

'Fine, fine,' I conceded. 'Don't let them burn the place down.'

'Go,' she said, shaking her head.

I left them all to it then, staying upstairs to get ready and see to Jo who wasn't coping at all. She just stared off into the distance as though she'd left her body and gone somewhere else and she was slowly wasting away because she wouldn't eat or drink. She couldn't sit up or speak or do anything other than stare at the wall or sleep. But I wasn't going to question it. She had every right to behave however she pleased but I was going to be there with her every step of the way.

Christian and I near carried Jo to the funeral. Her parents were there of course and sat beside her while she stared at the coffin, tears rolling down her face, her body shaking in grief as the minister and a parade of people said lovely things about Benny.

Jo sat in a club chair in the corner of the coffee room after the service while people milled around drinking tea and eating the cake and biscuits, catching up with old friends and family, discussing the tragedy they'd had to accept, offering their condolences to Benny's heartbroken parents and then to Jo who barely registered them entering her personal space.

'Please come home,' Jo's parents begged her as the last of the stragglers left.

Jo just shook her head.

Her parents looked at Christian and me, lost, not knowing what to do or how to help her. I'd been that broken, I realised as Christian's hand slid into mine. It seemed so long ago but I realised how far I'd come because of the people around me. I would be those people for Jo.

'You want to come back to the café?' I asked her.

She nodded, tears welling in her raw eyes.

'It's fine,' I said to her parents. 'She can stay as long as she wants. I promise I'll make sure she's okay.'

They nodded reluctantly, not knowing what else to do. They'd been trying to get her to come home for days but she didn't speak, just shook her head. She barely moved from the bed, leaving only to use the bathroom. 'Thank you,' they said, before hugging me goodbye after we'd gotten Jo into the car.

The car dropped us out the front and Christian carried Jo down the laneway, through the back door and straight up the stairs.

I went in through the front door to check everything was still standing, still trading. Kelsey was standing at the front window with a dishcloth in her hand.

'Everything alright?' I asked.

'Yeah, I think,' she said.

'You don't sound too sure.'

'Well, I didn't want to say anything but there was this lady in here earlier asking for you. Not by name but she described you. I told her you were out and I didn't know when you'd be back and now she's standing out there on the street just watching the café.'

'Where?' I asked getting a better position to look out the window. Then I saw her across the road, leaning against a tree, just standing there. 'The blonde? That's who you mean, isn't it?' clarifying I wasn't going mad.

'Yeah, that's her. She was a real bitch too. I was going to phone Christian but your mum said to just let it be.'

'That's okay,' I said as a couple of Christian's guys walked over to her, had some words until her face scrunched and after a final scowl in our direction she waved over a taxi and was gone. 'Thanks,' I said, leaving her to wipe the tables.

'How's Jo?' Mum asked as I passed the counter.

'Not great,' I said. 'She wouldn't go home with her folks, so she's going to stay here. I don't really know what to do with her, Mum, she won't eat or drink or speak. I just don't know,' I said shaking my head.

'She'll be okay. She just needs time. There's some soup upstairs, bribe her if you have to. Even if she only has a few spoons. But you're doing all you can do, love,' she said, pulling me in for a mum hug.

Upstairs, Christian had put Jo on the sofa in front of the telly. I heated up some of Mum's soup and promised if she had a few spoons she could sleep again just as Mum said to and then I tucked her into bed.

Jo was sleeping in the next room while Christian and I stared at the television, not knowing what else to do with ourselves when Mum stuck her head in.

'Benny's parents are here to see Jo,' she said.

Christian and I shared a worried look. 'Send them up,' I said. What else could I do?

I met them and at the top of the stairs and took them through to the kitchen where Christian already had the kettle on to boil and cups lining the bench top.

'Jo's sleeping. She's not doing very well to be honest and I'd rather not wake her,' I said to them as Christian handed out the coffees.

They nodded quietly, wrapping their hands around their coffee cups, clearly not doing too well themselves.

'Have you eaten?' I asked.

Benny's mum shook her head but didn't speak. I heated some casserole and insisted they eat while I went to check on Jo.

Jo was awake, staring at the wall. 'Benny's folks are here to see you,' I said, waiting for a reaction that didn't come. 'Jo, they said it's important. They need to talk to you. Do you think you can get up?'

She shook her head.

'Can you at least sit, do you think?' I asked, not wanting to force her too far.

She nodded and I helped her sit with pillows propping her up.

I brought in Benny's parents while Christian fetched them some kitchen chairs. I was going to leave them alone but Jo reached for my hand so I sat on the bed with her.

'I'll go check on downstairs,' Christian offered.

'Stay. Please,' Jo whispered, so he sat beside me, his hand resting on her leg in supportive comfort.

'Jo, honey,' Benny's dad began, his voice shaky. 'We need to talk about the house.'

Jo only nodded.

'What about the house?' Christian prompted.

'Well, Benny wrote his will after he bought the house but never updated it. I suppose no one thinks to when they're 27, so we're still listed as the beneficiaries so there's the mortgage and things. We're happy for you to have the house and everything, of course, but we just can't cover the costs. It's too much.'

Jo nodded again.

'Jo?' I prompted quietly.

Jo shook her head, 'I don't have any money,' she said, tears overflowing from her eyes.

'It's okay,' I patted her hand, understanding even when she'd had her job, she'd never contributed to the mortgage, Benny didn't need her to even though it must have been high, the house is beautiful.

'I could help,' offered Christian.

She shook her head. 'I can't go back there.' She looked up at me, her eyes pleading, her broken soul begging for something. Help? I wasn't sure, I could only imagine.

'It's okay, Jo, you can stay here. Do you want Christian and I to sort out your things?'

She nodded. 'But this is where you live.'

'That's okay,' I told her. 'There's plenty of space in the living room for a bed. Actually, we don't need the living room really, do we? We have all of downstairs.'

She just watched me in that childlike way of shock.

'You could move in with me,' Christian said quietly.

Now I looked at him with shock.

'I mean it,' he said. 'Jo can stay here and you can move in with me. Not right away. Stay as long as Jo needs you.'

I looked at Jo, not sure what to say or what to make of it and she nodded. Confirming which bit I wasn't sure, but knowing her, still deep inside, buried beneath all her grief, my friend was telling me to go forth, run to that kind and lovely man.

'Okay,' I smiled. 'We'll do that, then.'

I could see he wanted to take me in his arms, whoop with joy, something, but he didn't. It wouldn't have been appropriate. So he just smiled, and nodded. We'd whoop later.

'We've already taken the few things we wanted to keep,' Benny's Dad said. 'Jo's welcome to anything there, we'll donate whatever she doesn't want.'

'Thank you. We'll have everything sorted for you on the weekend,' I said, knowing Benny had been a good earner and that the mortgage on that lovely house must be quite the strain for a grieving family.

'Thank you,' said Benny's mum, choking on the sob in her throat, tears glistening in her eyes. Then she hugged fragile Jo, telling her, 'You'll always be a part of our family. Call us anytime,' she sobbed.

When they'd finished their goodbyes, Christian showed them out.

# Chapter 22

I boxed and labelled Jo's personal items, some items I knew were sentimental, pictures, trinkets from romantic getaways, that sort of thing. I put a selection of clothes into a suitcase ready to transfer into the wardrobe upstairs at the cafe, while boxing the rest for her to sort out after I moved. Christian organised for a van to collect the boxes and take them all back to the café where we made space for her things in the basement amongst Mrs May's clothes and stolen treasures.

'Have you heard anything more?' I asked Christian, referring to his inquiries about Henry Mayberry.

'Not yet, but I should soon. Any day now,' he said, kissing the top of my head before heading back upstairs.

Jo was in a medication assisted sleep. Christian's doctor said it helped with people who'd been through such a big shock and the funeral had been so hard on her. It was the only way her poor body could cope. So we let her be and had some leftover casserole in the kitchen.

'I miss you,' he said between spoonfuls.

'What do you mean, I'm right here,' I said, suspecting exactly what he meant.

'I know. And don't get me wrong, I'm glad you're here for Jo and I'm not complaining at all, but I miss waking up with you. I miss just hanging out with you. It's too quiet.'

'That's all?' I asked, even though prompting such a conversation when there was nothing to be done about it was dangerous.

'Well, I miss that too,' he said, raising his eyebrows in jest. 'But mostly I just miss you.'

It was the sweetest thing anyone had ever said to me. I'd never imagined any one could actually miss me. Miss the sex, yes, but me? I didn't quite know what to do with this type of affection. Other than roll it up in that beautiful ball of love that came with Christian.

'She'll start getting better soon the doctor said,' I told him.

'I know. And really, it's fine, no hurry,' he said reaching for my hand and softly rubbing his finger across it.

Monday morning and the troops arrived one by one. Mum laden with Tupperware, cakes and muffins for downstairs, soups, casseroles, lasagne and apple pie for upstairs. She disappeared upstairs and sorted out the meals into the fridge, gathered her emptied Tupperware containers that I'd cleaned and left on the bench and I suspected checked on Jo before eventually coming down and wrapping an apron around herself.

The old lady was in her booth, halfway through her tea when Kelsey arrived smiling ear to ear which I suspected had something to do with the date she'd had with my brother Saturday night. She changed out of her office clothes and into her café clothes ready to help with the lunch rush. 'That blonde chic's outside again,' she said, as she organised herself.

'What's she doing?' I asked. How crazy was this woman? She was starting to freak me out with her obsessiveness, especially now I knew the brooch was probably real after the loot in the basement. But I didn't know what to do about it. I didn't want it if it belonged to her great grandmother but what if it didn't? What if she was just some crazy con artist trying to snake me out of Mrs May's lovely brooch? I needed answers and I knew finding out more about Henry Mayberry was going to give them to me. He was the key, I just knew it.

'Nothing. Just standing there like before. Who is she?'

'No one. Well, we're fine as long as she doesn't come inside. But don't you go walking back to work on your own. I'll get you a taxi,' I told her.

'It's okay, after her giving me grief the other day, Christian is making me come and go with one of his drivers.'

'Of course he is,' I smiled as I heard footsteps on the stairs before Jo came around the corner.

Jo had dressed and showered but her eyes were bloodshot, her face was pale, she was skin and bones and needed a good feed. I wasn't saying anything, though, she was up and that's what counted. She'd slept for a whole week. Anything was an improvement from that.

'Coffee?' she asked.

Kelsey, a little dumbfounded, took a second to comprehend she was the coffee maker. 'Long black,' I said to Kelsey who went about making coffee.

'Have you replaced me already?' Jo asked.

'Of course not,' I laughed. 'A gift from Christian, one of his Junior Accountants,' I said, raising my eyebrows.

'You're kidding?' she said. 'That man's insane.'

'I know,' I smiled, loving every bit of his insanity.

Kelsey brought over Jo's coffee and I handed her one of Mum's muffins. 'Sit,' I told her.

She looked around the empty café as though it were full and she was looking for an empty seat. Before she could choose, the old lady was standing in front of us. She took the coffee out of Jo's hand, grabbed her elbow and led her to her booth where they both sat silently for the rest of the day. Mum replaced the old lady's pot of tea and before long, switched Jo from her long blacks to a pot of peppermint tea. I sent out their favourite sandwiches at lunchtime and they stayed there in the booth in contented silence until after they had one of Mum's cupcakes. Then the old lady kissed Jo on the head and said, 'All will be okay,' and left. Jo nodded and went upstairs to bed.

That became the routine of the week. The old lady and Jo in the booth and Kelsey behind the counter and the Blonde Bitch watching from across the street until one of Christian's people, tipped off by Kelsey's driver I suspected, shooed her along. What she was watching for I had no idea but it was making me uncomfortable and Christian had started sending a car to take Mum home at the end of the day. She didn't mind too much. She felt like a celebrity.

On Saturday I woke up to find Jo missing from the bed. She was in the living room watching cartoons. 'You okay?' I asked, sitting on the other end of the couch and snuggling my feet under the throw rug she was using.

'I think I am,' she said with a half-smile. 'Vivi's tomato plant's looking a little sick, you're not taking very good care of it.'

'I've been busy. Maybe you could see what you can do. You have a much greener thumb than I do,' I said.

'You're not turning into Vivi are you?' she asked.

'Shut up,' I said, kicking her. 'You know a plant was never going to last long with me.'

'I think the point was you were supposed to put in the effort,' she said.

'Yeah, yeah.'

She shook her head. 'Fine, I'll give it some water later. You don't have to stay all day, you know. You can go see Christian if you want.'

'Don't be silly, I'm fine here.'

'He must miss you.'

'He'll live,' I smiled.

She smiled in return. 'It's okay, though. Why don't the two of you go have lunch or something? I can raid that sad looking DVD collection in the corner.'

I nodded. I didn't want to burst with excitement in front of her but I missed Christian. I missed his smell. I missed his voice. I missed feeling safe and loved with his arms wrapped around me. He'd popped in a couple of times for lunch but he had work to do too. He was busy with meetings and property stuff so those few visits were way too quick.

I waited until the cartoon had finished and went to shower. I messaged Christian with only the word, lunch?'

He replied almost instantly with, 'Hell, yeah.'

So after making sure Jo had food and water and moving all the vodka, Valium and sharp objects well out of reach, I wished her luck with my sad DVD collection and left her with the container of cupcakes on the coffee table.

Christian lived in the Old Regent Hotel. On the top floor. I'd not yet been invited and after the ostentatious Audi, I could only imagine what awaited me. But I looked forward to another insight into the man that I had fallen for. You could tell a lot about a person from their home, the books they read, the things in their fridge, the linen on their bed and I wanted to know more about Christian, who he was, what lay deep beneath the surface.

I'd wanted to wear something pretty for him, maybe sexy, but really I didn't have much and I was riding the scooter across town anyway so I just wore jeans and a loose top with my hair pulled back and just a dab of makeup. I probably could have walked, it really wasn't that far, maybe twenty or thirty minutes on foot and it was a beautiful day for this time of year but I didn't want to waste a single second and I'd only have arrived sweaty and gross. He didn't need to see that just yet. Besides, I was under strict instructions to be careful now the Blonde Bitch had taken up residence in the front of the café and walking across town with Sam didn't sound as nice, so I gave him a wave on my way out and he followed me on his own bike, way too tough for a scooter. I'd told Christian it was unnecessary but even though I hadn't seen the Blonde Bitch outside all morning, Christian insisted it meant nothing and the thought of her lurking in the shadows watching us made my stomach turn.

Christian was waiting on the footpath in front of the hotel when I pulled up, a big grin breaking across his pensive face as he spotted me.

'Hey you,' he said, pulling me to him as a shiny black BMW slowly rolled past and he shared a look with Sam who was standing in the shadows.

'Hey,' I smiled, kissing him as we both pretended not to see the car.

He nodded to the receptionist as we passed and headed straight for the lifts. Inside, he swiped his key card to access his floor and we stood, waiting for the lift to ascend, the tension becoming palpable despite the only contact being our hands.

Inside his suite, the door was barely closed, my bag barely on the entry table before he had me up against the wall, his mouth and hands roaming, groping, devouring me urgently as though starved, finding all my pleasure zones before scooping me up and carrying me to his bedroom.

On the way I caught only a glimpse of the giant flat screen TV, black leather couch, coffee table covered in papers, before he placed me as gently as a china doll onto his enormous bed, which looked like a hotel bed but was as lush as a cloud from heaven, it was like laying on a pocket of air.

Christian took his time reacquainting himself with every part of my body, expertly eliciting guttural, primal noises I never knew I was capable of as again and again he made up for missed time.

When he was finally finished, I lay stunned, speechless, panting, drained, sated, and ridiculously, utterly alive. He ran his fingers down my spine, barely touching, leaving a trail of goose bumps as he went, sending intense sparks of pleasure throughout my body, making all the right parts tingle and sing with glee.

Christian went to freshen up in the ensuite and I shrugged

into his discarded shirt, not bothering to button it and padded out in search of the kitchen and some water.

As I wandered through the living room, I got the full effect of the testosterone explosion that had occurred in the decorating. There was no personality, no colour, no life.

I found my way to the kitchen with its black marble bench tops and top of the line appliances that sparkled and shone, putting everything Mrs May had to shame. It seemed to be the only room that had received any renovation.

I opened the fridge, leaving fingerprints on the brushed chrome door. There wasn't much inside other than half a carton of milk, umpteen bottles of spring water and a bowl of grapes.

I grabbed two bottles of water and popped a grape in my mouth as I felt Christian's feathery touch on my shoulder, sending bolts of electricity throughout my body.

'We don't have a restaurant yet, so I've ordered some pasta from Giorgio's, is that okay?' he asked as he found a bottle of wine in the fridge door.

'Giorgios?' I asked. 'Giorgios don't deliver,' I told him.

'I asked them really nicely,' he said as he opened the bottle and poured two glasses.

'So, what do you think?' he asked, handing me a glass of wine. 'Of the apartment,' he clarified.

'It's not what I expected. Not after the Audi, the way you dress, this doesn't look like you at all.'

He looked around, taking it in. 'I guess I always thought it temporary. It never really felt like home. Mum had the kitchen redone but I haven't really done anything else, I suppose.

Ordered the couch and bed online. I didn't really care what they looked like, just that they were serviceable and comfortable.'

'Well the bed certainly is comfortable.'

He grinned naughtily at the mention of the bed and what we'd just done in there before adding, 'It does mean you get free reign to do as you please, I suppose,' he grinned. 'If you still want to come live here? You can make any changes you want,' he offered eagerly.'

'Of course I still want to move in. I'm sure I can do a little something with the place,' I smiled.

He smiled. 'Good, because I like you here wandering around in nothing but my unbuttoned shirt,' he said, nibbling my ear, his hands sliding over my body, igniting a whole new fire.


'So, tell me about Mrs May, how did you meet her, anyway?' he asked, as we lay side by side, our bellies full of Giorgio's Fettuccine Puttanesca, our sex drive momentarily sated.

I knew right then it was time to put it all out in the open. Christian had a right to know if we were going to live together in the near future, if we were even going to have a future.

'Well,' I began, apprehensively, not wanting him to know any of it. Feeling like it happened to a whole other person. Wishing none of it had ever happened at all. But then, if that had never happened, I wouldn't be lying beside Christian. I'd still be living my miserable old life. Or did I just miss the original turn off to this life? Would our paths still have crossed in another serendipitous way?

I took a deep breath, started again. I knew I had to tell him everything and there were no halves to something like that. I wanted him to have all the information before he ran like the wildebeest during migration. 'You might not like the story that goes with me meeting Mrs May,' I said, trying to prepare him.

'What's that supposed to mean?' he asked, propping himself up on an elbow.

'Okay, here goes,' I said, too afraid to look at him as I spoke, staring up at the ceiling instead which only reminded me of that horrible night that now felt so long ago. 'I was in a dark place. A really dark place. I did something stupid, Christian,' I said as a tear ran down my cheek.

'Hey,' he soothed, catching my tear.

'You don't understand,' I said. 'You might not love me any-more,' I told him.

'I will love you till the day I die, Ainsley, nothing you could ever say could change that,' he said, wiping another stray tear.

'I tried to commit suicide,' I said, pausing, letting it sink in. He didn't respond so I went on. 'I was in a really dark place and I just wanted it to stop. I didn't know how to make it stop,' I said as he gathered me to his chest and let me sob.

Once I'd stopped crying I gave him the facts, the way my brain misfired, the misinterpretations that compounded the darkness, how my mother found me unwashed for days, every dish I owned on the sink where they'd been for weeks, the layers of dust and debris. I told him of the pit so deep and dark and lonely I never thought I'd find a way out. How I couldn't face getting out of bed some days so I just skipped work and hid under the covers. How Sergeant Jack would come by for milk, I now sus-pected a false pretence to check on me. How it all hurt so bad, the pain so vile and all-consuming I couldn't breathe and I just didn't know how to make it stop.

Christian didn't run. He didn't throw back the covers and haul my crazy arse to the lift. He wrapped me in his strong arms so tight it felt like a cocoon.

We lay there for some time, silent, safe. Christian sniffed and he took one arm away from me to wipe a tear.

'Don't cry for me,' I told him, pulling back to face him, one hand on his chest as I wiped a tear from his cheek.

'I can't help it. I hate that you were so alone, that there was no one there to hold you, to make sure you were okay.'

'But I am okay,' I assured him, looking into his beautiful deep sea-green eyes. 'I have you,' I smiled.

'Yes,' he smiled back, drawing me to him. 'Yes, you do.'

Why is it all the truths come out when you're naked? After my afternoon confession, we talked about our families and what it was like growing up, how Christian survived his brother's shadow and his father's contempt. I spoke of never fitting in, never finding a place I could be me, until now, with the café and with Christian. And then, for one last time before I returned to Jo, we made each other forget all the crap, all the chaos, all the past as though we were the only two people existing on the entire planet.

I walked in the back door, a smile on my face, almost floating on air. The light was on in the basement. I didn't remember leaving it on and was about to pull the cord and turn it off but though I should check Jo wasn't down there.

'Jo?' I called as I went down the stairs. 'You down here?'

But there was no reply. Had she found Mrs May's loot?

I finally got to the bottom and found Jo slumped in amongst a pile of her open boxes tears streaming down her face as she sat in the middle of the mess holding a picture of her and Benny in her hands.

'What are you doing?' I asked her softly, not wanting to spook her.

'I just needed a jumper,' she whispered. 'I opened the wrong box,' she smiled through her tears.

I sat in amongst the boxes with her and scooped her into my arms.

'I miss him, Ains,' she whispered.

'Of course you do,' I soothed.

I let her cry for a while before I said, 'Why don't we go upstairs and eat something.'

She nodded and scooped up the pile of clothes folded beside her. 'Can I bring Benny?' she asked hopeful.

'Of course you can.'

She smiled and hugged me with all the things in her arms, 'Thanks, Ains, thanks for everything.'

'No problem, Jo Jo.'

She smiled, 'You haven't called me Jo Jo in a while.'

'I haven't been drunk in a while,' I laughed.

'Are you drunk now?' she asked suspiciously.

'No,' I smiled. 'It just felt like a Jo Jo kind of moment.'

'I like it,' she said.

Upstairs, I cleared some more space for her in the closet and she put Benny on a cupboard in the living room where he'd always be with us and we heated up some casserole and apple pie.

As we were shovelling the last spoons of pie and cream into our mouths, Jo said, 'You know, you might well be drunk, Ains, I just don't think it's from booze.'

'What's that supposed to mean?'

'It just means, that whatever The Ferret did to you today has you glowing and giddy like a drunk schoolgirl.'

'Shut up,' I giggled as I felt a blush cover my face, taking her plate to the sink.

# Chapter 23

We spent Sunday in front of the television, eating popcorn, watching old movies and talking about boys. Benny's name brought tears to Jo's eyes but we talked about him anyway, we talked about his silliness and his boldness. He was quite a character and his spirit was enough to leave a hole in the lives of everyone he knew. But talking about him felt good. I could see it felt good for Jo, too.

Jo was back behind the coffee machine on Monday so I called Christian and told him to keep Kelsey. Colour was coming back into Jo's face and life was coming back into her eyes, slowly but surely.

'Some people here to see you, Ains,' Jo called around the corner, disappearing back to her station before I could ask who.

I took the sandwich I'd just finished toasting out of the press, plated it and took it out with me.

'What are you doing here?' I asked Christian's sister as I handed the plate to Mum to take to its owner.

'Wait,' Lydia called as I was about to walk back into the kitchen.

I stood, silently, waiting for her to say whatever she had to say, for one of her companions, Andrea or Alex standing sheepishly behind her to say something.

'We just want a minute. To apologise,' she said.

Again, I stood waiting, arms crossed over my chest.

'Can we sit somewhere? Please?' she begged.

'Fine,' I said, pointing to a booth. 'Jo, can we have some tea?' I asked.

Jo nodded and I followed the girls to a booth. Luckily the lunch rush was over and that had been the last sandwich on order.

There was an awkward silence hanging over the table as I assessed each of them and they got to properly assess me until Jo brought over a pot of tea. I didn't even care what they liked, they got what Jo brought. They didn't comment or complain and poured from the pot into the pretty tea cups.

'We're really sorry, Ainsley,' Lydia said. 'I don't know what we were thinking to be so horrible and you had every right to be mad. You and Christian both.'

I nodded, sipping the French Earl Grey. I damn well knew I had every right.

When I didn't say anything, Lydia went on. 'It was just a surprise, that's all. We hadn't seen Christian in so long and everything was so tense. Anyway, I don't know what we were thinking and we wanted to apologise and maybe get to know you better, set it all right.'

I nodded. 'Thank you. But it's really not me you should be

apologising to. Christian is a good man and he loves you and you crushed him. That's who you should be apologising to. Not me. I have to get back to work,' I said, getting up to leave.

'Wait,' Lydia said, grabbing my arm. 'You're right. Are you both free for dinner?'

'You'd have to ask Christian,' I said, leaving them to the remains of their tea.

When I bravely went out a little while later, Mum was clearing their table. I breathed a sigh of relief and got on with my day of cleaning up and watching Sam shoo the Blonde Bitch away across the road.

Jo and I were out the back, hanging tea towels on the line when Christian came around the corner.

'Hey, ladies,' he smiled, giving Jo a friendly peck on the cheek and me a not so friendly peck on the mouth. 'How was your day?' he asked.

'Good,' Jo replied.

'Interesting,' I said.

'On that note,' Jo smiled. 'I'll leave you to it,' and she took the empty washing basket upstairs.

'Interesting, hey?' Christian asked as we made our way inside, locking the door behind us. 'Interesting doesn't have anything to do with my sister and her entourage, does it?'

'Hmmm...' I smiled. 'Perhaps. So does that mean they came to see you, too?'

'It does,' he said, stopping me at the bottom of the stairs, pulling me to him, pressing me against the wall with his body as he kissed me deep until my knees began to buckle. 'Hello,' he smiled.

'Well hello, yourself,' I said, my hands feeling the strength in his chest as I kissed him again. 'So what happened with Lydia?' I asked as we went upstairs and into the kitchen.

'She was impressed with you, with how you stuck up for me and didn't crumble under the glare of a Harrington.'

'I was impressed with me too,' I laughed. 'It's a good glare.'

'She wants to have dinner. She sat in my office with her entourage and begged for us to have dinner with them before they go back to Melbourne.'

'I know. I told her it was up to you. It was you she needed to apologise to and make amends with so dinner is also up to you. What did you tell her?'

'She's buying, at Assagio's tonight,' he smiled.

'Very good, then,' I said kissing him quickly.

'But I need to go home and get changed. Want to come with?' he suggested.

Jo was laughing at a Friend's rerun in the lounge room so I asked if she'd be okay.

'Of course I will, it'll be nice to have the place to myself. Go,' she said. 'Stay the night even and then I can have the bed to myself and maybe I'll get a decent night's sleep,' she laughed.

'I told you you could have one of the rooms upstairs,' I smirked.

'No way I'm sleeping in one of those beds.'

I laughed. 'Me either. Who knows what's in those mattresses. I just want to pretend that whole upstairs doesn't exist.'

'That is a good plan. Now go, leave me to this big beautiful bed.'

There were plenty of leftovers in the fridge for her so I threw a change of clothes in a bag and left with Christian.

Even though the water was running and my head was under the nozzle as I enjoyed washing off the smell of cheese toasties, I heard the door open.

'You know,' Christian called. 'We have a little time before we have to meet them.'

'Is that so?' I asked, pulling the curtain aside.

'Yes it is,' he smiled. 'That's so indeed and I believe I owe you a debt of gratitude for defending my honour today?'

'You make a very good point. So why are you still wearing your shirt?' I asked, raising my eyebrows as he quick as lightening near ripped his clothes from his body and joined me under the nozzle.

He put his hands either side of my head on the tiles and his mouth and body took what he needed to get through the evening ahead as my body happily obliged, accepting the searing pleasure that rippled through to my core.

It took some moments before I could feel the water from the shower raining down on the bottom half of my body, before my senses came back to Christian's brightly lit bathroom, Christian's body still leaning against mine as he, too, slowly came back to reality with a grin on his face.

He nuzzled my neck, whispering in my ear, 'You're amazing,' then he kissed me, rinsed himself off and left me to do the same as I watched his beautifully naked body leave the room.

'You look happy, Cookie, really happy,' Lydia smiled when we got to the restaurant.

'Cookie?' I asked, trying to suppress my smile.

Christian looked at me, trying not to smirk.

'I am happy,' he said, to his sister, 'I'm really happy, Lids,' he said, squeezing my hand.

'So tell me what Christian was like as a kid?' I said, hoping to lighten the mood.

'Serious,' she smiled happily. 'Always serious, always building stuff and counting his monopoly money. He'd steal Jaz's teddies and conduct presentations in his room. It was no surprise he got his degrees in architecture and business management in record speed.'

'You actually have a degree in architecture?' I asked, surprised. I thought he just did business things that sons of billionaires take on when the time comes. I knew he dreamt of designing the little beachside fantasy he had for us but I didn't know he was actually qualified to do it. Every day there were more layers to this man.

He simply nodded.

'He was good, too,' Lydia added. 'He used the first wave of his trust fund to buy a property and build his own country cottage and it's simply gorgeous. It really is,' she smiled.

'A country cottage, too?' I asked.

'It's a long way from here,' he smiled. 'Perhaps we'll go there some time when Jo's better.'

'Who's Jo?' asked Lydia.

'My friend, she brought us tea earlier,' I told her. 'Her

boyfriend just died, she's staying with me for a while until she's feeling right again.' Christian squeezed my hand.

'So, how is it being back?' I asked Lydia and her entourage, changing the subject again. 'Christian said you've all been overseas until recently,'

'It's nice,' Lydia said. 'An adjustment but it's nice. I missed home, I'm glad to be back.'

The night went on like that, superficial catching up between a brother and sister and everyone else getting to know a little about each other and sharing in some good food and a laugh or two which was nice. It lightened the air. Alex was still a little quiet but by the end even she was smiling.

'It's like you're a whole different person,' she said to Christian as we were getting ready to leave. 'I don't mean that nastily,' she added. 'I'm just saying.'

'It's okay,' Christian smiled. 'I feel like a whole different person. And hey, I never did say sorry about my behaviour that day at the hotel. It was unacceptable and I'm sorry.'

'Its fine,' Alex said, waving it all off. 'But thank you,' she added appreciatively.

He nodded then turned to his sister and hugged her, 'I missed you. It's good to see you,' he told her quietly.

'I missed you, too,' she smiled. 'It's good to have you back, the real you. I knew you were in there somewhere.'

'Well, you can thank Ainsley for bringing me back,'

'That we will,' she smiled, hugging me before Christian hustled me into his Audi, his usual chauffeured town car waiting at the kerb for the girls.

'So why don't you do any of the designing for the business?' I asked Christian on the way home.

He shrugged. 'Dad never thought I was any good, well, not good enough for his buildings anyway.'

'Is that what you'd rather be doing?'

'I like seeing something go from a drawing to a finished product. But it's been a long time.'

'What would you like to design?' I asked, refusing to let it drop.

He shrugged. 'Resorts and the like, like what we do, but warmer, homelier, beautiful architecture, ecofriendly maybe, definitely full of hidden amenities that make you go wow,' he said, his face lighting up as he spoke.

'You could, you know.'

'Could what?'

'Do it. Go out on your own. If you wanted,' I said.

He shrugged and we pulled into his secure car park right next to the lift.

'Someday, Ains, someday,' he smiled, tilting my chin so that my mouth met his in a soft but deep kiss.

'So, Cookie huh?' I asked as I straddled him on the bed and even in the cover of darkness I could see him blush.

He flipped me over fast, pinning my hands above my head, his mouth diving on to mine in an attempt to distract me. I pulled my mouth away as best I could while pinned underneath him.

'Uhuh, no fair. You have to tell me,' I smirked, mustering all the core strength I could and in his brief moment of weakness, I flipped him onto his back, pinning his arms, although really, I had no strength in comparison to him. 'Tell me,' I said, hovering above him, just enough to tease him.

'Fine,' he conceded. 'I was three, I got into a bathtub of blue dye our housekeeper Margot had ready to dye some of Tom's stained clothes, in turn dying myself blue before running through the compound imitating the Cookie Monster from Sesame Street. Margot called me Cookie after that and everyone else followed.

I dove onto his mouth and rewarded him for opening up. 'I like Cookie,' I smiled when I came up for air. 'I like Cookie a lot,' I said, making my way down his body

Monday night Christian arrived just as we'd finished cleaning up and were about to head upstairs for the night. His arms were laden with takeaway food, which smelt amazing and our stomachs instantly groaned.

'Is she still out there?' I asked.

'Sam moved her on earlier.'

'Good. Then you best bring that upstairs,' Jo smiled, nodding to the food.

With our bellies full and the last of Mum's apple pie in the microwave, Christian put a photograph in the middle of the table.

'What's this?' I asked picking it up to see the photograph of Henry from the paper.

'It's the original photograph. Larger, you can see more desert. Not sure it's any more helpful though.'

'Why is there a gun to his head?' Jo asked.

'No idea,' I told her, only slightly fibbing. I suspected it had something to do with the basement full of stolen jewels but I didn't want to involve her in the details until I knew for sure what the hell was going on. 'Is this all they found out?'

'Pretty much. That and there's no record of Henry's death,' Christian said.

'Really? So he could still be alive?'

'I guess. Who knows? His death may have been registered under another name or not recorded at all, especially if they'd buried him there in the desert.'

'I suppose.'

'Besides, where would we even start? It's just a photograph of a desert. It could be anywhere.'

'No,' Jo interrupted. 'I know this place. Those trees, they're Joshua trees. They grow in the Mojave desert. Benny had photos and endless stories about them from when he went to Vegas and went out to the Grand Canyon. You go through the desert to get there.'

'Vegas?'

'Yep. Vegas baby,' she smiled. 'Although, I think that desert goes into California and some other places, too.'

'Vegas, huh? I know someone up there who will know for sure.' Christian said, thinking. 'Probably doesn't help us much though, it's a big desert. Where would we even start?'

'I don't know,' Jo said. 'But if there's a chance Henry is alive, you have to go find him. What if he's been waiting and waiting for Ana to come and find him or trying to find his way back to her all these years?'

'Well look at you, you old romantic,' I smiled. I still hadn't been able to tell her about the jewels in the basement. I didn't want to tell her until I knew the truth. To find the truth, I had to find Henry but I couldn't just leave Jo, not now. Henry had waited this long, he could wait a little longer. 'But we can't go, anyway. There's the café and, and stuff.'

'What stuff?' she asked. 'Me? Don't be ridiculous. I'm going to be fine. Did you see me chatting to customers today? Totally on the mend,' she smiled.

I looked at Christian waiting to see what was ticking over in that brain of his. 'Looks like we're going to Vegas,' he smiled. 'I'll sort it all out and let you know,' he said, kissing the top of my head and gathering up his things.

I walked him downstairs. 'Can we really leave Jo?'

'Not sure we have a choice. She's right, what if he's been waiting all these years? What if he's stuck or something? Or even if he's dead, don't we need to find out how and why and solve all these mysteries once and for all?'

I nodded, kissed him long. 'You're a good man, Christian Harrington.'

He smiled. 'You make me a good man, Ains.' He kissed my head and left.


I daydreamed about jetting off with Christian all morning, going on an adventure together to find out what happened to Henry Mayberry. It was all very romantic.

My arse vibrated with a message from Christian just after the morning rush had dissipated. 'All set, we leave Friday,' the message read. I relayed the information to Jo. Thankfully Mum hadn't arrived yet, much to the disappointment of the morning coffee drinkers who'd been getting used to their muffins. I would have to remember to mention that to Mum, perhaps it would soften the blow when I told her I was off to Las Vegas with Christian.

Mum eventually walked in laden with her Tupperware, just as Jo was talking about how naughty and fabulous this trip could be for Christian and me.

'What trip?' Mum demanded.

So much for cushioning the impact with some flattery over her baked goods. I looked to Jo for support but really there was nothing anyone could do to help me here. 'Christian and I are going to Las Vegas to look for Henry Mayberry.'

'Who's Henry Mayberry?'

'Ana's husband.'

'Didn't he die? Isn't that what you said?'

'Well, we thought he had, but it turns out there's no record of his death. The photograph that had run in the paper was taken in Las Vegas. It's the last place he was seen alive. Christian thinks we might be able to find him or at least find out what happened to him,' and hopefully solve the mystery of my jewel filled basement, I thought to myself.

'Well why do you need to go, can't he go on his own?'

'Muuum,' I whined.

'Don't mum me, Ainsley. I'm not sure you're really in a position to be gallivanting to the other side of the world with a boy.'

'I told you, Christian is not a boy and he's not just some guy.'

She huffed and went to find a plate for her cakes.

I was busy with toasted sandwiches when Christian stuck his head into the kitchen. 'Ains, you got a minute?'

I looked up concerned. 'Course. What's wrong?'

'I have to cancel Vegas. Dad's had a heart attack and needs me to go up north and oversee the development he was working on. I leave this afternoon.'

'What? Is your Dad okay? How long will you be gone?'

'Dad will be fine. He won't give in that easy, but he needs to rest. I don't know how long I'll be gone. I'll be back as quick as I can,' he said, looping a finger inside my apron and pulling me to him.

Ripping off my gloves, I wrapped my hands around his neck, moulding myself to him as I fell into his kiss. 'How long before you have to leave?' I asked.

He laughed, 'Too soon.'

'What's going on?' Jo asked, walking in.

'Christian has to go up north for work, his dad's in the hospital.'

'Oh shit, hope he's okay,' she said. 'What about Vegas?'

'It'll have to wait,' I told her.

'Shame,' she said, turning to leave.

'Wait,' said Christian. 'Why don't the two of you go? I'll set you up with my contact and you two can find him, see some sun and have a break while you're there. It'll be good for you both. Get some distance from blondie out there.'

'I dunno,' I started.

'Seriously, Ains. Go on, you don't need me.'

I looked at Jo and she had a hopeful look in her eye. I couldn't refuse, after all she'd been through. He was right, it'd be good for her to get away, to get some fresh scenery.

'What about the café?'

'I'll get Kelsey and her friends in. Your mum loved being the boss last time, it'll be fine,' he said optimistically.

'She'll have reorganised the whole bloody place by the time we get back.'

Jo laughed, 'Probably. So does that mean we're going?'

'I guess so. We're going to Vegas,' I squealed.

'No need to be so excited,' Christian said sulkily but smiling.

'Awe, I'll miss you,' I said, kissing his cheek.

'Yeah, yeah,' he said, laughing. 'I'll get it sorted. Stay out of trouble.'

He left the kitchen and Jo and I started a happy dance, which of course attracted my frantic mother. 'What now?' she demanded.

'Christian can't go to Vegas,' I told her.

'Oh, thank God,' she said, relieved.

'So Jo and I are going instead,' I said, smirking.

'Heavens above, what next?'

'You get to run the café and boss Kelsey and her friends around while we're gone,' I told her.

Her face lit up, 'Really? Me? In charge for all that time?'

'Yep. Just don't burn the place down, Mum. Now get back to work, both of you, people need their food or there'll be no café to run.'

'Yes, Boss,' they both saluted, laughing and went back to work.

# Chapter 24

A hole grew in the pit of my stomach the moment Christian's plane took off. I continued to serve customers and make toasties, forcing a smile onto my face, all the while I felt the hole stretching and gorging the further away he got, the further away from phone and internet contact, at least for a while anyway. I was already calculating how long before he landed and could call me, till I could hear his voice and know everything would still be okay.

'Stop it, Ains,' Jo instructed as she handed me a batch of orders, clearly sensing what was rumbling about in my head.

'Sorry, can't help it, you know.'

'Yeah, I know,' she said, patting my shoulder and heading back out to the front of the café.

I had plenty to do to keep me busy, ordering in enough bread, ham and cheese, tea and coffee and everything else Mum would need while Jo and I were in Vegas. I had lists to make for Mum and contact details for suppliers should she need them and the lunch rush to contend with, so I got on with it. I tried not to think about how far away he was and that soon, when Jo and I flew out, he'd be even further away and not contactable at all.

We stopped mid-afternoon for a much needed pot of tea. I'd taken to the French Earl Grey as my tea of choice, I'd been trying so many trying to match Mrs May's but I just couldn't find the right blend. I flopped into a chair. 'What am I even going to pack for this trip, I don't think I can keep pilfering from Mrs May's supply of clothes from the 70's,' I whined.

'Well I suppose we should go shopping, then,' Jo said, her face lighting up just a little for the first time in a while.

'We could go tonight,' I suggested. 'After we close up. The mall's open late enough. We can pop into Myer or DJ's, get something to eat, go to the Richmond for a bevvy, what do you think?'

'I think that's a fabulous idea,' she said, clinking her tea cup to mine as a customer walked in. 'I got it, you sit,' she said, going to serve the customer.

The mall was quiet enough for us to stroll into Myer's without any pushing and shoving and wander through the racks without the masses. We picked up some maxi dresses and sun-dresses, shorts and drill pants mostly off the final clearance racks. The pickings were slim this far into the new season but we managed enough to stock my lagging supplies.

We were wandering through the designer racks when poor bored Sam that Christian had insisted come with us just in case of any trouble asked, 'Will you be alright while I run to the bathroom?' He looked around first at the near empty store to make sure there would be no surprises.

'Of course. There's no one here. We'd spot her a mile away, go, relieve yourself,' I said, waving him off.

Jo and I continued wandering through the racks of clothes we couldn't afford laughing like regular people then I saw her. 'Shit, Jo,' I said, dragging her into the Charlie Brown racks.

'What?' she cried.

'She just bloody came out of the fitting rooms, didn't she?'

'Are you kidding me?'

'No, I'm not.'

We hid behind the gowns up against the wall, slightly obscured by a large display. 'What do we do now?' Jo asked.

'I don't know. We can't go looking because she could be any-where.'

Just then my phone vibrated. 'Hello,' I whispered.

'Ainsley? It's Sam,' he said as though I didn't have caller ID.

'We're kind of busy, Sam. Where are you?'

'Geez, I just went to the bathroom. How'd she get up here so fast?'

'She was in the fitting room. That's what happened. Now we're trapped.'

'Where are you now?'

'We're buried in the corner of the Charlie Brown racks, amongst the gowns. We can't see her now. We can't move.'

'Okay, I can see the Charlie Brown section but not you so don't move, stay where you are, if I can't see you, neither can she. She's scanning the floor. She has people hovering around the escalators and the lifts. There are too many eyes watching the floor, they'll see me as soon as I move. Right now, I'm still out of their sight line.'

'Wait,' Jo said. 'I worked here one Christmas when I was at Uni. There's a service elevator near here. This used to be women's lingerie and I remember helping out in the docks one shift and bringing up the racks. Can you see where Sam?'

'I see it. The entry way is next to Leona Edmonston. Sit tight and I'll let security know what's happening. We need to get you out without any fuss or endangering their staff.

We waited, too afraid to breathe or move, an itch going unscratched on my leg.

'Okay, you're good to go. They're even helping us out with a diversion over the other side but it'll only be enough to turn their heads for a few seconds. You won't have long to get to that elevator. Nick's down in the loading dock waiting for you. Go with no one but Nick, do you hear me?'

'We hear you. Thanks, Sam,' I said as some shelving collapsed over the other side in Miss Shop causing a hell of a racket.

'That's our cue, let's go,' I said to Jo and we ran between the racks to the gap in the wall that led to the storage area and the freight lift hidden in there.

'Shit that was close,' Jo said, doubling over to catch her breath as the cavernous lift took us down to the loading dock.

When the doors opened, Nick was waiting, gun drawn and shuffled us into a car. 'Sam doesn't want you going straight back to the café so I'm taking you to the Richmond as planned. He'll meet us there,' he said, driving down North Terrace then right onto Charles Street, parking illegally before shuffling us the few steps down the mall and up the stairs to the Richmond bar. We were halfway through our drinks by the time Sam found us. 'I followed them until I was sure they went home. Christian wants you to stay at his place tonight.'

'We can't do that,' I said thinking it was all a bit much. 'We don't have any stuff and we fly out in the morning. I don't even have a key,' I said.

'Lucky I do, then,' said Sam. 'It's not up for negotiation. Once you're in for the night, Nick and I will go and get your bags. They'll be in the car when it comes to get you in the morning. I've picked up noodles for you already. Mr Harrington said they're your favourite, so there'll be no need to leave.'

'Fine, fine,' I groaned.

'Are you kidding me?' Jo whispered as we walked into Christian's apartment.

'I know, it's like all the testosterone from the entire city threw up in here,' I laughed.

'My God, you're not kidding,' she said. 'It's a great space though.'

'To do with as I please, so I'm told.'

'Really?' she asked, her eyes wide with excitement.

I left her to sleep in one of the spare bedrooms while I went to lie on that beautiful bed of Christian's where I could still smell him and fell asleep feeling safe with a huge smile on my face.

'Ooh fancy!' Jo grinned as we stood on the sidewalk with our luggage at four in the morning as a shiny black Mercedes pulled into the kerb.

'That really wasn't necessary,' I messaged Christian as we drove to the airport, thinking a regular taxi would have been just fine. He replied with an uncharacteristic smiley face, which left me concerned he wasn't done.

The driver handed me an envelope as we were getting out of the car and while standing in the check in line I opened it to find a Qantas Club membership card.

'Fool,' I mumbled. Then I checked the booking code on the print out. 'We're in business class?' I mumbled, shaking my head but somehow not surprised. I suspected it was the only way Christian knew how to fly. I messaged him, 'You're mad!'

He replied with, 'I love you. Fly safe.'

I gave him a smiley face and a few xx's.

Five hours into the flight from Sydney to Los Angeles and I was starting to feel pretty grateful for the business class airbeds. It was just a shame I couldn't send Christian a more appreciative message.

'Remind me to thank that man of yours when we get back,' Jo said, accepting a glass of what looked like Baileys from the hostess.

I raised my eyebrows at her drink.

'What?' she asked. 'It's a nightcap,' she smiled. 'I'm trying to adjust my body clock.'

Not a bad idea really. I ordered a Baileys for myself and went to the bathroom to get ready for bed.

After a short stopover in Los Angeles, we finally arrived in Las Vegas, much fresher than most. Another uniform clad man awaited us after baggage collection holding a sign with my name on it. He led us to a town car, the heat already fast building to scorching.

We gawked shamelessly out the window as we drove down the strip, grinning ridiculously from ear to ear.

Jo nudged me in the ribs as we passed the MGM. I nudged Jo as we passed the Bellagio. She nudged me back as she gazed up at the Eiffel tower standing proudly in front of the Paris Hotel and then there was the Venetian on the right as we drove into a driveway hidden by a large moat and a forest of bushy trees.

'Here you are, then,' announced the driver as I looked up past the shiny façade to the wonky, neon-lit timber sign hanging purposely askew above, proclaiming we were at Stranded. I hadn't heard of it but as we got out of the car, the driver added for our benefit, 'Brand new, this one,' he said, looking at the doors longingly.

While the valet unloaded our bags, we stood, looking around the drive so well hidden by an enormous forest of dense trees and shrubs, creating a buffer from the noisy neon-lit strip. The drive itself was laid with cobblestones, the valets dressed in black pants and untucked white shirts and gold vests. It felt as though we'd stepped into a whole other place than the fancy, neon-lit, glowing strip we'd just been on, like a little paradise, like we'd become stranded on our own little island.

'Can you believe we're here? In Vegas?' I said to Jo.

'Are you kidding!' she replied, her face positively glowing, her smile wider than it had been in a really long time.

The driver closed the boot and I went to pay or give him a tip or something but he batted my hand with the money away. 'No ma'am, Mr Harrington has taken care of it.'

'Oh, okay,' I stammered. 'Well, thanks.'

'My pleasure. Just call if you need anything or when you're

ready to go back to the airport,' he said, handing me his business card.

'You're Miss Donovan, then?' asked the valet when he'd finished stacking our bags onto a trolley.

'Yes,' I answered apprehensively unsure why the valet would know my name.

'Very good,' he replied. 'We've been expecting you.'

Jo and I shared a worried look. 'Why would the valet be expecting us?' she whispered.

'I don't know,' I whispered back as we followed the valet into the reception area where he waved his hand at one of the many people milling about while we stupidly gazed around at the marble floors that looked like sparkly sand on the beach, the mahogany reception desk, the gold covered staff and crystal chandeliers. It was like a hidden oasis.

A beautiful lady with long caramel-coloured, perfectly highlighted and hot-rollered hair teetered over to us on her Louboutins with a huge glossy red smile stretched across her face. 'Hiiiiiii,' she smiled. 'Welcome to Stranded. I'm Cass, I'm head of guest services here at the hotel. If there's anything at all that you need while you're here with us, please don't hesitate to ask. Now, which one of you is Miss Donovan?'

I raised my hand a little as though I were in a classroom.

'Very good, then,' she said, handing me her card, 'We're very pleased to have you here with us.'

'Thank you,' I said. 'But please, call me Ainsley and this is my friend, Jo.'

'Ainsley, of course,' she smiled brightly. 'Very nice to meet you, Jo,' she said, shaking Jo's hand.

'Okay,' she continued. 'Here are your keys. Go all the way to the top and to your left. Marco has already taken your bags up.' She went on to give directions to the pool, the restaurants, bars, the breakfast times and finished with, 'and if there's anything you need, a car, tickets to a show, anything at all, any time, please don't hesitate to call me. My personal cell is on the back of the cards I gave you.'

'Thank you,' I said, not really sure what else to say. It was a lot to take in, a lot of information and a lot of over the top niceness. 'Don't we need to check in, sign something, hand over a credit card or something?' I asked as she was ushering us to the nearby bank of lifts.

'No, no,' it's all been take care of...'

'By Mr Harrington,' we both interrupted.

She smiled, pressed the up button, wished us a lovely stay and left.

Jo and I were silent as we ascended in the cube of shiny gold and mirrors that was the lift. I don't know about Jo but my mind was numb, frozen, stuck in awe and amazement. We'd only just planned this trip earlier in the week, how had Christian even had the time to organise all the extra special treatment.

'Why are we up so high?' asked Jo as the lift came to a stop.

'Don't know. I suppose booking so late, maybe that's all that was left?' I proposed as we walked down the hallway with its lush green carpet, so lush it was almost a crime not to take off your shoes and wiggle your toes in the plushness. 'Well, here we are,' I announced, unlocking the door with the swipe card.

We stood in the marble floored doorway, staring at the opulent room before us. A floor to ceiling window sat directly opposite, the view of the strip and all its landmarks framed in glass. Beautiful art hung on the walls, a plush sofa, which sat in the middle of the room faced a huge television. There was a kitchenette to the side and a couple of doors that I guessed were bedrooms and bathrooms. It had to be some sort of mistake. This was way more penthouse than hotel room.

'Maybe they have us mixed up with someone else?' I suggested. 'I've seen that happen on the TV and then the poor schmucks have to be kicked out later to make way for a whale and his snotty wife.'

'A whale?'

'Yeah, the big gamblers, they call them whales. I saw it on the telly.'

Jo nodded, comprehending it all slowly. 'Well, I suppose we should make the most of it then before they kick us out hey?'

'But what if they charge us? We can't afford five minutes in a room like this.'

'I bet Christian can and hasn't he prepaid it all?'

'I suppose but I don't like to take advantage.'

'You're not. They can't charge us anyway. It's their mistake, not ours. We're just innocent victims. Just don't raid the mini bar and we'll be fine,' she smiled, suddenly full of wisdom.

We each picked a room and had just dropped our bags down when the doorbell rang. Yes, doorbell, not just a knock like a regular hotel room. I met Jo in the living room. 'That'll be them coming to kick us out now, I hope you didn't bother to unpack anything,' I laughed.

I opened the door to find a uniformed man with a big smile

and a food trolley. 'Good afternoon,' he smiled. 'Here's your lunch, Miss Donovan,' he said, wheeling his trolley in.

'Thank you, but we didn't order any lunch,' I told him.

He looked at his paperwork to check and said, 'Mr Harrington ordered it, ma'am. Where would you like it?' he asked moving forward into the room.

'The table I suppose,' I said and he went about unloading cloche covered plates onto the dining table and wrapped desserts I was too far away to see into the fridge and poured two glasses of champagne from the trolley. When he was finally done he came over, handed me the bill to sign, refused a tip and handed me a note card in an envelope. 'From Mr Harrington,' he said, then bid us farewell and a lovely stay.

I opened the note, it read, 'The PI guy, Russell Whittington, will meet you in Gilligan's at eight am. Don't line up, I've booked you a table. Miss you. Love you xxC

I looked at his note, reading it again, tracing my finger over the words, his xxC, even though they would have been transcribed from his email by some admin person at the hotel, it felt like he was so far away and those words were my only connection to him, his declarations of love, making my heart ache and making me strong at the same time. It'd been so long already, too long, since I'd heard his lovely voice or felt his strong arms around me, I wanted to cry.

Jo patted my shoulder, 'Come on, let's eat,' she suggested and I realised in comparison to Jo, I should stop being a baby.

I smiled gratefully and followed her to the table where she'd already removed the cloches to reveal amazing towering cob salads.

Sitting on the couch after stuffing ourselves with salads and sticky toffee puddings and finishing the champagne, we looked out the enormous windows at the strip below, our eyelids getting heavier and heavier by the second. If we didn't do something, we'd be asleep by two and awake at midnight. We needed to adjust our body clocks.

'We have to go out,' I declared.

'No, we don't,' Jo replied sleepily.

'Yes, we do,' I confirmed. 'Come on, move,' I prodded her.

'But why?' she groaned.

'I read somewhere you need sunlight to beat the jetlag. We can sleep as soon as we've had dinner,' I promised.

'But that's hours away,' she whined.

'It has to be done to beat the jetlag,' I insisted. 'You'll thank me tomorrow, I promise. Come on, get changed and let's go.'

She finally moved with a large sigh.

'And no laying down in there!' I called as we went into our separate rooms to freshen up and change out of our travel clothes.

'What now?' I asked Jo standing on the other side of the moat and mini forest that kept Stranded sheltered from the strip, keeping the whole oasis in the desert theme alive and true. 'Which way?'

We looked side to side, up and down the strip, blinded each way by famous landmarks, floating balloons, Eiffel towers, distant turrets, roller coasters hanging off the side of buildings, giant circus tents and masses of people pushing to gather in front of what I guessed were the Bellagio fountains.

'That way, then?' I suggested walking towards the hordes of people.

We saw what we could of the fountains, went up the escalators towards Planet Hollywood, picked up some frozen cocktails in giant yard glasses, giggling like twelve year olds as we headed back to the street and letting the ridiculousness and the heat overwhelm our senses as tequila worked its way around our bodies.

We walked back to sit on a bench in front of the fountains after the crowds had dissipated. 'It just doesn't even seem real that we're here, does it?' Jo asked.

'I know, it's so surreal,' I agreed as the water began another choreographed dance in front of us, bringing back the crowds.

'Can you feel it?' I asked Jo.

'Feel what? The tequila?'

I laughed, 'No! The history, the life, the spirit of those who've come before?'

She sat a moment and smiled. 'Yeah, it's like an underlying pulse, isn't it?'

'Do you think he's out here somewhere?' I asked.

'Who? Henry? Maybe,' she said.

'What if he doesn't want to be found? Doesn't want to see us? What if he's moved on, built a whole new life, has a whole new family? That happens, you know. Or maybe he's so old he's forgotten who they are or who he is?'

'And what if he hasn't? What if Ana really is the love of his life like everyone says?' Jo countered.

We both sat thinking quietly for a minute. I was wondering about Henry, what had happened to him and what we'd find when we met Russell Whittington, PI, in the morning and if we really would find Henry. If there was to be some incredible movie style happy ending to all of this or if disappointment was all that lay in wait. I wasn't sure I could take the disappointment. But he was old, it was definitely a possibility. There were so many possibilities, so many ways it could turn out, few of them good.

'Shall we have some food and give up for today?' Jo asked as a couple of supersized, super loud Americans blocked our view of the fountains.

'Yeah, for sure. I don't think my poor little brain can take any more of this in,' I laughed, slurping the last of my drink up the straw.

We got burgers from a restaurant named for a world famous chef who only actually passed through town a couple of times a year and then gave up. We went back to our enormous suite, our rooms and collapsed into our perfect beds, as lovely and soft as pockets of air just like the one at Christian's place and slept like the dead until the sun peaked through the curtains and our wakeup call echoed throughout the suite.

# Chapter 25

A hostess led us to a table in Gilligan's buffet followed by stares and glares of queued and waiting customers. It was a busy restaurant, I gave up wondering how Christian managed to get things like exclusive tables in wait your turn venues or worrying how much such a thing cost and just followed the waiter to our table.

The PI guy was waiting, head down, playing with his phone when we approached. He wore colourful board shorts and a slightly wrinkled powder-blue, button-through shirt as though he couldn't decide whether he was on holidays or doing business. It soon turned out he was all business and the board shorts were just to throw people off. He was tall and broad with dark floppy hair and well-maintained, two-day growth on his deep-tanned face and spoke with the slightest hint of an Aussie accent. In another time and place he may have even been pretty sexy. In fact it was a bit of a waste on Jo and I, which was a shame.

'Ladies, good morning,' he said, standing after we thanked the waiter. 'Russ Whittington,' he introduced himself

'Ainsley,' I said, shaking his outstretched hand. 'This is my friend, Jo.'

'Pleasure,' he said. 'Sit, please,' he insisted, waving a lady over to pour our coffee.

'Christian sent me a copy of the photo. I've finally gotten someone over at the paper to dig out the original and scan it through to me. The one you had was too grainy to work with, but the new one is perfect. It's going through my facial ageing system right now, might even be ready by the time we finish breakfast,' he smiled, quite pleased with himself. Rightly so perhaps, it sounded like quite a complicated business.

'So, who is this bloke anyway?' Russ asked.

'No one. Not really. Just an old friend of a friend,' I told him.

'This is a lot of effort for no one. For a friend of a friend,' he commented dubiously.

'He might be no one. He might be lost. He might be in trouble. But once he was the love of my friend's life and he needs to know she died and left him a son,' I said, leaving out the mysteries they'd left behind that I hoped finding him would solve.

'Ah, that makes a bit more sense, then,' he said, shovelling in some more eggs before guzzling his coffee like it was the only thing keeping him upright. Which, going by his slightly dishevelled appearance, it possibly was.

We were just finishing the last of our eggs when his phone beeped. 'Got it,' he declared. He turned his smartphone towards us, 'This is what your Henry Mayberry would look like today. What do you think?'

I nodded, taking in the greying hair and the wrinkles, but he still looked like the cheeky Henry Mayberry in the original photograph that had been printed in the paper. It was really quite clever what Russell had done. By the smile on his face, he never got sick of being appreciated either.

'So, what next?' I asked.

'We show it around, see if anyone recognises him.'

I nodded as though that made perfect sense, as though wandering up and down the famous Las Vegas strip showing people a picture was easy. I was sure it wasn't going to be that easy.

'Right, you ready?' Russ asked as soon as our cutlery hit our plates.

'Um, I suppose so. Can we finish our coffee?' I replied for us both, not realising we'd be traipsing behind him on this photo flashing escapade.

Russ waved over the waitress and asked for the bill.

'It's been taken care of by Mr Harrington,' she smiled sweetly, collecting our plates and scurrying away while Jo and I rolled our eyes.

'We could have paid for our own breakfast,' I grumbled to Jo as I collected our things.

'Don't be so ungrateful,' she smirked, nudging me.

Russ threw a decent tip down on the table, anyway and we followed him out into the casino.

'Right, let's get started then, hey?' he said, putting his game face on.

We were quickly swallowed by the void, by the people, the noise of people beginning their day of gambling, some still going from the night before, some sipping cocktails even though I was still digesting my eggs.

We crossed the thick green carpet, passed waitresses in shiny gold crop tops that looked shrink-wrapped to their bodies.

'Don't they look just like the meter maids on the Goldie?' asked Jo as one passed with thick blonde hair cascading down her back, twisting to stare at Russ.

'Wow, they really do, flirty smirks and all,' I joked.

We nearly bumped into a craps table with all our gawking and were promptly admonished by Russ. 'Would you two watch where you're going before you get us thrown out?' he huffed as a handsome, Hugo Boss suited man came out of a door hidden by a leafy mural and walked straight for Russ.

'Maaaaaate,' the man crowed in a poor attempt at an Aussie accent.

Russ laughed, grabbed the man's hand, slapping him on the back. 'How are you, D?'

'I'm alright,' he said. 'Bit early for you though, ain't it?'

Russ laughed conspiratorially. 'Workin' today,' he said. He nodded to Jo and me and introduced us. D shook our hands, his hand was strong and sure and even though he was beautifully handsome and clean cut, I could tell he was a man you wouldn't want to mess with.

Interrupting our pleasantries, a woman screamed *'Bastardo!'* scurrying across the casino floor in a fabulous, low cut, skin tight, LBD with a cowl neck perfectly accenting all she had to offer. She was young, dark with long glossy black curls and big brown eyes, her mascara smudged into black smears under her eyes as she hobbled on one sparkly, strappy Manolo, the other she held in her hand, the heel hanging loose.

Jo and I looked at Russ and D trying not to laugh, trying to decide which one was the *bastardo* in question. They were smirking at each other and, as the woman and her crazy eyes were almost upon us, two far burlier Boss-clad blokes stepped out and stopped the woman with a gentle hand gesture as D opened the secret palm tree covered door and ushered us through.

As soon as the door closed, the boys burst into raucous laughter. The kerfuffle with the woman continued on the other side of the door as she shouted at the bouncers and called after whichever *bastardo* had wronged her. D slapped Russ on the back and shook his head with a look of amusement, bewilderment or admiration, I couldn't quite tell.

'Let's find somewhere quieter, yeah?' he suggested.

'Thanks, mate,' said Russ as we followed D down a brightly lit, utilitarian corridor, a far cry from the opulence and sparkle we'd just left on the other side of the door.

We passed a group of showgirls kitted out in their feathers and sequins. 'Hey, Russ,' they cooed in sing-song form as they passed.

I looked to Jo whose eyebrows were stretching up to her hairline in amusement. 'Who is this guy?' she mouthed.

I shrugged my shoulders. Clearly he was a ladies' man. I just hoped he was as good a PI.

The office D took us to, really just a multi-use alcove with a desk, nothing fancy or official like you'd see on the telly.

Russ didn't pay any attention, he got down to business showing D the picture on his smartphone and telling him Henry's story in the hope something might spring to mind.

'Nah, mate, doesn't look familiar.' He shook his head as he looked at Henry's picture a moment longer, as though double-checking with his own mind. 'Check with Mish, though. She knows everyone and has that steel cage memory. If anyone will remember him, it'd be Mish.'

'Mish?' Russ asked, then sighed.

'Come on, you're not afraid of Mish, are you?' D laughed.

'Come on girls,' Russ demanded as though we were children.

'Mish should be on the floor. Jonesy's in town,' D called as we walked away.

'Great!' Russ groaned, storming ahead.

We traipsed along behind Russ like groupies, every woman we passed nodding wantonly at Russ before looking us up and down with disgusted glares. It was doing nothing for our self-confidence.

We stormed across the casino floor as though on a military mission towards a perfectly sculpted brunette, long legs, long chocolate hair, perfect cheekbones, perfect chic outfit clearly worth more than my last car, showing just enough skin but not too much. She was talking to one of the staff but waived them off as soon as she saw us.

'What do you want? Who are they? Parading your girlfriends in front of me now? Classy, Russ.'

'This is work, Mish. Can you be professional just for a minute? Please?' Russell begged.

She actually hmphed but didn't protest any further or leave

so Russ went on and showed her Henry's picture. 'Do you know this guy?'

'Nope,' she said, without any further elaboration.

'You sure?'

'Of course I'm sure,' she snapped.

'Okay, then. Thanks,' he said, slightly exacerbated by the whole exchange.

'You!' Exclaimed a wild bulldog of a man, short and stumpy, as round as he was tall, his face wrinkled and mean, hurtled towards us.

'Shit,' Russell groaned.

'Now you've done it,' Mish whispered with a sadistic grin. 'Jonesy,' she soothed. 'Russell's just leaving. Aren't you, Russell?'

'Yeah, yeah, thanks,' he mumbled as we all quickly walked away.

'Sorry about all that,' Russ apologised sheepishly when we were back out in the bright hot sun. 'Maybe you should just wait for me by the pool? I'll come find you later with an update.'

'Fine by me,' Jo declared and we left the Casanova to it.

# Chapter 26

We had picked up some cute bikinis from Jetty Surf on our pre-departure, shopping trip, before we'd headed into Myer. It was the wrong time of year for bathers and the pickings were slim but to be honest, I never really thought we'd use them. We were coming here to find Henry, not sit by the pool.

Jo emerged from changing in the bathroom with a coverall dress with tropical green leaves on it. Mine was a boring, plain white cheesecloth. Her face was beaming with anticipation and I realised how much she might need an afternoon in the sun by the pool after everything she'd been through of late, so I put my concerns about wasted time aside and got into the spirit. We were in Vegas after all.

We bought sunhats and sunscreen from a beach fashion store amongst a mall of shops we passed and headed to the pool.

The morning was stretching towards lunch time, the sun beat down like a wicked hot poker but already people were stretching out on sun lounges like corpses baking in the sun around the enormous, swirling pool, proudly displaying their feminine wares as the men pranced around like peacocks.

We found a pair of sun lounges towards the back, away from the waterfall at one end and all the squealing attention seekers, where we wouldn't be on show with our pale legs and not quite supermodel physiques. We smothered ourselves in sunscreen and ordered some salads and margarita slushies and laid back, letting the goodness of the sun's UV's stroke our skin and soothe our souls.

'So what's with Russ do you reckon?' I asked, sipping my margarita.

'Do we want to know?' Jo asked, laughing.

'Yeah, probably not!'

'That was one crazy-eyed woman, though, wasn't it?'

'Oh my god! And that bloke!'

'I do wonder what he did to piss him off,'

'Who he did you mean?'

She laughed, 'A who for sure. Wife or daughter, you think?'

'Or both?'

'Hell no!' Jo exclaimed. 'Well I hope not, anyway!'

We giggled for a while at the thought of Russ causing havoc all over town as the tequila weaved its way throughout our bodies.

'So, you and The Ferret?' Jo said. 'Who'd have thought you'd be so serious about The Ferret?'

'Shut up,' I laughed. 'Honestly, though, I really didn't think I'd ever get to feel this way about anyone.'

'What? Ever?'

'Yeah, I never thought I would. I thought it just wasn't on the cards for me.'

'Really? But you're amazing,' Jo said.

'Awe thanks, right back at ya. But not that long ago, I didn't think there was anything left for me in this whole world.'

'Oh yeah, forgot about that. Hon, are you okay now?'

'I am. I'm good. Thanks to Ana and mum, you and Christian. I can't believe how it's all changed. How much I now have to live for. On that day, I could never have even imagined life could be this good, couldn't have come up with it if I dreamed it. But goodness, I can't even get started on Christian.'

'Awe,' Jo said, misty-eyed.

'Sweetie...' I said, my heart breaking for her.

'No, no, I'm okay. I promise,' she insisted, waving the man over for more Margaritas.

'Really,' she continued. 'I'm so happy for you. I really am. It's just, I miss it. I miss it all. Having someone you know is there to catch you when you fall no matter what. Benny was my person and I miss him and I don't think I'll ever find it again.'

The waiter arrived with our drinks and some snacks to keep us going.

'I don't know if there's another man you could love and share your life with like you did with Benny,' I said. 'I don't know any of the rules, clearly. But I do know that things get better. That love comes in all different ways at all different times and someday, when you're not even paying attention, it's just better. Never the same but that's sometimes okay, too. And until that happens, I am going to be your person. I know it's not the same as Benny but I'm here for you, always.'

'I love you,' she said. 'I really don't know how I would have gotten through these weeks if it wasn't for you and Christian. I just don't know. You guys kept me, you kept me together. You kept me whole when I just wanted to be nothing.' Her voice was catching. She took a sip of the margarita. We both did. It was all I could do to keep my own tears at bay. 'I don't know how I'll ever repay you,' she finished.

'This is what friendship is,' I told her. 'You magically appeared right when I needed you,' I told her.

'No,' she said. 'When you needed me I was in bloody Fiji with that manipulative, arse of a boss.'

'Hey,' I soothed. 'I really don't know if it'd have mattered if you were in Fiji, the office or at home. I was in a really bad place and I wasn't letting anyone in.'

'Well, whatever,' she said. 'I've learnt one thing over these months, life is far too short to not be present with the people most important to you. Nothing, especially a crap job, no matter how big your pay packet is or how it strokes your ego, is worth sacrificing time with your people.'

I reached over and squeezed her hand and wiped a tear from my eye before reaching for my margarita and taking a big drink until I got a brain freeze.

'Okay, enough of all this soul searching,' I declared, taking a big breath. 'We're in Vegas and there's so much plastic, drama and sin going on round this pool, it'd give that daytime TV a good run and we're missing all the gossip opportunities.'

Jo laughed and pointed to a skinny old man with bushy white chest hair whispering sweet nothings to an Amazonian blonde with the biggest knockers I'd ever seen and a bikini that should have been illegal in public.

'That's some impressive waxing she has there,' I laughed.

And that's how we wiled away the afternoon, gossiping about the bevvy of folk before us, those relaxing and those clearly getting up to no good. As I scanned the poolside, my eyes froze by the bar where a familiar tall svelte blonde stood.

'Jo,' I called, my voice quivering. 'By the bar at the entrance, is that…?'

'Who? Where?' Jo asked, sitting bolt upright.

I looked at her dumbfounded. How could she not have seen her? I looked back to where the Blonde Bitch had stood and she was gone.

'Where'd she go?' I asked.

'I think you're losing it, Ains. Do I need to call Dr Bailey?'

'Seriously. I saw her.'

'Saw who?' Jo asked.

'The Blonde Bitch.'

'Really? Here? She followed us here? How?' Jo asked, sitting up, paying attention.

Then I saw her again. 'There, by the bar, showing the barman something.'

'Shit. What's she showing him? What if it's a picture of us?'

'Maybe no one will recognise us in the bikinis and big sun hats and glasses? How'd she even get pictures of us, anyway?'

Russell perched himself on the end of my chair, making it bounce a little. 'What's up with you? You look like you've seen a ghost.'

'Just someone from home, that's all.'

'Where?' he asked.

'Over by the bar,' I said, explaining all about the Blonde Bitch, her obsession with the brooch and her stalking.

He twisted around. 'Is she still here?' he asked, twisting around like a pretzel.

I looked around too but I couldn't see her. 'Doesn't look like it,' I said as his final twist almost had him falling to the floor and making a spectacle.

Once we'd finally stopped giggling, he asked, 'How many of those have you had?'

'Not too many,' Jo giggled. 'Want one?'

'I think I need one,' he said.

'Good day, then?'

'Not very fruitful, that's for sure. But we'll try again tomorrow. Right now I think we need to get some food into you two,' he said. 'Come on, then,' Russ insisted. 'I've had enough trouble for one day, I don't need that man of yours giving me grief because you two got sloshed,' he said, leading us away from the pool which was now overflowing with people.

We walked the sandy marble streets of the hotel and made our way to the restaurant of yet another famous chef Russ insisted was the best in town.

'We need cocktails,' Jo sang to the waiter when he stopped at our table.

'No you don't,' laughed Russ.

'Yes we do,' I scolded. 'Suggestions?' I asked the waiter with a victorious smile.

'You look like strawberry martini kinds of ladies,' the very camp and very handsome waiter suggested.

'Strawberry martini's it is, then,' I declared as Russ added a beer for himself and a jug of water for the table to the order.

'So you really think it was the Blonde Bitch you saw earlier?' Russ asked after the waiter had left.

'Yes, I swear it was her.'

'Even with margarita goggles?' he asked.

'Yes, smarty pants, even with margarita goggles.'

As I said it, I saw a blonde head pass out of the corner of my eye and swung around to see an ordinary person going about their business.

'Now look at me. I'm jumping at every bloody blonde I see,' I said, slumping in my chair with frustration.

'I think you two can stay with me tomorrow,' Russ said. 'I don't like the sound of this Blonde Bitch following you all this way.

'Speaking of coming all this way,' Jo interjected. 'What happened today?'

'I worked all my charm on the waitresses, the hostesses, the security staff, showing Henry's photo, describing how he'd come to be in Vegas in case the story rang a bell that they could match to a face. But no one knew him. No one knew his story. He wasn't in the wait staff or the entertainment staff. He wasn't a regular gambler or a local anyone recognised. It was a complete dead end,' he said, exhaustedly sipping his beer.

'No,' Jo giggled as another round of martinis arrived with our food. 'That's all nice to know and everything but what was with the crazy shoeless chick, the showgirls and the fat bloke ready to blow a gasket?'

Russ blushed like a schoolgirl. 'You ladies don't need to know any of that sordid information,' he said, offering no more and attacking his beef ribs like a caveman.

'Fine,' Jo sulked. 'We'll just make up our own conclusions, then,' she smirked.

Russ shook his head and kept eating.

'So,' Russ said after we'd finished eating in silence and the waiter had taken our plates. 'Clearly this one has her indulgent man at her whimsy, what about you?'

I nearly choked on my cocktail. Jo was speechless for a moment and then said, 'My boyfriend just died. So nope, no man here.'

'Shit, I'm sorry,' said Russ. 'Well don't I feel like a jackass?'

Jo shrugged. 'You weren't to know.'

The waiter returned, 'Another round?'

'Perhaps something stronger this time to finish up. Maybe some of that cognac,' he looked at me for approval or something. I just shrugged and nodded. Sounded fine to me.

'So where is the great Christian Harrington, anyway?' he asked as we sipped our cognac. 'Why'd that man of yours send you all this way alone?'

'He had family business.'

'Ah, sounds ominous.'

I shrugged. I didn't know what it sounded like. I only knew hearing his name sliced away at my insides as they ached to see him, to touch him, smell him, hear his voice tell me ridiculous things that made me think I could take over the world, that I could go all the way to Vegas and find Henry just because I wanted to and it would end with streamers and parades and a Disney-style happy ending.

'It's a sore subject. She misses him,' Jo said for me as Russ raised his eyes with curiosity at my pained and thoughtful face. 'She's prone to the dramatic,' Jo added. 'Straight out of the loony bin, you know.'

That made me laugh so hard I almost spat my fancy cognac across the room.

'Good God, what has that bloody Christian Harrington sent me?' laughed Russ. 'So tell me,' he said, changing the subject from my craziness. 'For this Blonde Bitch to have followed you all this way, there must be more to this story than just a lost love and a brooch.'

'You know, you're right, Russ, I don't even know the rest. Why are we here finding the story of a lost love and a single fancy brooch?' Jo asked.

I looked at them trying to figure out how to not tell them or maybe I should, maybe they deserved to know? 'Henry Mayberry was a famous jewel thief,' I told them.

'The eggs right?'

'Not just the eggs. There's more. Lots more.'

'What?' Jo sputtered.

'Those crates in the basement next to all the stuff we brought back from Benny's, they're all packed with teapots filled with jewels and money. Christian did some research and it looks like it's all stolen and the last place Henry Mayberry was seen was here in Vegas in that picture with the gun to his head.'

'Oh my God,' Jo said breathlessly.

'Shit,' Russ stammered, taking a long sip of his cognac.

'Sorry,' I said. 'I probably should have told you everything.

But I didn't want you to get into trouble if or when it all came out.'

'Oh, tell him how your friend was a famous madam,' Jo said, trying to lighten the mood.

'You're kidding, right?' Russ said.

'Nope,' I shook my head. 'But you might need another of those cognacs for this story,' I said, waving over the waiter.

We ended the night on a lovely light note telling unexpected stories from nice old ladies then we farewelled Russ in the foyer and took our vodka, tequila and cognac-filled bodies to bed.

# Chapter 27

We waited on the eerily quiet street for Russell. We'd ordered up eggs for breakfast, we didn't need to be delaying this search for buffets and conversation. We weren't even up for conversing with each other and just stood quietly watching the street.

Jo yawned and tapped her foot. We'd both popped painkillers with our eggs and drank a gallon of water but we were still suffering terribly so we stood in comfortable silence and watched the double-decker bus making its way down the strip towards Freemont Street strangely empty bar for the ghosts of the night before. Soon it would be filled with people and chugging at snail speed like the rest of the strip, once everyone woke and cured their hangovers. But for now it was just the few early birds off on day tours and us ready for the day's searching.

Russ ambled slowly up the street as though he hadn't a care in the world. 'Ladies,' he addressed us by way of good morning when he approached. 'Ready?'

We both grumbled in reply and he dared laugh a little as we followed him up the street.

'I know some people working today up this way, so we'll start at the MGM, my mate's sister's working cocktails on the floor and I've a mate on valet up at the Luxor, so we'll do New York-New York and Excalibur in between and just hope we hit on something. I really don't fancy having to scour every single casino. Not all of them will be as helpful as the ones we've been to so far, so hopefully one of these will come through.'

We nodded and he shook his head and kept walking.

We walked under the shiny lights of the MGM and into the beautiful foyer, too tired and too sore to admire it properly, blindly following Russ in a haze. My eyes hurt to look around so I just focussed on Russ' back, on the wrinkles in his shirt, wondering if he even owned an iron. I paid attention though as he led us through an archway made of an aquarium, water and thousands of brightly-coloured fish ready to collapse on our sore heads. Jo was as impressed by it as me. I knew because she grabbed my hand and we both instinctively walked a little faster.

We hurried behind Russ, jumping at the high-pitched screeches of wild animals. Thunder roared all around us and we practically cowered under the table we arrived at in the family friendly cafe. Russ and the waitress were in hysterics.

'They'll have some cheese sticks, lots of coffee and juice,' he told the waitress when he'd stopped laughing.

The waitress left giggling, bee-lining for her buddies who were trying to hide their sniggers behind their skinny little hands.

'Now you two stay here until I get back,' Russ instructed. 'Do not move! You hear me?' You have my number if you need me, so does Stacey but please behave and don't make a scene.'

'Fine, fine,' Jo said, waving him off. 'You go find Henry and we'll wait here and eat,' she said, smiling tightly as our coffee arrived.

I sat silently sipping my coffee, too tired to talk, watching a monkey watching me from a fake jungle opposite. This was the weirdest place I'd ever been.

Eventually Stacey brought over our cheese sticks covered in marinara sauce and even though we'd not long eaten breakfast, suddenly I was starving and as soon as we started shovelling those disgusting babies into our mouths there was definitely no talking.

As our first batch of cheese sticks was nearly gone, inhaled even, Stacey brought us some more, refilling our coffee.

'Better?' she asked.

We both nodded, too busy stuffing our faces to actually speak.

'So, how do you guys know Russ?' she asked with that ridiculous look in her eye people all over Vegas seemed to have whenever Russ was mentioned. It was sad and pathetic. Did they not realise it? Did they not feel any shame for letting themselves be reduced to bumbling bimbos by a man?

I smiled at the poor sap and thought I should throw her a bone. 'My boyfriend hired him to do some PI work,' I told her, watching the look of relief ease across her face.

'Oh right, the photo he showed us of that old guy?'

'Yeah, that's it.'

'So where is your boyfriend? Why isn't he traipsing about after Russ?' she asked suspiciously.

'He's not here,' I said. 'He had to work, so it's just us,' I said, nodding in Jo's direction, wishing she'd leave before the cheese sticks got cold.

'And do you have a boyfriend?' she demanded from Jo.

Jo's eyes instantly shone with fresh tears. She was far too hungover for inappropriate questioning from a stranger. This girl was getting way too nosy and way too personal and I was way too hungover to keep my manners intact and I blurted, 'No, he's dead. He died a month ago, so you don't have to worry, neither of us are after Russ. He's all yours.'

The girl's face fell, went a little grey and she hurried off. I was just glad I could get back to the cheese sticks and my fresh cup of coffee even though I knew I'd been horrible to her.

'That was really mean,' Jo said, smiling.

'I know. I didn't mean to, but seriously, what's wrong with these people? He's not Brad Pitt and he's a scoundrel.'

'Scoundrel?' she smirked.

'Yes,' I laughed. 'A dirty rotten scoundrel.'

Russ returned as we were just finishing the last of our cheese sticks. He flopped into the spare chair and although some other girl had been to refill our coffee since I was so mean to Stacey, Stacey now hurried over, cheery as the sun, and poured some coffee for Russ who barely acknowledged her.

'Any luck?' I asked him.

'None,' he said looking as dejected as he sounded.

'I've been talking to all the right people and nothing. No one knows him. We may never find him, you know that, right?'

'We will, I just know it,' I said.

'Ever the romantic,' Jo groaned as she stood. 'Where to next?'

'New York-New York,' Russ said, throwing some money on the table.

'I could have paid,' I said.

'Ah, it's okay, I'll add it to your boyfriend's bill,' he smiled, draping an arm across each of our shoulders as though he were Hugh bloody Hefner. If looks could kill, that Stacey he winked at on the way out, would have shot us a billion times dead with a machine gun.

We left the MGM and walked across the overpass walkway to New York-New York, the morning sun already dazzling with its stinging heat.

Just inside the doorway was an oxygen bar. 'Sit,' said Russ. 'It'll help with the hangovers.' He looked to the guy manning the bar and said, 'Don't let them out of your sight,' he told him. 'Bear's a bouncer by night, so don't mess with him,' he told us and he went down the escalator into New York-New York.

'He's taking this whole protection thing a bit too seriously, isn't he?' I said to Jo.

'Not really, Ains,' she said. 'If that Blonde Bitch has followed you all this way, then shit, it really is that serious and I'm glad Russ is being a little extreme. Although,' she said, leaning in and whispering, 'I don't know this wanna be hip hop dude here would be much use in a showdown.'

'Hey,' called Bear. 'I do just fine. Now sit still and be quiet,' Bear instructed with a smirk as he tried covering our giggling mouths with oxygen masks.

Not much can happen when you have an oxygen mask strapped to your face, so it leaves you with a lot of thinking time and I was struck as I watched people going down and coming up the New York-New York escalators just how far I'd come. It was only months ago I'd tried to take my own life. Only months ago I had nothing. I was lower than I'd ever imagined possible with no visible way out. No one in my corner to pull me out of the dark, no light shining from any of the dark corners engulfing me.  And now, I was here, in Vegas, the bright morning sun streaming through the windows, almost blinding us and my heart was now so full of love and happiness and I was so grateful I'd messed up and failed at the whole ending my life thing. Glad I had found this new, amazing life, which I'm sure I'd have found if I'd just called my mother for help in the first place instead of sinking all alone, I thought as Bear turned off the machines and took off our masks.

Jo stood, stretching like a cat.

'Where are you going?' Bear demanded quickly.

Jo looked at him surprised. 'Nowhere, just stretching,' she smiled, amused.

'Good. Sit. Russ said you weren't to move and I wasn't to let you out of my sight,' he said, slightly panicked.

'Fine, fine,' Jo smirked.

I was laughing at their exchange when I glimpsed a streak of blonde out the corner of my eye, coming in from the walkway that joined the MGM to New York-New York and I instantly froze, muttering, 'Shit!' as I saw the Blonde Bitch's mountainous brother lean into his sister and whisper something in her ear.

'What?' demanded Bear.

'It's them,' I whispered. 'Don't look, geez,' I groaned as they both turned. 'Bear, do something. Where are those masks?' I begged when he didn't move.

Bear fumbled and scrambled as he covered us with his scrawny body trying to put on my mask. Jo got frustrated waiting, snatching hers from his hand and was strapping it on herself just as Russ came up the escalators in front of us and the Blonde Bitch and her mountainous brother were almost right beside us.

My eyes connected with Russ'. I tried conveying the trouble, looking to the side where the Blonde bitch and her brother were passing by, walking right towards him as though in slow motion.

Russ' body stiffened, his face scowling as he tried to figure out what was going on and he walked right into the Blonde Bitch, their bodies smacking into each other.

'Hey man, what are you doing?' The Mountainous Brother demanded, stepping in with a heavy hand on Russ' chest.

Russ barely flinched, just hung his head and mumbled, 'Sorry man, really.'

'Yeah, well, just be more careful,' he grumbled as they stomped to the escalators without as much as glancing in our direction.

Russ headed out to the walkway towards the MGM as the Blonde Bitch turned, taking one last long look at Russ' retreating back before she was swallowed by the dark of the casino.

'Go that way, Russ will find you,' Bear said, pointing towards the other walkway leading to the coloured turrets of Excalibur.

'Thanks,' we both muttered.

'For everything,' I added as Jo grabbed my hand and practically dragged me across the walkway and into Excalibur.

A timeshare rep pounced on us as soon as we got through the doors. Clearly she needed her eyes checked if she thought we had any money for things like timeshare properties. She prattled on a million miles a minute none-the-less and I looked at Jo with my eyebrows raised and she just shrugged. She was right in her silent communication, we should just go with it until Russ found us, it was better than wandering aimlessly around the foyer, so we just nodded politely and let her get out her well-practised spiel.

'They have no money,' Russ finally spat condescendingly at the woman from behind us.

The woman stalked off in a huff.

'Vultures,' he groaned, leading us away from the timeshare people by the elbows.

'So that was definitely her back there?' Russ asked, once we were a safe distance from prying ears.

We both nodded.

'And the guy? The meathead, who's he?' he asked.

'Her brother,' I told him.

'Right,' he said frustrated. 'Let's get this done, then. The sooner you two are off the street, the better.'

Russ was desperate, he was snapping at people, shoving Henry's photo in front of their terrified faces. 'Have you seen this man?' he demanded from anyone passing by, scaring old people and mild-mannered tourists.

He stopped a knight in full armour, complete with a pastel-coloured maiden at his side. Almost begging, he showed them Henry's picture, asking if they'd seen him, telling his story, explaining, 'He might look older or younger we don't know how he's fared over the years,' he said, the dejection showing in his shaky voice.

The knight gave a blunt and regal, 'No,' not breaking character for a second.

His maiden was about to say the same, but paused and instead said, 'Hang on, isn't that the guy that sits out on the walkway playing his harmonica for money?'

The knight took a closer look and in a regular American accent said, 'You know, I think you're right. But the guy out there,' he said, indicating the walkway we'd just come from with his head, 'is much thinner, older, greyer.'

'We just came from there, we didn't see him, just a guy strumming a guitar,' Russell told them.

'He comes around six or seven, catches the dinner crowd.'

'Thanks, man,' Russ said.

'No worries,' the guy said. 'You should come see the show when you've sorted all your business,' he said, handing us three passes to the Excalibur show for the next night.

Russell nodded and thanked them for the tickets before they hurried off, back in character, delighting passers-by.

'Right, then,' said Russ after the knight and his maiden had left. 'Let's get you two off the street. We'll come back later.'

We hurried, heads bowed, sunglasses on, all the way down the strip, arms linked, dodging tourists to our oasis in the desert, our poor feet begging for mercy.

# Chapter 28

We got into the room and I ordered up burgers for lunch. Russ went to the window and looked out as though he could see things on the street from that high up and then closed the curtains as though those on the street could see us.

'Do you think they know why we're here? Do you think they know about Henry?' I asked.

'Maybe,' said Russ. 'Depends who they asked and if they were feeling friendly.'

'So Henry could be in danger? He could be heading out to the walkway right now, none the wiser. Shouldn't we be there when he gets there to warn him or something?'

'It's okay, Ainsley, he'll be fine. It took us a lot of time and effort and begging to find him remember and we had a photo and people know me, they won't talk so easily to a stranger.'

'You're right. I'm overreacting, aren't I?'

'Little bit,' Jo agreed.

'It's just, we've come so far. I don't want to lose him now, not after everything.'

'I know, I know,' said Jo patting my hand.

We ate and then camped out on the sofa under Russ' watchful eye for the afternoon watching American TV, waiting for the clock to tell us it was time to go.

I poured a glass of water, my hands shaking so much I almost spilled it all over the bar. 'This is crazy,' I said.

'We're going to find him, Ains, we will, just breathe.'

'Yeah, yeah,' I smiled, finally getting myself together.

At six thirty we headed back out onto the walkway with our fingers crossed. He had to be there or we were going to have to start looking the suburbs. I couldn't even fathom how that would work. We had to find him before it went that far.

'Stay right by my side, both of you,' Russ instructed as we started walking down the strip. 'I want to feel you both, every step, you hear me?'

'Yes, Russ,' we both mumbled.

I saw him smirk but he never took his eyes off the street as we hustled along.

We heard the harmonica before we saw him. He'd drawn a little crowd, generous people happy to put coins and notes of all denominations into his hat. It looked like he did alright. But he was thin, bony thin. He clearly didn't get enough food, bathe often enough, shave often enough or spend much time buying clothes. I felt guilty for having all of Mrs May's money when Henry clearly needed it. I mentally ran through how much was in my bag. It was all his, whatever I had.

Russ was about to speak to him but I put up my hand, stopping him. 'This part is mine. I need to speak to him, for Ana.'

'Excuse me,' I said, squatting beside him and whispering so passers-by wouldn't hear. 'Are you Henry Mayberry?'

His hollow eyes shot to me, widening like saucers with panic.

'It's okay, I'm not the police or anything,' I told him, slowly. 'Actually, I'm a friend of Ana's, of Stasie's.'

'My Stasie?' he asked breathlessly.

I nodded as his eyes filled with tears. 'Is Stasie okay?'

I shook my head, my own eyes filling with tears. I no longer wanted to be the bearer of bad news to this frail old man. But it was my job. I owed it to Ana.

'What happened?' he asked softly as people moved on now he'd stopped playing.

'She was sick. She passed away in her sleep a couple of months ago. I'd have come sooner but she'd said you died. I didn't know you were anywhere to be found.'

'That was our plan,' he said. 'If I got caught.' He looked at us warily. 'You know the story I'm assuming. If you've found me, you must know?'

'Yes, we know,' I smiled.

He nodded and continued. 'The plan, if I got caught, was Stasie was never to return to the café. She was to disappear into the suburbs, change her name and tell our child when it was born that I'd died in the war. I don't even know what she had. Was it a girl or a boy?'

'You had a son. His name is Mitchell.'

He nodded. 'I was supposed to go to her. I promised her I'd always find a way back. But I couldn't. I couldn't get enough money for food, let alone airfare. They stole my passport and I couldn't exactly go to the consulate for another one. I was stuck.

I was stuck in this bloody, godforsaken, hot hell pit for all of eternity,' he said, angry tears spilling out of his eyes.

'Did she live okay? Was she and the boy okay? Did they have a good life?' he asked, hopeful.

'Yes, they seemed to. I'm sure your son would like to know you're still alive.'

'No. He mustn't know. There'd be no way to keep the truth from him. He must never know what we did. Who his mother really was. You cannot ruin his memories of her. Her beauty would be tainted if he knew the truth. He'd never forgive her. He was never to know about the jewels and things if I wasn't there to protect him. What happened to it all?'

'I have them. Ana left the café and everything in it to me.'

'You must have been a good and trusted friend to her,' he said, placing his hand on top of mine. 'Thank you. It is a comfort to know she had someone she trusted around her.'

'I could send you the jewels, the money, all of it. It's yours. It could help you get home or you could sell them for food and somewhere to live. You wouldn't have to sit out here every night,' I offered.

He smiled. 'No, that's okay. Pretty things are no good to me now. They need to go back to where they belong. There's a journal in the last crate I sent. I always sent it in the crates so I didn't have to carry it home. You give it to the police, they'll know what to do with the jewels.

'I really don't mind being out here amongst the people. It's a small comfort in a lonely world. I'd always hoped someday Stasie might pass by,' he said wistfully. 'But she never did,' he said, tears silently falling down his face.

'I think she was always waiting for you, too,' I told him, remembering all the years she'd sat on her verandah as though waiting for someone.

'There was no way to contact her, to let her know where I was,' he said. 'I don't know what she changed her name to or where she went. It didn't matter though. It was better this way. I didn't want to disappoint her. How could she see me like this?' he said, waving his hands in the air. 'And now it's too late,' he cried.

'Please,' I begged him, not knowing what else to do. 'Will you come back to our hotel, have a shower, something to eat and then we can figure what to do next?'

He shook his head. 'There's no point. No point to any of it without my Stasie.' He sobbed into his hands before raising his tear stained face and playing something sad on his harmonica.

'We have to do something,' I said to Jo and Russ. 'We should at least get him some clothes and food.'

Russ nodded. 'Come on.'

We went in to one of the takeaway food stalls just inside Excalibur. I ordered as many bottles of water as we could carry, as many containers of food as I thought safe, no point buying too much if they were going to go bad before he ate them. We picked up some clean clothes from the souvenir store, planning to go to the nearest shopping centre in the morning to buy proper clothes and groceries but for now we just wanted to get some clean clothes on his back and some nutrients and fluids into his frail body before it wasted away completely.

The walkway was silent when we returned. Just the soft hum of people drifting on the air. The harmonica had stopped. 'Why isn't he playing?' I asked, terrified he'd run off and we would never be able to find him again.

But at the top of the stairs we could see him still sitting on the walkway where we'd left him, his head hanging to one side, the harmonica in his hand hanging limp. I dropped the bag I was carrying, water bottles rolling across the walkway and ran, pushing people out of my way until I reached him. Russ and Jo running right behind me. But it was too late. Russ checked his pulse but it was no good, we were too late. He was gone. Henry had died. All alone on a walkway.

'We were just here,' I cried. 'How could it have happened? He was just fine. One of us should have stayed,' I cried. 'One of us should have stayed,' I mumbled again as I fell to Henry's side. 'I'm sorry, Henry, I'm so sorry,' I cried.

Russ went across to the entry of Excalibur to ask one of the security team to call an ambulance and we waited with Henry. I sat beside him, holding his hand as I knew Ana would want me to. I knew it took some time for a spirit to leave someone's body and before he left to find his Stasie, I wanted him to know he wasn't alone anymore.

The ambulance took away Henry's body. I told them there was no family and handed them a wad of Mrs May's money to cover any costs. Another homeless man sat further down the walkway still lightly strumming his guitar. We gave him Henry's food and water and went to leave.

'Hey,' called a police officer who'd come to investigate.

We turned, hoping it wasn't us he was calling but he was looking right at us and we froze on the spot.

'Russ, is that you?' asked the officer.

'Yeah, man,' Russ replied, exhausted.

'This anything to do with you?'

'Why? Does it matter?' Russ asked.

'I heard from D you've been all over looking for some old guy, this him?'

'Maybe.'

'Right, then, until we get the results, we best have a chat, hey?'

'Really? Come on, man,' Russ begged.

'Sorry, man, procedure. You guys were the last ones with him according to those tourists over there.'

'Bloody tourists,' groaned Russ. 'Fine, fine. Come on, then.'

'Great,' I said to Jo as we followed Russ who was now happily chatting to the officer. 'As if everything so far wasn't enough, now we're going to be arrested for murder. Mum's going to kill me.'

'Don't be so dramatic, Ainsley, we're not going down for murdering Henry. It won't take them long to figure out it was natural causes,' Jo said.

'I hope so,' I told her.

'It's a bit exciting, though,' she gushed. 'Best holiday ever, you know.'

'I think you've lost your mind,' I laughed.

I looked up and saw the Blonde Bitch and her mountainous brother standing at the end of the walkway watching us. I gripped Jo's arm like a vice. Jo gripped Russ' arm and he screeched like a little girl. The two cops flanking us demanded, 'What's going on? What's the commotion?'

'Nothing, man,' Russ assured them as we all passed the

Blonde Bitch and her brother, our eyes locking, passing as though in slow motion.

Then it was over. We were on the street below being guided into a cop car and they were nowhere to be seen. My heart was pounding, my mouth was dry and I was pooling sweat in uncomfortable places.

'You girls okay?' Russ asked.

We nodded, mumbling incoherently.

'Well, you're fine now,' he assured us.

'Yeah, for now,' Jo groaned.

'They can't get up to the penthouse. I'll let D know to keep an eye out for them and we'll go straight back to the hotel when we're done with this and then you can get your flight home sorted.'

'If we ever leave,' I sulked. 'They're going to put us in jail, I just know it.'

'They're not putting us in jail,' Russ smirked. 'They'll get their answers, sort out the paperwork and we'll be on our way before the parties start for the night.'

'Whatever,' I said, like a five year old. 'I'll be saying I told you so when they take your mug shot.'

'Told you she has a flair for the dramatic,' Jo laughed, nudging me.

We sat in an empty room at the police station with the officer and some cups of terrible coffee. Russ explained the whole story to the officer who didn't look like he believed a word of it. Eventually he wandered off and left us to snooze in the hard plastic chairs.

When he returned, he was almost laughing. We were bleary-eyed and in desperate need of food and sleep. 'Alright,' he said. 'Coroner says it looks like natural causes and I did some searching and turns out you're right about his story. Who'd have guessed? Any idea what happened to all the stuff he stole?'

'Nope, not a clue,' said Russ. 'Not even his dead wife said a word.' Which wasn't a total lie. She hadn't said a word about any of it to anyone.

'It was a broken heart, wasn't it?' I said to Jo and Russ as we climbed into a taxi.

'What?' Jo asked.

'Henry, he died of a broken heart,' I said again.

Jo put her arm around me, 'Yep, I'm pretty sure he did.' She looked up at me with tears in her eyes and I realised just how hard this all must have been for her, so I squeezed her.

'Thank you for coming. I know all this can't have been easy.'

'Thank you for having me. It's been a bloody blast and believe it or not, it's helped,' she smiled tightly.

'Okay, enough melodrama,' Russ interjected. 'We need drinks. Bloody lots of them. That man of yours is still running some sort of tab at that hotel?' he asked as we got out of the taxi in front of the hotel.

'Seems to be,' I said.

'I'd expect nothing less. Let's go, we'll be safe enough there and I need a drink or ten,' he said, leading the way.

Russ had a quick chat with D, then we found a table in the garden bistro. Trees and plants all around us, a blue sky painted above. You'd swear we were at a little beachside café in Noosa if the casino floor wasn't just metres away. We sat under a fully grown tree draped in sparkling fairy lights, people going about their business around us, barely even noticing, the tree, us, the craziness of it all. But then that's Vegas.

Russ ordered the best Russian vodka they had in honour of Ana and Henry. He downed three shots before we'd finished sipping our one. 'Don't look at me like that, I have cop shop cooties,' he said, throwing back another shot.

It didn't take Jo long to get with the groove and Jo was matching Russ one for one. I kept my intake light with the help of Dr Bailey's nagging voice in my ear and the last threads of my hangover still hanging on.

Every time Russ threw back a shot, he banged his shot glass on the table, crying, 'za lyoo-bóf' in terrible Russian and after a couple of shots, Jo was doing her own poor imitation of whatever Russian phrase Russ had gotten off his phone translator. Eventually Russ gave up on the Russian altogether and started toasting 'To love,' 'To Ana,' 'To Henry,' and whatever else he thought up.

As the contents of the bottle disappeared and the banging and shouting grew louder, other patrons threw daggers our way, passers-by laughed and the staff appeared unsure what to do and to be honest we weren't really looking our best after spending half the night at the police station. It'd been a long day, our hair was scraggly, our clothes wrinkled and no doubt a little sweat caked from the hot Vegas sun. We looked a little more than worse for wear but still the staff kept a safe distance, apologised to the few annoyed patrons, moved them to another bar or comp'd their drinks, but they never asked us to be quiet or to leave which was very strange. I wondered if we were really that frightening or just that shameful.

As Jo's speech began slurring into indecipherable mumbo jumbo, it was time to call it a night. 'Come on you drunks, we gotta go before they kick us out.'

'No, no, not yet,' Jo whined.

'Yes. Come on,' I said, leading her up by her elbow.

'You're such a spoil sport,' she complained.

After some more slurred refusals and much debating, I eventually got them both standing. There was no way Russ was going to find his way home when he could hardly find the walkway so I insisted he come up with us. He could have the sofa. It was definitely big enough.

Finally in our suite, I barely had to push Russ with my finger to have him collapse on the sofa. I took off his shoes, threw him a blanket and left him to it. Jo was already face down, fully clothed on her bed, so I also removed her shoes and pushed her under the covers before going into my own room and collapsing on my bed and quickly falling into a perfect, vodka-fuelled sleep, the events of the day far enough away to be analysed another day.

# Chapter 29

The shards of light forcing themselves into my bedroom through the smallest gaps in the curtains, felt like daggers slicing my eyeballs into pieces. My head was compressing under the weight of a wrecking ball and my insides felt as dry as a sponge left outside in forty-five degree heat for a month.

I put one, oh what the hell, two, Hydralite tablets into a glass of water. When I'd drunk them, I did the same with a Berocca with which I washed down a couple of Panadol.

I lay staring at the ceiling, swearing never again as we all do in such a situation. But slowly, bit by bit, the pain in my head eased to manageable and I forced myself to shower, in the dark though, I'm not a masochist.

When I came out, all that was left of my hangover was my swirling stomach, desperately trying to process all that vodka with no food inside to absorb any of it.

Russ was sitting at the dining table in a spare dressing gown, tucking into a plate of eggs and bacon, apparently fresh as a daisy after the night before's indulgence. Two more plates covered with cloches waited on the table. I selected a chair on the other side of the table and was about to take the cover off my eggs when the door to the suite burst open.

'What the fuck?' Christian boomed into the room.

It took me a few seconds to process that Christian was standing in the marble foyer of the hotel suite. My Christian. Right there. But it was only seconds before I was racing across the room and smacking hard into his arms which instantly wrapped around my body as though that's what they were designed to do, burying his face into my neck like a magnet drew him there. He felt warm and safe and perfect and I breathed him in.

He pulled away from me, his face full of thunder. 'Ains, what the fuck is going on here?'

I looked across the room to where Russ sat shovelling eggs into his mouth at the dining table in his robe and realised what Christian had seen. The two of us, Russ and I, in our robes sitting down to our eggs. It all looked a little too cosy and suddenly I was having to hold Christian back. I didn't think for a second he could take Russ but by the tensing in his arms, in his whole body, I suspected he'd try anyway.

'Christian, it's not what it looks like. This is Russell Whittington, the PI guy.'

'I know who Russ is, why is he here, in a robe, looking like he spent the night?' Christian demanded, rigid as a board.

'Because he did.' I watched his face about to explode and held his face, forcing him to look me in the eyes, drawing his attention away from Russ. 'On the couch, Christian. We had too much to drink downstairs. We were all worse for wear so Russ slept on the couch.'

He watched my face for any sign of a lie, but there wasn't one to find and he gave up questioning me and pulled me into his arms, sighing into my neck, 'God I've missed you,' he whispered.

Jo wandered out of her room, her bed hair looking like something Medusa would sport, make up smudged all over her face. 'What's going on?' she asked. 'Christian, is that you?' she asked, squinting at him.

'Holy shit, how much did you lot drink last night?' Christian laughed.

'Them, way too much. Me, I wasn't so bad.'

'Yeah, why is that?' Jo asked, holding her head.

'Not sure really,' I shrugged. 'Maybe my nagging shrink in the back of my head keeping me somewhat on the straight and narrow,' I said, taking Christian by the hand to the dining table and pouring him coffee.

Jo looked at her eggs, screwed up her face and declared, 'I'm going back to bed.' I smiled as she softly padded back to the bedroom.

Christian pulled her eggs to him and tucked in while Russ filled him in on everything that had happened.

'Well, thanks for looking out for the girls,' Christian said, shaking Russ' hand as he stood up to leave.

Russ went to the guest bathroom and put on his wrinkled clothes, raised a hand in farewell and that was it. After everything we'd all been through together, he was gone and the space around us felt emptier for it.

We took our coffee to the sofa. Russ had folded his blanket and left the space as though he'd never even been there. Really, I was quite impressed at how well he bounced back from the vodka bender. But I guess that's the kind of fortitude one has to develop when they live in Vegas.

'What are you even doing here?' I asked Christian now we were alone and the reality of him being there finally sank in.

'I missed you,' he said, draping his arm across my shoulders and pulling me into him, kissing the top of my head.

'But what about your dad's project?'

'I quit,' he said, his whole body tensing.

'What? Why?'

He didn't answer, his body staying tense, fury pulsating through his rigid body.

'Christian, what happened?' I asked, instantly worried.

'Nothing, Ains, just forget it.'

'No. We're a team. What's going on?'

He sighed heavily. 'There wasn't anything for me to do on the project. Dad had it all sorted, work had been distributed and taken care of. It was just a reason to split us up. You and me. He said it was a good chance for me to get some space and some clarity, to be around people who knew and accepted me for who I was. He thinks you're just after my money. He couldn't imagine anyone as nice and lovely as you actually wanting to be with me for any other reason.'

Tears pricked my eyes as his handsome face fell, his broken, sad eyes glistened. How could his own father be so cruel, make him feel so utterly worthless when he was one of the most amazing people I knew? How did hearing that not break your soul?

'Then I walked in here,' he said in a whisper. 'And I wondered if he was right, if I'd just been fooling myself this whole time.'

He looked at me, sad, broken, terrified, defeated. Every one of the worst emotions I knew, clouding his beautiful eyes. I pulled his mouth to mine, showing him how wrong his dad was, how wrong they all were. I loved him. I'd missed him every day. I hung on to him, desperate, afraid, never wanting to let him go.

'Don't ever think that. Never. I love you Christian Harrington. I love you for your kindness and your sweetness, even your craziness. I love you and I'm not going anywhere. I don't even know how to breathe without you anymore.' I wrapped my arms around him and snuggled into his warmth, breathing him in, 'I love you so much it hurts. When you weren't nearby, when I couldn't call you or see you anytime, I thought my insides might explode. My heart and soul are connected to you. Being away from you hurt. I ached inside wanting to hold you. It was one of the hardest times I've ever known not being with you. It wasn't on par with... Well you know, but I didn't like it and I don't think I could do it again.'

I felt him nod. 'Promise me, Ains, you won't ever try anything like that again. No project, no family stuff will ever be more important than you. I'd leave it all in a heartbeat to be with you if you needed me. Promise me you know that. I couldn't survive losing you. I couldn't.'

'I promise,' I said looking into his eyes, his beautiful soft eyes, no longer broken as his lips softly brushed mine in a sweet, gentle kiss as though our mouths had known each other forever.

'Ains?' he asked as he pulled away.

'Yeah?'

'Will you marry me?'

'What?'

'Will you marry me?'

'Really? You want to marry me? Are you sure?'

'I've never been so sure of anything in all my life. I can't imagine ever living without you. It would make me deliriously happy if you would be my wife.'

I blushed, tears racing to my eyes as I smiled. 'Yes.'

# Chapter 30

'So how's today?' Christian asked, placing a stupidly enormous diamond on my finger.

'For what?' I asked staring at the ring, in complete disbelief that Christian's proposal was planned, not spur of the moment, that he'd gone to the trouble of buying an incredible ring and everything

'To get married,' he said, with a cheeky smile.

'Really? Today? Here in Vegas?' I asked

'Why not?'

'Other than my mother will kill me and Dr Bailey might have me committed as soon as we return, there is not a reason in the world to stop me marrying you today, Christian.'

He smiled like the happiest, proudest man I'd ever seen and in that moment I felt more loved for every single ridiculous part of me and happier than I'd ever thought humanly possible. I couldn't believe that this man was going to be my husband before the day was done. *How did I get so lucky?*

While Jo continued sleeping we grabbed some lattes and a taxi and went to get a license.

I couldn't help grinning like a fool as we sat on the couch afterwards.

'So,' he said, a little sheepishly. 'I have this for you,' he said, handing me a black AMEX card with my name on it. 'Use it for anything you and Jo might need for today, dresses, shoes, whatever.'

'Christian, I don't need this,' I said, afraid to ask when he'd gotten around to organising such a thing. 'I don't need a fancy dress or fancy shoes or to get my hair done. I'd marry you right here in this room in my pyjamas, I don't care. I just want to be married to you,' I smiled.

'I know,' he smiled back. 'And I love you for it. But it's not necessary. Just because we're getting married in Vegas, there's no reason why you can't still be a princess.'

He put his finger on my mouth as I was about to protest some more. 'Don't even try,' he smiled. 'The girls on the concierge will help you with anything you need. I'll take care of the rest and see you later,' he smiled, kissing me quickly before leaving.

I sat on the couch staring at the black AMEX card with my shiny name printed on it. He'd have to change it now, I thought, by the end of the day I'd be Ainsley Harrington. I smiled at the thought. How did it even happen? I wondered as I watched the colours sparkling from the heavy diamond on my finger.

'What are you doing?' asked Jo.

I showed her the credit card, 'He asked me to marry him. It's to buy dresses and stuff for you and me.'

'What?' she asked, her eyes big, a huge stupid grin stretching across her face as she grabbed my hand to look at the ring, her mouth hanging open.

'Yep. I'm getting married,' I said, as much as a reminder to myself as to Jo. 'Today. Did I mention I'm getting married today?' I said smiling.

'You're kidding me, right?'

'Nope.'

'Shit! Your mum and Dr Bailey are going to have you committed, you know that, right?'

I laughed, 'I said the same thing.'

'Good, so you know it's crazy, then?'

'Yep. But I'm still going to marry him.'

'Good,' she winked. 'So I suppose we better scrub up and go get some dresses then,' she said, suddenly full of life.

Jo sculled a cold cup of coffee as she passed the dining table and headed straight for the shower, while I sat on the couch continuing to stare at my shiny name on the very black AMEX card, running my finger over it, feeling the bumps, not really sure what to do with it.

Once we were both ready and Jo was fully caffeinated and stopped staring at me stupefied, we went down to the concierge.

'I need a wedding dress, can you point me in the right direction?' I asked the girl behind the desk.

'Of course, Miss Donovan. Did you have any designer in mind?' she asked.

Jo and I looked at each other and back to the girl, 'Vera Wang, of course,' we sang.

The girl laughed. 'Of course. I'll have a car take you to Bridal

Couture. I'll let them know you're coming and they'll take excellent care of you,' she smiled.

A moment later, a uniformed driver found us in the foyer and led us out to a town car that drove us to the bridal shop.

The town car pulled up in front of the bridal shop. A very small blonde waited out the front beside skinny wannabe hip-hop star bouncer dude, Bear.

'What's he doing here?' I asked Jo.

'I don't know,' she said, her face cautious and curious.

As we walked up to where the lady waited, I eyed Bear out the corner of my eye. I looked at the lady and felt instantly frumpy in my cheap maxi dress.

'I'm Dawn, welcome,' she said, holding out her hand.

'Ainsley,' I said, shaking her outstretched hand. 'This is Jo,' I introduced.

'Come, come,' she said. 'Let's get started.'

We all eyed Bear suspiciously as we passed. 'What are you doing here?' I whispered when I was close enough.

'Your fella sent me. Told me not to let you out of my sight.'

'You can't come in there,' I hissed.

'Too bad, I am. Your fella said and Russ said, so I am.'

'Russ?' I asked. 'Of course,' I said to Jo before Bear could answer. 'Russ has told bloody Christian everything.' I rolled my eyes theatrically, 'Come on, then,' I said to Bear.

I froze inside the door. The room was full of racks filled with beautiful gowns. They weren't covered in plastic and crammed onto racks like I'd seen at home, they were free and lovely, just waiting to be found and loved.

'What's wrong?' asked Bear concerned, his eyes darting about the empty room.

'Nothing. Look at them.'

'Look at what?' he asked, scanning the room.

'They're beautiful, you idiot,' I scowled at him, shaking my head.

Dawn led me to a fitting room. Waiting in front was a whole rack of Vera Wang dresses. I reached out, lightly touching one, a smile so big spreading across my face. They were the most beautiful dresses I'd ever seen.

Dawn chuckled good humouredly, even though she'd probably seen it a thousand times. 'Which one would you like to try first?' she asked.

'Oh goodness, how do you choose?'

'Why don't you start by telling me what you had in mind?'

'Simple. Not too fussy but still classy and elegant.'

'Well, that we can do,' she smiled, taking a dress from the rack.

Dawn secured me into the dress. I stepped out to the viewing room where Jo waited on a couch with a glass of champagne. I raised my eyebrows at her questioningly, wondering how she could possibly stomach champagne after all the premium vodka she'd drunk the night before. She should have the hangover from hell. In fact, she'd had the hangover from hell only two hours ago.

'It's free,' she mouthed, taking a sip while Bear scowled uncomfortably beside her.

I shook my head, laughing. 'Well, what do you think?' I asked, turning to face the mirror.

'You look amazing, Ains,' she said. 'Not sure the tiers are really you though,' she said.

I studied myself in the mirror. The dress was amazing, a strapless lace bodice that flowed down to a tiered lace and tulle skirt, a black ribbon around the waist. It was sensational, more than I ever could have imagined. But Jo was right, the tiers weren't really my style and a little busy for what I had in mind.

I told Dawn. 'No problem,' she said as we walked back to the fitting room. 'I think I know just the one.'

Fastened into the next dress, I already felt different, alive, transformed. I walked back into the viewing area and Jo sat up, her face lighting up.

'Ains,' she gasped. 'That's it. It's perfect. You look, you look amazing,' she said breathlessly. 'Doesn't she, Bear?' she asked, nudging him.

'Sure, sure,' he nodded. 'Amazing.'

Smiling, I turned to the mirror. The dress had a simple, classic, lace bodice that met with a white ribbon, the skirt falling like that of a Grecian goddess. I stepped into a strappy pair of Jimmy Choos and Jo and I stared for just a little bit in awe of the beauty that is Vera Wang.

When I'd put my dowdy maxi dress back on and returned to the viewing area, Dawn handed me a glass of bubbles, turning to Jo, saying, 'Now, what about you?'

Jo clapped her hands together excitedly.

Dawn smiled, 'You know Vera has this beautiful blue dress I think would look amazing on you.'

'Yes, yes,' Jo cried, racing after Dawn while I sat with my glass of champagne beside Bear who stared off into the distance as though he was wishing he was anywhere else.

Jo returned with a midnight blue, three quarter, satin dress with a V-neck. She stepped into some sparkly, strappy Jimmy Choos, gasping at her reflection.

'Jo, you look amazing,' I told her.

'Can I have it?' she asked hopefully.

I laughed, there was no question but I nodded anyway and she did a little celebratory dance on the viewing platform.

Jo stumbled out of the car. We were giddy from too much champagne and high on Vera Wang. Leaving Bear carrying our parcels and dress bags we headed for the lifts giggling like schoolgirls.

'Ma'am, excuse me,' the girl from the concierge called as she hurried to catch us, poor Bear laden down with our goods trying to position himself in front to protect us but really not much good with his arms so full.

'Hi,' I said to the girl.

'Oh, I'm glad I caught you. Mr Harrington has asked that you go to the spa. I'll have someone take your gowns,' she said, smiling at Bear and clicking her fingers at someone standing nearby who relieved Bear of all our purchases.

The spa was empty except for the staff who were in a corner sipping coffee. They all put down their cups as we walked in and scurried to their stations.

'Hi, I'm Melanie,' a far too perky, all American cheerleader type greeted us. 'Follow me,' she said, heading down a hallway.

'I might just wait here,' suggested Bear with a look of fear in his eyes.

'Righto, then,' Jo laughed, hooking her arm through mine and following Melanie to the change rooms.

'Pop on your robes, then go down the hallway to the lounge. Help yourself to some cucumber water and someone will come find you in just a little bit, alright?' she smiled.

'Sure, thanks,' I said.


We each stretched out on day beds with big icy glasses of cucumber water looking out the big floor to ceiling windows overlooking a little atrium oasis with big, lush, tropical trees with little fairy lights, brightly coloured shrubs and a pond. Croaking of frogs in the pond drifted in through the open windows and instantly, the last remaining remnants of stress, from my journey to now, the café, Mrs May dying, the loneliness, all of it along with any snippets of anxiety from being about to marry Christian, the most incredible man on the planet, a man I surely didn't deserve, knowing my mother and Dr Bailey were going to kill me, all of it evaporated out the window, disappearing into that beautiful oasis where the trees chewed it up and made it clean.

I could see Jo felt it too, the last of the lines around her eyes were fading, her face was smoothing and that old glow she'd once been famous for was finally returning, bringing with it a little more colour and life.

There was no time to ponder my life and improved emotional state for long or to even comment on them to Jo before a perky advertisement for clean living dressed in a crisp white coat came to whisk me away to another kind of heaven.

The next couple of hours went by in a blur of scrubbing, buffing and massaging heaven. Deliriously content, I followed Miss Perky into a large room filled with nail tables and pedicure stations. The room would usually have been a bustling hub of energy, I was sure, but not today. There was just Jo on a recliner, her feet sitting in the little tub at the base, a cocktail in hand.

'Helloooo, there,' she called.

'Well, hello yourself,' I said, climbing onto the chair next to her, letting my feet fall into the tub now filling with warm water.

'Well don't you look all buffed and shiny?' she smiled.

'Right back atchya,' I said as the lovely Melanie handed me a bright yellow cocktail.

Melanie returned with a tray of chicken and mayonnaise ribbon sandwiches and I realised how starved I was. I shovelled sandwiches while a girl began on my feet and another started putting rollers in my hair.

As I was shoving my third sandwich in my mouth Jo said, 'I have a surprise for you.'

'Me? What sort of a surprise?'

Just as I asked, the girl working on my toenail cuticles switched on a lamp beside the little bath as the overhead fluorescents dimmed and music began thumping out of the overhead speakers.

'Jo, what did you do?' I asked.

She smiled like a Cheshire cat as five of the buffest, most beautiful men I'd ever seen danced their way through the door into the middle of the floor.

'You got me strippers?'

She laughed. 'Not just any strippers, baby, these are The Thunder from Down Under, all home grown goodness.'

'How did you do that?' I asked as the men began gyrating in front of us.

'Melanie knows someone. I charged it to our room. Christian won't mind, will he?' she asked, with a cheeky grin.

'Christian will kill you,' I laughed.

'It will be so worth it,' she smiled naughtily as the men bent down and ripped off their pants in choreographed unison.

One would think they were safe from the usual stripper shenanigans with a manicurist and footbath between them and a bunch of male strippers, but if you thought that, you'd be very wrong. Lovely manicure girl carried on as though there were no half naked men in the room, right up until she smothered my feet in cream, wrapped them in gladwrap and went to the other side of the room to eat my sandwiches.

The near naked men in front of me needed no further invitation. Using his balancing skills I had one man millimetres from me in a second, feet balancing on the edge of the foot bath. He took my hand and dragged it across his glistening, tanned six pack while Jo squealed with delight beside me.

Dancing man took my hand and rubbed it over his thigh while one of his dancing buddies straddled Jo, which stopped her laughing at my discomfort.

I threw my head back laughing as the dancing man climbed up to balance his feet on the arms of my chair and fake gyrated over me. When I lifted my head back up I saw the Blonde Bitch in the doorway trying desperately to get past Bear and I froze.

'Hey, you okay?' Dancing Man asked.

'Yeah, yeah,' I said, trying to smile.

'Hey, I'll stop if it makes you uncomfortable.'

'Sorry, it's not you, just some trouble over at the door, but it's sorted now,' I smiled as the Blonde Bitch glared at us then stomped away. Bear nodded to me that all was now well and I returned my eyes back to the sight before me.

Dancing Man gave me a final move before he joined the rest of his buddies who'd been tantalising poor Melanie and her staff (although poor Melanie looked pretty pleased about her tormenting) and finished off their dance.

'Yoga or pilates you think? That gives them that balance and flexibility?' Jo whispered.

I looked at her and burst out laughing. 'Christian really will kill you, you know?' I laughed.

'What he doesn't know, won't hurt him,' she said, smugly.

'You think red-faced Bear over there's keeping this to himself?'

'Hmmm, you leave Bear to me,' she winked.

'And the room charge?' I smirked.

'Hmmm...' she pondered, much less cocky.

The Thunder from Down Under team came over, kissing us each on the cheek, wishing me luck and they were gone. The manicurist came back to sort out my feet, another cocktail appearing in my hand as the hairdresser began removing the rollers from my hair and another girl began buffing the nails on my hands.

A few cocktails later and we were giggling like schoolgirls as Melanie and her crew told secret stories from the trenches.

Which socialite liked to discuss her conquests and details of her sex tapes as though the staff were invisible. Which A-list actress demanded a bowl of red jelly babies to be on hand and then continuously wrecked her nails as she scoffed them. Which super hunk was secretly gay and loved a good mani pedi. Which much loved star groped the girls and was continuously told this was not that kind of massage place. They never gave them away by name of course but there were enough details to piece together who was who. It's amazing how people forget their manicurists have ears. It was great for our entertainment though.

'You're all done,' my manicurist smiled as the blue light of the nail dryer was finally switched off.

'Come, I have your dresses in the change room,' Melanie instructed.

We shuffled down the long hallway in Melanie's efficient wake. 'I know it's not the most glamorous dressing room,' she apologised as we returned to the ladies change rooms.

'Its fine,' I assured her.

She smiled gratefully. Some more of the girls came and began disrobing us and putting us into our gowns, careful not to mess with our freshly painted nails, perfect makeup and finely coiffed hair. At times like this, there's apparently no room for modesty.

'Do you want to see?' Melanie asked when we were finally done.

I nodded, a lump suddenly filling my throat. Keeping all the words I wanted to say at bay as my heart pounded and tears filled my eyes. This was it. I was really going to marry Christian Harrington. After everything that had happened, I was going to end the trip with something good, something amazing and beautiful and I just didn't know, couldn't understand how a person got so lucky. I was terrified it was all just a mirage and the wind would blow and it would be all gone. I'd be alone. Again. I couldn't do that again. I couldn't live my life without Christian.

Jo squeezed my hand and I knew everything would be okay.

We walked back to the manicure room with its 360 degree mirrors 'Oh my,' Jo and I both whispered at the same time.

'Goodness,' I said, taking a better look at myself in the mirror. 'You guys do good work.'

Melanie and her team smiled proudly while Jo and I stood staring, speechless, the whole room silent for just a beat before my face broke out in an uncontrollable, ridiculous grin. 'I'm marrying Christian Harrington today,' I said to no one in particular.

'Yes, yes you are,' Jo grinned stupidly. 'She's proof that tides do change and dreams do come true,' Jo told those watching.

'Ladies,' called a security guard standing beside Bear at the bottom of the stairs where Bear waited still looking terrified.

'Ooh, it's time,' Melanie squealed as though it was her wedding.

'Aaargggh,' I mouthed to Jo who squeezed my hand, looking as excited and terrified as I felt.

'Come, on,' she said, hooking her arm through mine. 'Let's get you married to The Ferret,' she joked and we both burst out laughing.

'Come on, Bear,' she nudged as we reached the stairs. 'Stop your gawking and get busy protecting us. We both saw that Blonde Bitch earlier and I don't want her anywhere near our Vera Wang, so get going.'

# Chapter 31

Hitching my dress up with Jo's arm linked through mine we followed Bear and the other guy, apparently a mate of Bear's named TJ, much burlier and far more serious looking than Bear, outside and around the outer area of the pool to a strip of sand hidden between big lush trees.

A red carpet had been laid over the sand and we followed it through the bushland to a dock on the other side where a paddle steamer waited in a manmade river in the middle of the desert, kayakers and canoers and fisherman continuing to go on with their business oblivious to us as Bear helped Jo and me up the gangplank.

As soon as we were on board, the boat started up, humming beneath us. We stood at the front, looking out to the horizon to where the river curved in the distance around the lush, forest filled island in the middle.

Bear brought us glasses of champagne, still wearing his terrified look. My guess was Bear rarely saw this side of weddings and was more familiar with skanky female strippers and other tacky bachelor party goings on.

'What is this thing?' Jo asked Bear as we chugged along the river.

'It's usually a gambling boat for high rollers and their friends. There's a fancy buffet, lots of booze and all the regular tables. It sails around the lake a few times a night and they all stumble off around midnight. This whole river is for high rollers and their families to play in.

'Then why are we here? What did Christian do?' I asked, worried he'd finally gone too far.

Bear laughed.

'What?' I asked, pretty sure I hadn't made a joke.

'Mr Harrington can do whatever he wants. I don't know why you're so surprised. It's the advantage of owning the place.'

'Excuse me?' Jo and I demanded in unison.

Bear stared at us. 'Really? You didn't know?' he asked.

'That Christian owns a Vegas hotel? No!'

'Well, not him himself. It's a Harrington hotel but Mr Harrington did the building of it. Was here for months. That's how he knows Russ.'

'Right,' I whispered as the steamer finally began to pull up to a dock on the other side of the island. Did it matter that I didn't know? Probably not. I couldn't possibly know every Harrington Hotel, right? It did explain a lot though, the penthouse suite, the exceptionally nice staff, not being thrown out of bars when we should have been, it was all making sense now.

'Are you okay?' Jo asked as Bear and TJ helped us walk down the plank.

I nodded, suddenly lost for words.

She stopped at the bottom, turning to hug me.

'It's just so surreal,' I said. 'I can't believe I'm about to marry Christian. Do you think I'm completely mad?'

'Yes! Totally and utterly bonkers. But in the best possible way,' she smiled. 'But he loves you so much his face nearly explodes with happiness every time he looks at you. You're perfect together. So really, I think you're the luckiest woman alive right now.'

I hugged her. 'I love you. I couldn't have done any of this without you.'

Bear cleared his throat behind us.

'Okay, let's go,' I said, smiling at Bear whose eyes were remarkably shiny.

Bear led us up the beach, along more red carpet while TJ kept his eagle eye on the empty beach. The sky was filled with colour, pinks, orange, reds and then, stepping out of the trees, his head bowed as he read something in his hands, to stand beside the celebrant was Christian looking like he'd stepped out of an Armani ad in his very dapper tux. It was ridiculous to think that he was my man. Soon to be my husband. It took every ounce of energy not to push Jo out of the way and run to him. Christian looked up from whatever he was reading and his handsome face broke into the biggest smile.

'Okay, you ready?' Jo asked.

'Ahuh,' I mumbled, afraid to blink, afraid that if I lost eye contact with Christian, he'd be gone, nothing but a figment of my imagination.

'Let's do this, then,' Jo squealed.

A string quartet sitting in the shade of the trees played the traditional wedding march as I followed Jo to the front of the aisle where Christian waited with a dishevelled Russ by his side.

Bear and TJ stood awkwardly behind us, fidgeting as the celebrant began. Whatever he said never made it into my head. The second I looked into Christian's beautiful green eyes, I was lost, mesmerised, drifting off to another place where no one else existed. I couldn't speak, I couldn't move. I was marrying the most incredible man I'd ever known and it was more than I could have dreamt to have had this man, looking like a prince from a fairy tale, standing beside me, loving me as much as he did. All I wanted now was a pen to sign the certificate and for all these people to be gone so I could fall into his arms.

Jo nudged me, bringing me out of my perfect bubble and nodded to the celebrant who said, 'Do you want me to read some basic vows or do you want to say your own?'

'Our own?' Christian asked, looking at me for confirmation.

I nodded even though I hadn't considered doing so and had no idea what I would say. I'd just expected the usual vows from the celebrant but before I could protest, Christian began speaking.

'Ainsley, ever since you looked at me with that sweet, beautiful face and chastised me for my bad behaviour, I've thought of nothing else but marrying you. I couldn't imagine for a minute spending my life with anyone else. You are the love of my life, my air, my soul, my purpose for breathing and I will spend every minute of the rest of my life trying to be worthy of your love.'

Tears filled my eyes, threatening to overflow. All I could do was say whatever I felt.

'Christian, I've never fit in anywhere. I've never been comfortable with who I am. I've never felt strong or worthy or beautiful but with you I feel all of those things. With you I can be me and you love me. I think of you when I wake and before I go to sleep. I want to make sure you're fed and covered and as happy and safe and as loved as you make me and so for the rest of my life I'm going to make sure you know how amazing and perfect you are and show you every day, how much I love you.'

Russ moved behind me, taking Jo in his arms. I turned to see if she was okay and she smiled through her tears, her shoulders shaking with sobs. 'Are you okay?' I asked quietly. She had been so close to finding her own happy ever after with Benny and this must have been killing her.

She nodded, 'Shut up and get married.' She smiled.

So we did.

'I now pronounce you, husband and wife. You may kiss your bride,' the celebrant said.

I melted into Christian's arms, our mouths moulding together as though they'd been made for each other, as though our souls were finally, forever fused as one.


Bear, TJ and Russ looked ridiculous as they joined Jo and the musicians showering us in rose petals, a chosen photographer capturing the fun and laughter for another time.

'My God, I love you,' Christian declared as rose petals rained down around us.

Bear and Russ heartily shook Christian's hand, pumping it hard to exert some testosterone amongst all the rose petal throwing, before hugging me.

Jo congratulated us both. 'I'm so happy for you,' she whispered, squeezing me too tight.

We drank some champagne with our friends and laughed as the sun set around us. Then they all turned to walk back down the beach to the paddle steamer.

'Where are they going?' I asked Christian as they all walked away laughing and joking with each other, their shirts now untucked, Jo's dress blowing in the warm evening breeze.

'Somewhere else,' he winked. 'I don't know,' he added when I raised my eyebrows at him. 'Russ said he had some tickets to some show with knights.'

'Ah yes, the Excalibur show we had tickets for. Did Jo mind?'

'No, she seemed fine. I thought it was better than having her sit around all night by herself while I have my way with you,' he said, leading me through the grove of trees.

I giggled. 'You can't talk like that anymore. I'm your wife now. You have to use your manners.'

His eyes darkened with a naughty look, his mouth turning up at the corners, 'Oh sweet wife of mine, I don't think I'll ever have manners when it comes to having my way with you,' he said, raising his eyebrows in jest.

I shook my head, 'Where are we going, anyway?' I asked, thinking surely we should have been on the boat with the others.

'You'll see,' he smirked.

Hidden amongst the trees was what looked like a traditional log cabin, all alone in amongst the acres of bush.

'Ah, but not just any log cabin,' he said proudly, scooping me into his arms and carrying me across the threshold.

'Geez, you don't do anything by halves, do you?' I said taking in the opulence of the room, as grand as any hotel suite and appointed with any and all comforts you could imagine.

He grinned as he kicked the door shut and pulled my mouth to his.

Christian kissed me like he couldn't get enough, couldn't get close enough. He undid my dress while he carried me into the bedroom, it slid off as he laid me on the bed and started, clumsily removing his jacket, tie and shirt unable to wait a second more and climbed onto the bed.

He wasn't wrong about having his wicked way with me, either. It was so wicked and naughty, I couldn't even describe it but by the time we were done we were far more intimately acquainted and exhausted, panting side by side, grinning ear to ear.

'I think I like this being married business,' he said, smiling at me.

'It certainly suits you,' I said, snuggling into him.

'I'm bloody starving though. You?'

'I could eat an entire buffet.'

'Not sure there's a buffet out here, but I'll see what I can do. You're going to need to recoup some strength, I know that much,' he said, kissing me and trailing his thumb across my jaw, sending goose bumps to all the right places.

He left me, my head buzzing, returning only seconds later with a bottle of champagne and glasses.

'To us,' he said, clinking my glass.

'To us,' I agreed as he draped his arm across my shoulder.

'Why didn't you tell me you owned the hotel?' I asked while we waited for our food.

'I don't. My family does. I don't have much to do with it, anymore. International properties fall under Tom's portfolio,' he said sadly. 'Besides, I quit remember. I own nothing now. But I made some friends while I was here,' he smiled.

'How long were you here?'

'Nearly a year during the planning, then on and off for months at a time while it was being built and then for the first few months after it opened to make sure everything ran okay.'

'It's a pretty nice hotel. You did good.'

He smiled proudly. 'Thanks. I actually designed most of it. We just didn't tell Dad. I let the architects and designers here get all the credit.'

'Are you kidding?' I asked, amazed, horrified that he had to hide something he should have been proud of. 'This place is incredible. How could you not take credit, tell your Dad? Surely it's proof of how talented you are?'

He smiled and kissed my head. 'If Dad had known any of the ideas were mine, he'd have canned every single one regardless of their actual merit. It's okay though. I'm proud of what I did. Besides, you better hope I'm this talented now I'm unemployed,' he winked as the doorbell rang.

'What did you get us?' I asked, joining Christian at the dining table where our food had been laid out.

'Nothing but the best,' he said removing the cloches.

'Burgers? Classy,' I laughed, even though I was pretty glad to see the enormous burgers surrounded by big fat fries.

'Not just any burgers, my sweet, they're Kobe beef with brie, caramelised onions, egg and applewood smoked bacon,'

'Yum,' I groaned, pulling out a chair.

'Ah, but that is not all. My wife asked for a buffet, she shall have a buffet,' he said, kissing the top of my head as he removed two more cloches, one containing a giant tower of onion rings and another of chicken wings.

'We'll never eat all that,' I said, laughing. 'And, I'm going to stink,' I said, shoving an onion ring in my mouth.

'We'll stink together, then,' he said, having one himself before having a good swig of champagne and getting comfortable to eat his burger.

I was so hungry I didn't speak until my burger was gone, until I'd devoured half a dozen chicken wings and made a good dent in the onion ring tower.

'How you doin'?' Christian asked, smirking.

'Mmmm... better,' I groaned, my stomach achingly full.

'Good. I have plans for you,' he smiled, taking my hand, leading me back to the bed.

If I hadn't known every inch of his body before, I knew it then. I explored every bit. I knew what made him tense, what made him groan, what made him cry out in ecstasy. He knew mine too, probably better than his own going by the time he spent exploring and devouring. I was glad we had no neighbours to consider.

I woke with the sun streaming through the window and Christian's arms wrapped tight around my body. I could have lain there forever. It was perfect. His strong tanned arms keeping me safe. And after all that had happened with Ana, the Blonde

Bitch and her entourage, with Benny and Henry dying, I needed to feel safe.

# Chapter 32

'Good morning,' Christian moaned in my ear.

I smiled, feeling his very special good morning as his hands began roaming, my body responding, how I didn't know. I should have been far too exhausted to move, but he had a way and my body reacted of its own free will as he brought about the toe curling ecstasy I'd now never have to live without. He was mine. Forever. I couldn't wait to begin living our lives together.

Thankfully he'd packed a bag for me so I showered and dressed and was looking forward to my first day as Ainsley Harrington. The red light on the phone was flashing when I came out of the bathroom so I checked the message. It was from Jo. 'Call me when you're up, I need food and details.'

I laughed and phoned her.

'Good morning Mrs Harrington,' she answered.

I chuckled. 'Well, good morning.'

'So are you and your husband going to be bonking all day or do you think you might return to the mainland and manage brunch with your dear friend?'

She was in fine form today. She was definitely getting back to her old self and it made me happy. I looked over at Christian who was drinking coffee and reading the paper. I committed the sight to memory and hoped every morning began this way. I covered the mouthpiece and asked him if he was up to brunch and he nodded.

'Yep, we'll be there in an hour. Is that soon enough?'

'Yep, see you then. Hey, do you think Christian could do something about that queue?'

'I'll see what I can do,' I said, fearing she was getting far too used to this life of luxury.

Christian made a call and organised a table at Gilligan's for breakfast. He asked and just like that, he received. He must have made some very good friends when he was here. We really could have just queued, I said, not wanting anyone to go to any trouble, but he was having none of it.

We didn't have to wait for the paddle steamer to chug its way back along the river. There was a speedboat docked on the beach waiting for us and Christian drove it over to the main dock like he did it every day. He left me with a waiter at the entrance to Gilligan's and went upstairs to check some emails, promising to only be a minute.

'Where's Christian?' Jo asked as the waiter led me to the table.

'He's just checking emails. I thought we could start with some champagne while we wait. Just us?'

'Awe, that'll be nice,' she said gratefully, laying her hand on mine.

'So,' she asked once our glasses were full. 'How's married life so far?'

'Bloody amazing,' I smiled.

She laughed, 'Well, you could glow a little less, people are starting to stare.'

'I'm sorry, Jo,' I said.

'Whatever for? For glowing? Don't be ridiculous.'

'This must have been really hard for you. I never meant to make things worse.'

'Are you kidding? I'm so stoked I could be here, that I got to see you marry The Ferret.' She winked. 'Yeah, it was hard. I missed Benny a lot. I miss Benny a lot every day, but I'm so happy for you,' she said, reaching across and holding my hand. 'You've no idea. I was so worried for you and now I see you with Christian and I know the universe has a plan for all of us, that it all means something. I don't know what its plan is for me or why Benny had to die, but someday it'll be better. Someday it won't hurt so much.'

I wanted to take away all of her pain and give her some of my happiness but I couldn't. I could only pour us more champagne and ask how her night of knights went.

'There was actual jousting and medieval food. We ate giant turkey legs with our hands and drank goblets of beer that kept magically filling. I swear, I didn't know if I was going to be able to walk back down the strip. I don't know who held who up, me or Russ, but somehow I woke in my bed, fully clothed, no sign of Russ.'

'Wow,' I said, 'Good night, then?'

'The best. Just what I needed. Lots of beer. Too much food and laughing and singing with no hoo-ha, if you catch my drift.'

'Oh, I catch your drift,' I smiled, glad she'd had such a good time and Russ had been a gentleman.

Christian eventually joined us and we ate. I thought I was never going to fill my stomach. The night before had used up every bit of fuel and I had quite a bit of replenishing to do.

'If it's okay with you two, I can get our flights changed to this afternoon. Unless you want to keep up with the festivities?' Christian said.

I looked at Jo for confirmation. I was done. I was over Vegas. So much had happened and it had ended on such a good note, I didn't want to change that. We both nodded and he sent the go ahead message to his assistant.

When his phone beeped a few minutes later, he told us we had a late departure out of Vegas so we went and changed into bathers and went to sit by the pool until it was time to leave.

It wasn't the same as last time. Christian had us hidden away in a cabana, away from any trouble, prying eyes and Blonde Bitches while we waited. No more enthusiastic people watching. I tried drinking a cocktail, but it didn't have the same anything. So we closed our eyes and just waited until Christian came for us, draping his arm across my shoulders and leading us to the car where he'd already had our bags loaded.

Nothing had turned out as we'd expected. I didn't know whether to laugh or cry as I sank down into my business class pod seat. We'd found Henry, but he'd died of a broken heart, then I'd married Christian, actually married him. I looked over to where he flipped through a newspaper and smiled. He was my husband for the rest of my life. My mother was going to kill me.

She was going to make me go live in that ward of Dr Baileys, I just knew it.

# Chapter 33

As we finally pulled up in front of the café we were all exhausted. It was late. We'd spent most of the day hanging around in the Qantas lounge in Sydney waiting to get on a connecting flight home. Of all days for the flights to be full, it was just my luck. But I had my husband and my best friend with me and knew life could be a lot worse. Jo and I made use of the facilities on offer while Christian worked on his laptop, putting together plans for his own business.

'Let me get those,' Christian said, reaching into the boot for our bags.

'It's okay, there's next to nothing in them, but thanks. We'll manage. You go make some space for me and I'll pack up my things.'

'Oh no, I'm coming in with you,' he said.

'Don't be silly. The Blonde Bitch will still be wandering the strip waiting for us to appear. Go home and make space for me,' I told him.

'Okay, I'll send a car back in a couple of hours,' he said, being careful not to be too pushy and make things uncomfortable for Jo.

'Sure,' I said, already having spoken to Jo and knowing she was fine with me moving tonight.

Jo left us and went to the back of the café to let herself in while I said goodbye to Christian, 'See you in a bit,' I smiled, before kissing him.

It was dark and quiet down the laneway. I really should get some sensor lights put in, I thought. Jo had left the back door open for me but hadn't worried about a light.  Lucky I knew the place so well now. I walked in and reached for the switch but someone grabbed my arm and kicked the door shut.

My brain went into overdrive. Who? What? Where was Jo? I called out to her but someone covered my mouth with a gloved hand that smelled of musty tobacco.

They dragged me down the stairs to the basement where I could see a light glowing. Jo sat gagged and bound in the corner, her eyes big and wide. I was shoved down next to her as they tied my hands. I finally got to look up and the Blonde Bitch stood over me, hands on hips, a smirk plastered on her stupid face.

'No bodyguard today?' she asked, with a smirk.

'How'd you get back so fast?'

'We left when your boyfriend showed up with body guards and got security to throw us out of Stranded. Figured you'd be back here soon enough and you would be much easier to find if we just waited you out.'

'What do you want?' I asked before her lackey tied a gag around my mouth, which made no sense at all considering I knew what they wanted and gagging me wouldn't help them get it.

'The eggs of course.'

'Well, you can have them,' I told her, fighting off the guy with the gag.

She looked surprised. Surprised I'd give them up so easily. But I didn't want them. I didn't want any of it if it was stolen. I definitely didn't want the stupid eggs if she wanted them so badly she'd do this.

'They're upstairs,' I told her, trying to get up.

'Fine, we shall go together. Watch the other one,' the Blonde Bitch snapped.

She followed me up the stairs, her hand pushing on my back to keep me going, my hands still bound as I led her into the bedroom. I nodded to the drawer in the bedside, 'They're in the black pouch,' I told her, not wanting her snooping at anything else.

The pouch was just inside the drawer. I'd moved the jewellery box to the back of the wardrobe for safe keeping but I'd taken the eggs out and put them in the pouch while I was figuring out if they were real and what to do with them. She removed the pouch and poured the eggs into her hand. 'Well, that was easy. Why was it so easy?'

'I told you, I don't want them. If they're your great grandmothers, then they're hers. If they're fakes, then you made a fuss over nothing. Either way, I don't care. They're not mine. They came with café when I inherited it. So if you want them so badly, have them.'

She smiled, pleased, proud, something more than recovering

a family heirloom warranted, but I didn't care. I wanted this business over and her and her crazy entourage gone before she realised there was more. That there was a whole basement filled with money and jewels but mostly I wanted her gone before Christian returned and decided to be a hero.

The Blonde Bitch left me in the bedroom as she went back downstairs. I followed but waited at the top of the stairs as she called out to her people from the back door. 'Come,' she called to them as though they were dogs.

They all ran up the basement stairs. 'We have what we came for, let's go,' she instructed them.

'What about the girl? Won't they call the cops?' one of the guys asked indicating the basement.

'Good luck to them if they can find us. Just leave her,' she said. 'They'll be fine, I'm sure. Eventually,' she smirked in my direction as she left.

I sighed with relief. It was too easy on both ends really. I wondered if they'd found the other jewels hidden in the teapots after all but it had all appeared to be undisturbed when I'd been down there earlier.

The basement. Shit! Jo! I had to make sure she was okay. I started running down the stairs, but I had no free hands to hold the rail. I was at my uncoordinated best and my foot caught on one of the stairs and that was the last I saw. I toppled down the rest and landed on my arm. I managed to mumble 'pomoshch,' to the empty room before blacking out.

'Shit,' was the next thing I heard. The voice was familiar. It was a man's. It was deep and velvety. Christian.

I tried to move but everything hurt. I tried to speak but only a groan came out. Christian scooped me into his arms, brushing some stray hairs from my face. Everything hurt. I had no sense of self-preservation when it came to falling.

We were heading out the back door when I finally gurgled out 'Jo.'

Christian stopped, clearly suddenly realising Jo was some-where. 'Where is she, Ains?'

'Base,' I gurgled.

I felt him give an order with only his head to whom I assumed was one of his security team or his driver or someone who I heard bounding down the stairs to the basement and next I knew we were being loaded onto gurneys at the emergency room and raced down a hallway with horrible bright lights.

Christian held my hand as the doctors moved around. He whispered in my ear that everything was going to be okay. But Jo was all alone. She'd been through so much. She couldn't be all alone now.

I mumbled her name and Christian squeezed my hand, 'It's okay. Sam's with her. She's going to be fine, she's mostly unharmed, just frightened.'

That was okay. She knew Sam. Sam was good people and I was just glad she was okay.

Eventually the doctors and nurses disappeared and left us alone. Christian kissed my forehead. 'I was so scared. I've never been more scared in all my life than when I saw you lying at the bottom of the stairs. My heart near jumped out of my chest. I should never have left you. Please, don't ever do that to me again,' he begged.

I tried to smile but my face hurt.

I heard people enter the curtained area but I couldn't move, everything still hurt. Then Jo was at my head, 'Ains, what did you do? What did she do to you?'

I tried shaking my head. The Blonde Bitch hadn't done this.

Then there were more people. They moved closer so I could see them, police officers. 'Can you tell us what happened, Ainsley?' they asked politely.

I tried to sit up, Christian helped but pain seared through my arm. 'She still needs to be patched,' he told them.

I lay back down annoyed, but tried to speak, 'I fell. She left with eggs, but I had no hands and I had to get to Jo.'

Jo stroked my hair. 'You fell coming for me, but I was fine. Bound and gagged, but fine,' she smiled.

I nodded, comforted that clearly she was alright.

I listened as Jo went through what happened with the police who listened quietly until she'd finished, then asked, 'These eggs, why are they so special?'

I looked to Christian for help, not knowing how much to tell them. If all those jewels belonged to someone else then that's where they belonged, I didn't want them. I nodded as best I could to Christian who smiled tightly, knowingly in return.

'They were stolen,' he told the officers whose eyes widened. 'Not by Ainsley,' Christian almost laughed.

'By who, then?' the police asked unsure.

'Henry Mayberry,' Christian and Jo said together.

'Henry Mayberry?' one of the officers asked, clearly having no idea who Henry Mayberry was.

The officers shared a disbelieving look after Christian told them Henry's story, then the other replied, 'Alright, then, we'll be back, don't go anywhere,' and they took their notebooks and left.

The doctor returned carrying a folder filled with test results. 'Everything looks fine. You were lucky, Ainsley, no serious damage, no broken bones or anything. But, um,' he looked at Jo and Christian and then to me.

'It's fine, you can say anything in front of them,' I told him.

He nodded. 'Did you know you were pregnant?'

My eyes nearly bugged out of my head. Pregnant? 'What? Don't be ridiculous,' I stammered breathlessly. I can't be pregnant. My mother and Dr Bailey were going to be pissed enough about me getting married in Vegas, but pregnant too? Shit, shit, shit.

I looked over to Christian and he was beaming like a lotto winner. Double Shit.

I looked to Jo who reached out for my hand, smiling.

I looked to the doctor to make sure he wasn't kidding and he was smiling too. Why was I the only one not smiling?

'You're only just pregnant by the looks of things,' he continued on. 'But I'm going to try and do some scans anyway, just to make sure everything looks okay in there after the fall, okay?'

I nodded dumbly. How had I not damaged anything? A teeny tiny, barely there baby and even that survived me falling down the stairs. Someone, somewhere in this crazy universe really wanted me to have this baby.

Christian held my hand, leaning over, he whispered in my ear, 'Breathe, Ains, it's going to be just fine. We can do this.' I could feel the smile and the support and the knowing in his voice and suddenly everything was okay. Knowing he knew I was panicking and didn't mind, was ready to help me through, made it all okay.

It was too early for an abdominal scan so I shooed Christian and Jo up near my head while the lady draped a sheet over my legs to do a vaginal ultrasound.

Then, there it was, up on the screen. The lady in blue was pointing to a little bean buried in the haze and Christian's eyes filled with tears. I didn't hear anything else the lady in blue said because it hit me, right at that moment, I had everything. I had Christian and now we were going to have a family. We were going to be perfect.

# Chapter 34

'You're both coming home with me,' Christian insisted when we'd finally been released from the hospital. 'No arguments, Ainsley,' he said, giving me a stern look.

'Fine,' I conceded. I'd like to have picked up a few toiletries and a change of clothes but Christian was not in an arguing mood.

'It still baffles me,' Jo laughed when we walked in. 'Where does one even buy this much ugly furniture?'

I giggled. 'Online, apparently.'

'Enough laughing at my decorating,' Christian smiled. 'We'll probably have to find somewhere new to live now I've quit so it's lucky I didn't go to any effort. Jo, your bedroom's over there, you'll find a change of clothes and things, go freshen up, dinner should be here in a few minutes.'

Jo raised her eyebrows at me and I just shrugged and followed Christian into what was now our bedroom.

On the end of the bed was a new white dressing gown, tracksuit pants, t-shirt and hoodie and a pair of pyjamas. 'How did you do this?' I asked, more out of curiosity than anything.

'Janelle who manages the front desk did me a favour. Freshen up, I'll see you in the dining room in a few, yeah?' he said, kissing the top of my head and leaving me to get changed.

Jo was dressed pretty much the same when I joined her and Christian at the dining table a little while later.

'I've organised for one of my guys to put some security into the cafe tomorrow, I don't want either you back there until he's done.'

'Christian!' I exclaimed. 'I can take care of those things myself, you know. Besides, that bitch won't be back. She got what she wanted and she's gone.'

'I don't care. I'm not discussing it. There's a few things you'll have to get used to now you're my wife.'

'Are you going to turn into one of those freaks who keep their women captive now? I'm not allowed to leave the house without you?'

He laughed. 'Absolutely not. I don't think anyone could keep you captive, Ainsley. But when it comes to keeping you safe, I will indeed do whatever I need.'

'Fine, then,' I huffed like a spoilt brat and reached for a container of Thai food.

'The police called while you were in the shower,' Christian said as we were getting into the car, early than my poor aching body wished. 'They caught the Blonde Bitch and her brother. The jewels really were her Great Grandmother's but they've been charged for what they did to you and Jo.'

'Good.'

'Don't you have to get to work soon?' I asked Christian as he got out of the car with Jo and I at the cafe.

'No. I quit remember?'

'But what about your new business and things, going it alone and all?'

'It can wait. Some things are more important than working. I'm not leaving you alone until I know everything's okay. Not after the fall and with the baby and everything.'

'Argh,' I groaned while Jo laughed at Christian's over protectiveness.

'Besides, I don't want you having to tell your mother everything on your own. I don't want you stressed.' Somehow I suspected he was going to keep this up until he had that baby in his arms.

The police were coming to collect the stolen jewels, so I was kind of glad he'd be there for that. I couldn't face seeing them go through all of Mrs May's things. I hoped they could find the ledger Henry sent in the last crate. I didn't want to hand over anything that belonged to Mrs May by accident only to have it all sit in a vault somewhere unclaimed for all eternity, or worse, given to someone it didn't belong to.

Christian did most of the prepping for the day's trade, insisting I sit and rest and he kept Jo on light duties, which was pretty funny to watch him trying to do manual labour. But he managed and Mum was bursting through the back door before we knew it, bags and arms full of Tupperware.

She started nattering on as only Mum in an uncomfortable situation could. She unloaded muffins and put cakes in the fridge and took casseroles up the stairs. When she came back down, I decided to just get it over with.

'Actually, Mum, you probably don't need to bring over the casseroles, anymore,' I started.

'Why ever not? Don't you like my casseroles, anymore?'

'I love your casseroles, but well, the thing is, I'm not going to be living here.'

'What do you mean?' she asked. 'Where on earth are you going to live? Are you coming back home? I'm sure that'd make your father happy, to know where you are.'

'No. Actually I'm moving in with Christian.'

She huffed as though the idea was ridiculous. 'Bit soon, isn't it? No offense to Christian. I'm sure you're a very nice boy,' she said to him, 'But Ainsley, are you sure this is a good idea? Shouldn't you discuss it with Dr Bailey before you do anything rash?'

'It's kind of a bit late for that, Mum. We sort of got married. In Vegas.'

She paled to a ghostly white. 'What do you mean you got married?' she asked, reaching over to the table to steady herself and lowering herself onto the chair.

'We got married, there's only one way that works.'

'Right,' she said, trying to comprehend.

'There's another thing,' I told her, not sure her poor brain could cope without exploding but figured it best to just do it all at once, like ripping off a bandaid. 'We're having a baby.'

'What!' she cried, the sound echoing all through the café.

'Calm down, Mum.'

'Is that why you got married? Because that's ridiculous. You didn't have to do that. Even I know that in this day and age, you don't have to do that.'

'Mum, that's not why we got married. We only found out about the baby last night.' I spared her the details of the hospital, the fall and being robbed by the crazy Blonde Bitch. That would have been way too much. I self-consciously pulled some hair forward to cover the bruise above my eye though.

'Right,' she said.

'Jo, can you get her a pot of tea and a muffin?' I asked.

Jo nodded, trying not to laugh and gathered up supplies for Mum who sat, staring into space, dumbfounded.

Then, just as I was calming Mum and even though the door was open, Christian's father and his entourage somehow burst into the café.

'Christian!' he boomed from the doorway.

'Shit,' Christian mumbled. 'How'd he even know we were back and how'd he get a flight so fast?' he said quickly.

I didn't pity him too much. I'd had to face my mother, now he had to face his father.

'Calm down, Dad or you'll have another heart attack,' he held onto the smile playing at the corners of his mouth.

'Don't you tell me to calm down,' he bellowed. 'What is this about you quitting your job and marrying, this, this, girl?'

'Do not refer to my wife that way,' Christian demanded calmly. 'There's no fake business trip you can send me on to keep Ainsley and me apart. Whether you like it or not, whether you believe it or not, I love her and she loves me and getting married is what people in love do.'

'She doesn't love you,' he spat. 'She loves your money, you fool!'

'Hey!' I interrupted. No one was going to call me a money grubbing whore and get away with it. I felt Mum right by my side and I knew she was thinking the same thing, whether she thought this marriage was a good idea or not. 'I love him you pretentious pig. I don't care if you think he is worthy or not. I think he is amazing. He's the kind of guy that runs through the rain in a fancy suit to make sure I'm okay. He brings me take-away and movies just so he has a reason to see me and he takes care of my friends even though he doesn't have to. He is the kindest, sweetest man I've ever met and I, for the record, I don't need his money. I have enough of my own and if you think you can burst into my café in the middle of a day's trade and bellow and holler insane notions about my motivations and slur my character in front of my customers, well, you have another thing coming. You can take your bad manners and your ridiculous ideas and bugger off,' I said, pointing to the door for affect as he stood, stunned to speechlessness. I bet no one ever told him off. When he didn't move, I added, 'Now would be good,' and nodded towards the door.

I closed the door behind him. He'd scared off all our customers anyway and I just needed some quiet. I just needed to block out the noise of the cars and the passers-by and even the air. I just wanted to hold Christian and tell him how much I love him. Him, not his money. I needed to breathe. I needed a cup of tea and I really needed one of Mum's muffins that were standing proud on the counter.

There was a knock on the front door of the café. We should

have re-opened already but we'd been so busy scoffing muffins and boosting our sugar levels we'd lost track of time. Christian went to open the doors and Jo rushed to man the coffee station but it was just the police.

Mum stared at them as though they were aliens. 'What are the police doing here? They better be here for coffee,' she insisted.

'Actually, no, they're here for another reason,' I said, not sure how much to tell her.

'Now what's going on, Ainsley?' She was getting her stern teacher voice going which was always scary, so I thought it best to just blurt it all out and let her process it with the rest of the day's news.

'The basement's full of stolen jewels. The police have come to collect them and return them to their owners,' I said, trying not to have too much fun with it.

'What?' she stammered. 'On top of running a brothel up stairs, that woman stored stolen jewels in her basement and thought it'd be a great idea to leave it all to you in her will? You, straight out of the hospital and everything. What was she thinking? That woman had no sense, no shame, no brains at all, I tell you.'

'In her defence Mum, the jewels weren't hers, her husband stole them.'

'Oh Christ,' she said, clasping her chest. 'The husband you just traipsed halfway around the world to find, I suppose.'

'Yep, that's the one.'

'Right, and did you find him? Is he going to be arrested for all this nonsense? Take away the café you've worked so hard for, we've all worked for?'

'No, he's dead now. He died just after we found him. We had to go to jail for a bit but it was just natural causes.'

'Jail?' she stammered. She looked like she was going to be ill. I forced in some more tea and made her eat a bite of my muffin but she just sat shaking her head. 'I knew this place was going to be trouble. It was too good to be true,' she said.

The old lady came in and walked up to the counter even though no one was there, completely ignoring Mum, pale and grey in the booth, fanning herself and the police standing in the middle of the floor holding their clipboards, wondering what to do. Jo saw her though and hurried over to make her pot of Russian Caravan tea and gave her a free muffin. The old lady nodded and went to her booth.

She finally caught sight of the police as she was passing but just looked them up and down, saying nothing and sitting in her booth.

A young, fresh out of the academy constable came in carrying a small cardboard box 'Where shall I start?' she asked.

Jo laughed, 'You might need a bigger box,' and the girl's eyes widened.

'It's all downstairs in the basement. You can't miss the crates, there's a journal in one of them and then there's the jewellery box in my bedside drawer,' I told them, too exhausted to bother with more details.

'Come, I'll show you,' smiled Christian.

'No!' cried the old lady from her booth. 'No, no, no,' she said waggling her finger as she walked over to us, her homypeds squeaking on the floor.

She'd barely ever said a word so it took me quite by surprise.

Everyone else too, I suspected, seeing they stood, frozen like statues.

'Are you okay?' I asked her. 'What do you know about what's downstairs?' I asked suspiciously.

'Only the ones downstairs he stole but not the teapots, them he buy for Stasie. The jewels upstairs, he buy, except the eggs. Stasie liked the eggs. The others, she didn't even open the boxes, didn't care, they were for Henry to sort out. But he never came back,' her face clouded over with sadness.

'We found him,' I told her.

'Henry?'

'Yes.'

'Where was he? Why didn't he come back for Stasie?'

'He couldn't. He was stuck. He was devastated when I told him she'd died. Then he died, a broken heart, I think.'

She nodded. 'He loved Stasie too much. They were like a match, a pair, like soul mates. Just like you two,' she said, smiling at Christian and I.

I smiled at her, 'Thank you. I would have hated to give away Ana's personal things. Would you like something to remember her by?'

'No,' she said. 'I have my memories. Memories of the parties and the friends and the adventures. I don't need anything more,' she smiled to herself nodding.

'How did you know Stasie?' I asked her, needing to answer the final question.

'She was my best friend,' the lady said sadly. 'Then one day she was just gone. I never saw her again and it broke my heart. When I drove past to church one Sunday and saw you painting the window, I thought I must come see if it is Stasie but it wasn't but the place looked just the same, so I come and I remember,' she smiled.

I squeezed her hand, told her Ana's story and thanked her again for all her help. The police went downstairs to collect the jewels.

'I'll get a nice display made up for the teapots, hey? Maybe for behind the counter?' Christian suggested as he took me in his arms.'

'What about the café, Christian, do you think they'll take all this, too?'

'No, I spoke to the lawyer, the cafe was owned by Ana and Henry. They can't prove how they paid for it. The café will remain yours,' he insisted as the police left with the last of the jewels.

The old lady stood silently before me until I looked down.

'You keep café, yes?'

'Absolutely,' I smiled.

'Okay, then. I see you tomorrow.'

# About the Author

Writer, hiker, food lover, TV addict and book nerd. Tamara is fuelled by Doritos, chocolate sultanas and Shiraz.

Tamara writes a stories of adventure and love, where women overcome life altering obstacles and sometimes heart wrenching pain to find who they're meant to be, decide the lives they want to live and fall in love with beautiful men (because, why not). There's always a few bad guys to keep them on their toes and some secrets to keep things interesting.

If you'd like to be in the loop for what's happening in Tamara's world of books, get member only content, contests and behind the scenes info, join her newsletter on her website www.tamara-martinauthor.com